K.C. MILLS

Christmas in Spite of You

BLACK
ODYSSEY
MEDIA

WWW.BLACKODYSSEY.NET

Published by
BLACK ODYSSEY MEDIA

www.blackodyssey.net
Email: info@blackodyssey.net

CHRISTMAS IN SPITE OF YOU. Copyright © 2024 by K.C. Mills

Library of Congress Control Number: 2023919148

First Trade Paperback Printing: October 2024
ISBN: 978-1-957950-53-2
ISBN: 978-1-957950-54-9 (e-book)

Cover Design by Ashlee Nassar of Designs With Sass

10 9 8 7 6 5 4 3 2 1

Manufactured in the United States of America

Distributed by Kensington Publishing Corp.

Dear Reader,

I want to thank you immensely for supporting Black Odyssey Media authors, and our ongoing efforts to spotlight more minority storytellers. The scariest and most challenging task for many writers is getting the story, or characters, out of our heads and onto the page. Having admitted that, with every manuscript that Kreceda and I acquire, we believe that it took talent, discipline, and remarkable courage to construct that story, flesh out those characters, and prepare it for the world. Debut or seasoned, our authors are the real heroes and heroines in *OUR* story. And for them, we are eternally grateful.

Whether you are new to K.C. Mills or Black Odyssey Media, we hope that you are here to stay. We also welcome your feedback and kindly ask that you leave a review. For upcoming releases, announcements, submission guidelines, etc., please be sure to visit our website at www.blackodyssey.net or scan the QR code below. We can also be found on social media using @iamblackodyssey. Until next time, take care and enjoy the journey!

Joyfully,

Shawanda Williams

Shawanda "N'Tyse" Williams
Founder/Publisher

Noel.

"WELL . . ."

I was sweating, literally sweating, because this was the make-it-or-break-it moment. And I *needed* this—like really, *really*, needed this.

"Noel, open the email. Waiting isn't going to change the response." I narrowed my eyes at Simone, my very best friend, who, at the moment, was being a pain in my—

"Give me that," she demanded. Before I was able to object, she confiscated my laptop. Once she dragged it across the counter and I could no longer stall, I closed my eyes, waiting for the final nail in the coffin. *My coffin.* It was coming. I felt it by the way my stomach knotted.

"Hmm . . ."

Hmm. She said "hmm" and "hmm" wasn't good.

"They said no, didn't they?" My voice released barely above a whisper, and my heart sank to the pit of my stomach.

"Not exactly. They—"

I snatched my laptop back and read the email.

Thanks so much for the design layouts you sent. We are at the year's end and would like some additional time to review the layouts before we make our final decision. One of our executives will be in touch at the start of the New Year. We look forward to working with you and Happy Holidays.

Happy Holidays to you too, jerks!

"This said no, Simone." I slammed my laptop closed, and my shoulders deflated. But, as usual, my overly supportive best friend wouldn't allow me to sulk. She quickly rounded the counter and placed her hands on my shoulders.

1

"It's not a *no*. It's a 'we're too lazy to decide before the holiday. We'll be sending you a contract and more than generous offer the first week of January.'"

"Right," I groaned, not believing one word of the overly optimistic pitch. I stepped around Simone and entered my living room, flopping onto the sofa, where I lifted a pillow and covered my face to muffle the coming scream.

Once I finished, Simone snatched it from my face and loomed over me, arms folded over her chest. She had *that* look. The one that meant I was about to be lectured.

"Save it, please," I groaned.

"Absolutely not. You will *not* sit here and self-destruct *or* sulk—whichever of the two you're personally choosing at the moment."

"Both."

"Then, no and no. *Denied*!"

"You can't deny a person's self-destruction or sulking, Simone."

"Actually, I can." She sat next to me and inched closer. I lifted my head and allowed it to rest on her lap. "It's not the end of the world, Noel—just a minor setback. You'll be fine. Your business will be thriving in no time. You have to believe that."

"I do believe my business will thrive. Otherwise, I wouldn't have dumped all my savings into taking this leap of faith. I'm not the one who needs to be convinced. My mounting bills need that pep talk. If I don't start making money soon, I'm going to be homeless. I was really counting on this contract to hold me over until the first of the year. Now, what am I going to do?"

"You're going to put on your big girl pants and use what you have."

I glanced up at Simone, who was staring back in a way that meant I wouldn't like what she was about to say.

"No. Whatever you're thinking, don't think it because my answer is no."

"Can you at least hear me out first?" She smiled mischievously, and I groaned, lifting from my current position and shifting until I was seated with my legs tucked and crossed at the ankles in front of me. I flicked my wrist to signal for Simone to continue. She got up and traveled back to the kitchen, returned with my laptop, which she opened, and began typing something, turning it to me shortly after.

"Not happening," I declared when I realized what the plan was. I was looking at the Shared Space profile she'd created for me a few weeks ago. I'd agreed to consider it as a last resort, but . . .

"Why not? You need the money, Noel."

I frowned, shaking my head and pointing at the screen. "I know I need the money, but that's just weird." I shivered in a cringy manner at the thought of what Shared Space was.

"How is it weird?" She raised a brow in a challenge, and I untucked my legs and stood from the sofa, pacing.

"It just is. Having strangers in your house, with access to your things, is creepy. Like, what if it's some perv who goes through my drawers messing with my things or worse—*wearing* them? Or what if it's some crazy person who likes to use that app to get intel on their next victim and then starts—"

"Starts *what*, Noel?" Simone was way too amused while I was freaking out. My mind shifted to the worst-case scenarios.

"I don't know . . . stalking me or something. If you think about it, the idea is genius. They'll be in *my* home, sharing *my* personal space and having access to *my* things. They'll know *everything* about me, and that's just . . ." I stopped pacing and wrinkled my nose. "Weird."

"Was it weird that we used Shared Space when we traveled to Miami or LA last summer?"

I rolled my eyes and flopped into the corner of the sofa again. "No, because we're *not* weird, and it wasn't my place. It was someone else's."

"You get to screen whoever you allow to stay. You can do the whole background check thing to make sure they're not—"

"Crazy? A stalker? A creepy pervert who goes around the country staying in women's apartments?"

"You're so dramatic, but yes. You'll know if they have a history of anything that seems off."

I narrowed my eyes. "And what if *I'm* their *first* victim? Then what? No criminal record exists, and *bam*! Some strange guy named Newton is spending the week in *my* apartment, sleeping in *my* bed, wearing *my* favorite silk pajamas."

"Or, you pack your favorite silk pajamas for your trip home to spend the holiday with your family and skip past all applicants with the name 'Newton.'"

I shot her a narrowed glare, and she smiled wider. "Come on, Noel. It's a great idea, and you need the money. People pay really good money for these temporary rentals. It can help you with your bills until you get the official 'welcome to the team' email from all those lazy people who aren't doing business because of the stupid holidays."

"Hey, go easy on the 'stupid holiday' part. The holidays are our friends and are the innocent party in all this."

"Okay then, stupid, lazy people." We sat in a standoff, and I chewed my lip, struggling with the decision until I finally gave in. She was right. I needed the money, and it really wouldn't be that bad.

I hoped.

"Fine. But you're helping me box up all the important stuff I own, and you're helping me sanitize the place when I get back."

"Deal. Now, are you doing this or what? One click, and your place is officially available on Shared Space."

She lifted a brow again with her finger hovering over the keyboard. One touch and my life would be officially exposed to strangers.

I nodded, quickly squeezed my eyes shut, and turned my head. I couldn't watch.

Seconds later, I heard Simone's overtly amused voice, and my laptop close. "Done. Now, we wait."

Kanton.

MY ASSISTANT WALTZED into my office with an iPad tucked under one arm, phone in hand, with her eyes glued to the screen. She was dressed in her typical business attire. Today's ensemble was deep navy, wide-legged pants and a matching blazer, giving a sleek and professional look.

Her honey-auburn-colored hair was slicked back into a ponytail, exposing her thin lips and nose, manicured brows, and flawless makeup. Shelby looked like a corporate shark in heels, which she would one day be, but for now, she was my secret weapon. The woman who kept my life organized and running like a well-oiled machine. She was the fine line between keeping me from tipping over the edge and pulling it all together.

Without removing her focus from the device in her delicate hand, she navigated through my office, avoiding a collision with the furniture, and placed the iPad in front of me. I lifted it into view and leaned back, crossing my leg so that my left ankle rested on my right thigh.

"What's this?" I squinted at the brightly colored furniture and floor-to-ceiling windows, highlighting the interior and allowing for the perfect optics.

"A listing on Shared Space. Take a look and let me know what you think. These spots go insanely fast, and you're running out of options this close to the holiday."

Ah. My last-minute trip to Atlanta.

"What's Shared Space?" I wasn't familiar with the name and had made assumptions, but I needed to be sure what was meant by *shared*. I damn sure wasn't planning on spending a week with someone I didn't know.

"A modern-day co-op. People offer up their homes to others, short or long term."

"Offer, as in they leave, and the guest will be there alone?"

Her eyes snapped up to mine, and a smug grin eased onto her pretty face. "Of course. I know there's no way you would spend the week with someone you don't know. Lord forbid you be placed in a situation where you must ignore those pressing mergers and acquisitions long enough to be social."

I lifted one shoulder into a lazy shrug. "I can be social. I simply choose not to. I have a—"

"Ten-year plan. Yes, I know. Take over the world, and then you'll consider having a life."

My smile expanded. "I have a life, Shelby. It's just not what most consider ideal. I've built a solid foundation that I can hopefully pass down to my kids, which they, in turn, can pass down to their kids. It's called creating a legacy, something we as a community need to improve upon. My parents did it, and now, so will I."

"I know what a legacy is, Kanton, but you are aware that a social life is required to afford you the opportunity to meet the woman who will assist in creating those kids who you're building this legacy for, right?"

"I can always adopt." That wasn't the route I wanted to take, but it was fun antagonizing Shelby. She was every bit of the astute and tunnel-visioned businessperson that I was at times, but she had the advantage of sharing her life with someone who often softened her in ways that I wasn't.

"I'm serious, boss. All work and no play—"

"Keeps my portfolios growing."

"Kanton . . ." she warned with a sharp look that had my smile expanding again.

"I'm kidding. I want a family as much as you want me to have one. Just when the time is right. After I secure this deal, I'll consider slowing down enough to go on a date or two . . . *maybe*."

"You're insufferable sometimes."

"But I pay you handsomely, which is why you stay around to suffer. And for the record, I tried the relationship thing, remember? Jordan is currently packing her things, or at least, I hope she is, so that she can be moved out of my apartment by the time I return."

Jordan, who I had dated for all of three months before she conveniently moved in with me . . . without my knowledge. I returned from a business trip to find her things arranged in my place, and since I was trying to embrace a social life, I gave Jordan and me a valid chance at having a future. After living together for six months, I realized she and I were mismatched. Unfortunately, she refused to accept our differences wouldn't make for a happily ever after, and I was having a hard time detaching her from my life. It seems we had finally reached a common ground since she agreed to be out of my place before the first of the year.

"If she knows what's good for her, she'll be out before I return."

I handed Shelby a warning look. The last thing I needed was Shelby getting personally involved in Jordan's removal from my life, although it might be amusing to see the fallout. "Leave it alone. I have it covered."

She groaned and rolled her eyes, pointing to the iPad again. "Do you want the place or not? I need to accept the offer because my guess is it will be gone by the close of business . . ."

"It's nice but kind of . . ." I frowned, trying to find the proper terminology without being offensive.

"Quirky and eclectic. Yes, it's all that. Probably belongs to some artsy type, but the space has beautiful bones and more importantly, it's the perfect place for you to stay when it comes to closing this deal with Brighton."

"What makes you say that?"

"The unit is in his building." She smiled smugly, feeling accomplished. She knew me better than anyone, considering she spent more hours with me than her boyfriend. The opportunity to be in the same building as Brighton was golden. Nothing would prevent me from having access to him, not even a bout of bad weather, which Atlanta wasn't known for this time of the year, but I wasn't taking chances.

"Then there's your answer. Book it."

"Perfect." She extended a hand, and I leaned over my desk, passing the iPad back to her. Her fingers moved across the screen with expert speed. She tucked the device under her arm a few moments later and smiled.

"Done. You're officially booked for the week of Christmas. Which, by the way, I think is insanely crazy. Who the heck wants to work the week of Christmas? I would have loved to be a fly on the wall when you had that call with your mother."

"I do if it means closing a multimillion-dollar deal, and my mother was not happy at all. However, she'll survive. I need to convince Brighton that Global is the only chance he has of keeping controlling interest in his family's company. All I have to do is meet with him in person to prove how great this merger can be, not just for me but for his company and future business between the two of us. The Prestige Luxury brand is huge but in dire need of our help if they want to continue owning the monopoly on luxury hotels, apartments, and spas worldwide."

"Right, and while you're doing all the heavy lifting, which will make us all rich, I'll be with my boyfriend, hopefully, celebrating our engagement."

"He's proposing?" I arched a brow, and she smiled mischievously.

"If he's smart, he will. I've given him every opportunity to pick the perfect gift, which is a Tiffany True diamond that he will present me with on Christmas Eve at an intimate dinner we'll share in our cozy little cabin in Breckenridge."

I chuckled, shaking my head. "You've planned the entire thing for him?"

"Yes and no. I might have dropped subtle hints, but I'm leaving it all in his very capable hands." She winked, heading to the door. Then she paused and turned to face me just before leaving. "Once I have all the access information for the listing, I'll forward it to you. They don't send it until twenty-four hours before you're scheduled to arrive, just in case you change your mind. In the meantime, I'll finalize the reports you'll need to present to Brighton and his team next week. Should I order lunch for you today, or will you be going out?"

I drummed my fingers on the desk, mentally walking through my day, realizing I had a lot of work to do. "You can order in. How about—"

"Thai from ThaiSquared. Got it."

I chuckled at how well she truly knew me. "Perfect. Always on top of things. Thanks, Shelby."

"My boss pays me handsomely to suffer. No thanks necessary." She flashed me a smile before leaving my office, and I fired up my desktop to get my day started.

It was after nine by the time I made it home. I entered my apartment, placed my things on the kitchen table, then paused momentarily to fold my overcoat over the back of one of the chairs. Releasing a sigh to exhale away the day, I pulled open my refrigerator and removed a beer, taking it into the living room with me, where I lifted the remote and sank into the sofa.

I loved my life. There wasn't much to complain about. After graduating at the top of my class with a degree in business, I had the type of career most only dreamed of. By twenty-two, I started my first Global Restructuring Firm. By twenty-four, I had my first million-dollar account. At twenty-eight, I had already far exceeded my goal of being listed as one of the nation's up-and-coming corporate restructuring firms and financial strategists. I'd already obliterated my ten-year plan but still wasn't ready to slow down. Mainly because . . .

My phone vibrated with a call, and I groaned, seeing my mother's name flash across the screen. If I didn't answer, she would repeatedly call until I did. This was her thing, which had turned into *our* thing. She called, and I dodged her. She refused to let me rest until I answered at least once.

"Good evening, Mother." I kept my focus on the television as I mindlessly flipped through channels.

"Well, good evening to you too, my long-lost son."

I chuckled, lifting my beer and taking a healthy gulp.

"You know the address to both my residence and my office, Mother. I'm far from lost."

She scoffed. "You know what I mean, Kanton. It's the week before Christmas, and we don't have your flight information. Will you bring a plus-one to the gala, and if so, please send me her bio so I can be prepared."

I snorted at the thought of dating a woman who had a bio that my mother would approve of. There were plenty. I would bet my life my mother had several *bios* from women who met her standards of being qualified to date her son—none of whom would meet my qualifications of being interesting enough to entertain for longer than my mother's gala would last. She and I differed greatly in that area.

"That's easy. There are no arrival plans, which means no plus-one. I'll be in Atlanta next week, *working*."

"You absolutely *will not*, Kanton. Next week is Christmas."

"I'm well aware, Mother."

"Then what's this nonsense about you working? Everyone will be expecting you to be home for the holidays. We have a tight schedule as is, with our family dinner, Christmas Eve decorating, and the gala—which, by the way, has already raised over a million dollars that we'll be sending out to well deserving charities."

The Christmas dinner and Christmas Eve decorating performance would be captured by whatever newly hyped videographer my mother had hired to narrate the perfect story of our perfect family. Hard pass on that.

"I've already sent my donation from my personal and business accounts, but I won't be there. Sorry, but this deal is important."

"Our *family* is important, Kanton. What am I supposed to tell everyone when you don't show?"

I shrugged, not really caring. I was one piece of the perfect holiday puzzle. My mother didn't give a damn about seeing me. Well, that wasn't the complete truth. She loved it when I came home because she did love *me*, but this was more about me playing my part in a holiday creation that she would have flawlessly edited and then placed on her personal and charity websites. It was always about appearances.

"I'm sure you'll figure it out, and if you can't, that's why you pay your team of minions. They're very capable of drafting a speech for you to deliver to anyone concerned about my absence."

"It's not about that. I look forward to you being home for the holidays, Kanton."

"Seriously, Mother? You could not care less about me coming home beyond how it disrupts your perfectly laid plans. Unfortunately, you'll have to improvise this year. I won't be home."

"I suppose I can spin this one way or another, but I *will* miss you. Just know I'm terribly disappointed."

"I'm sure you are. As sure as I'm convinced that you'll survive. Good night, Mother. I love you. I have an extremely early morning tomorrow." I smiled into the phone, knowing that she was pouting.

Not exactly a lie. All of my mornings were early, which I would bet my life she knew, and that was why she didn't argue with me.

"Good night, Kanton. I love you, and if you just *happen* to change your mind—"

"I won't. I love you too, Mother."

She sighed again just before my phone went silent. I glanced at my phone, feeling a tinge of guilt that I wasn't going home for the holidays, but then again, it wasn't like it mattered. My family didn't function like most.

Instead of cozy nights with ugly sweaters and apple cider or eggnog in front of the fireplace, my parents and I would be dressed in the most expensive threads, posing for staged pictures throughout our home. To others, we appeared to be the perfect blend of love and privilege. But in reality . . .?

My mother was overly obsessive about our image, my father worked more hours than he spent with us, and I had only been conceived to complete their all-American image. It was nauseatingly taxing, and my number one reason for loathing the holidays, and Christmas more than the others because it was always the longest week of my life growing up with all the scheduled events and appearances my mother insisted on every year.

My friends were out playing, enjoying their vacation, while I was spending my time entertaining adults who didn't understand that I simply wanted to be a kid. Holidays were not fun, and I could do without any of the insanity of it all.

Noel.

"I CAN'T BELIEVE YOU'RE not coming. Aren't you feeling better?"

I squeezed more honey into my tea and then stirred the concoction to make sure it was blended well.

"I feel a lot better. I think I'm through the worst of it, but it's still not a good idea for me to be traveling."

And the fact that I can't afford the last-minute ticket.

"But you'll be alone for Christmas, which makes me sad."

"Mom, I'll be fine. I'll decorate, bake some cookies, and FaceTime you guys on Christmas Eve and Christmas morning. It will be just like me being there."

Lies. All lies.

"But, honey—"

"Don't, Mom. I promise I'll be fine. I'm feeling much better now, so maybe I'll head out later to find a tree."

Another lie. A tree wasn't a luxury I could afford at the moment, and I refused to put up one of those fake ones. Things were more than a little tight, and I also wasn't feeling up to leaving my place to go on the hunt for one, even if I could afford it. My town was overcrowded with tourists overdosing on Christmas cheer, and I currently didn't have any to offer.

"Noel . . ."

"I'll be fine," I declared as a final word, and thankfully, she accepted it.

"Okay, honey, but we can cover the ticket if you change your mind. I know they'll be expensive at the last minute, and with the new business and everything . . ."

I tilted my head back, pointing my face toward the ceiling, squeezing my eyes shut to curb the wave of guilt. My parents assumed that things were fine and my business was new but flourishing. I didn't tell them any different because, well, I was an adult and needed to handle things on my own. They were barely making things work on their end and didn't need to be concerned with me being an added expense.

"It will be expensive, and I would almost guarantee no flights are available. I'll plan a trip to visit soon, I promise. I'm really busy right now anyway with the new accounts and all . . ."

A tiny white lie that could be considered speaking success of my business into existence and not a false statement. Yep, I'll go with that. I didn't like the idea of lying to my parents.

"Oh, wonderful, honey. In that case then, I don't feel so bad. How about I send you something special? If I can get it in the mail today, you'll have it by the weekend."

"Sure, that would be great."

"Wonderful. I love you, honey. Get some rest, and make sure you're staying hydrated. It's important." I smiled into my mug and then lowered it.

"I will, Mom. I promise."

I ended the call just in time to avoid my mother hearing the coughing fit that grabbed ahold of me. I truly was feeling better, but the congestion and sore throat still gave me fits. The tea was helping, and the nighttime medicine made it easier for me to sleep. Hopefully, I will feel well enough in the next few days to try to decorate a little. I glanced at the plastic bins Simone had dragged out for me before she'd left.

Decorating would clearly help my mood. Being stuck at home, alone for the holidays, was pure torture. Simone was visiting her family. She'd offered to stay back to spend the holiday with me, but I couldn't ask her to do that.

She loved Christmas and her family as much as I did, and with her crazy job hours, she rarely got the time off to get home to see them. Her sister had also just had a baby, whom Simone was all too excited to meet for the first time. I refused to ruin their Christmas just because mine was officially ruined.

I lifted my tea and trudged to my room, climbing into bed after setting the tea on my nightstand. Once I was snuggled beneath my bedding, warm and cozy, I turned on the TV and decided to watch some trash. I'd usually be watching Christmas movies, but it was too depressing to see all the happy couples and families working their way through Christmas disasters, only to find their happily ever afters and Merry Christmases.

I sighed and tugged my blanket further up my chest, reaching for my tea.

"This sucks," I mumbled just before my phone vibrated next to me. I lifted it and pushed out a pout before answering.

"Please tell me you're not calling to tell me some funny story about how your dad forgot the eggs and had to go back to the store only to discover they were completely out, and now you can't make your mother's famous gingerbread cookies, and Christmas is officially ruined." I smiled. "Oh wait, that might not be such a terrible thing, the ruined Christmas part, that is."

"Wow, you've officially hit rock bottom. Instead of goodwill and cheer, you're all coal in the stocking and burnt Christmas cookies. Never thought I'd see the day, friend."

I scoffed. "Desperate times call for sour attitudes." I coughed several times and then lifted my tea to take a few tentative sips.

"Yeah, well, I'm not used to this from *you*. I'm going to need you to cheer up. And you sound terrible. I thought you were getting better."

"Oh gee, thanks for the compliment."

"Noel, I'm serious. That cough sounds bad, and you sound—"

"Depressed? Well, I am. This sucks."

"This is adulting. You are officially an adult having to make the tough decisions, which means no going home to Mommy and Daddy for the holidays, but you'll survive."

"Oh, that's cold, Simone, and will I survive? This certainly doesn't feel *survivable*. Also, I've been an adult."

"Well, yeah, you have, but the kind with a biweekly paycheck you could count on. Now, you're officially self-employed and having to figure things out on your own while hiding how broke you are from your parents. An entirely new level of adulting, sweetie."

"In between blessings. Not broke," I muttered. "And you're saying that like I should be excited. Again, this sucks."

"You should. Considering this is a new phase in your life. Noel two point oh. Big boss, taking over the world with your virtual staging and designs."

"Noel two point oh is officially broke. I want to bypass the upgrade and stay with the older model. Please and thank you."

"Too late. You're in this, which, by the way, is why I called. I wanted to make sure you canceled your booking. You've been a little distracted, so I wanted to ensure you didn't forget."

I did.

"Nope, didn't forget. Got it covered. I have up to twenty-four hours before arrival to cancel without penalty. I'll get it done. Girl, don't you dare believe him. Once a cheater, always a cheater." I frowned at the TV.

"Who are you talking to?"

"The TV."

"What are you watching?"

"*Second Chance at Love.*"

"Oh Lord, now, I know you've officially hit rock bottom. The entire month of December is usually reserved for you to have Christmas movies on repeat. The fact that you're watching trash TV means you're much worse off than I expected."

I grinned. "I'm fine, I promise. Just doing a little television sulking, but I'll be back to normal by tomorrow. Trust me. I've got big plans. I'm going to decorate my place and bake some Christmas cookies. I ordered everything I needed this morning and had the groceries delivered. See? Perfectly fine. I'm going to make the most of this horrible Christmas, even if it kills me."

"Let's pray it doesn't. I don't like people, so I have no interest in auditioning newbies for the spot of my *new* best friend," she groaned, and I smiled brighter.

"Not that anyone could ever compare to me . . ."

"No, they wouldn't, which is why you can't let this sucky-ass Christmas kill you. Promise me."

"I promise. Tell your family I said hello, and Merry Sucky-Ass Christmas. And kiss the baby for me. Send me pictures. Lots of pictures. Oh, and video. I'll be living vicariously through you this week, Simone. Don't let me down."

"I won't, but I have to go. It's time for eggs and eggnog."

"Oh, that sounds interesting. And *dangerous*. Not a good combination."

"It's usually a breakfast thing, but my flight didn't get in until after lunch, so we're doing it now. Trust me, it's not a good combination, but Mom's big on themes. Pray for me."

"Nope. No can do. Misery loves company, and I, my dear friend, am currently miserable."

"You're horrible."

"This week I am, but you love me." I felt my eyes getting heavy. The medicine was kicking in. "Gotta go. I feel a nap coming on. The drugs are officially doing their job."

"Okay, but before you take that nap, cancel the booking."

"Right. Doing it now. Promise."

I reached for my laptop, suffering through another round of coughing as I powered it up.

"Noel, I'm serious. Make sure you cancel. If you don't, you'll have to pay that penalty and return the money to the person who booked, or worse, they'll show up, and *that* would be fun."

"Yep, got it. Doing it now." I yawned and rubbed my eyes, which felt very heavy.

It didn't take me long to log into the customer portal and pull up the one booking I had. My chest felt tight, having to move through the steps to cancel. I really needed the money. It wasn't much, but at this point, every penny mattered. Either way, I didn't have a choice. I wasn't going home for the holidays, which meant my place wouldn't be empty.

I navigated through the cancellation screens and moved through the steps. While my request processed, I set my laptop beside me on the bed and slumped down farther, snuggling beneath my covers. I peeked at the screen several times to ensure it was still processing. At some point, I yawned, and my eyes closed. My computer dinged, and I glanced at the screen long enough to see an email pop up from Shared Space, which meant they had my cancellation. Now, it was time to sleep. The medicine had won this battle, but I wasn't putting up much of a fight.

Kanton.

"**I**'D LIKE TO extend a special thank-you to all of you. I'm one man, which means my abilities are limited, but with a team like the one I have, we are unstoppable. It's because of your hard work and dedication that Global is so profoundly successful."

I lifted my champagne flute, and so did my team. We were small but mighty, and I meant every word. My drive and tenacity for business got us started, but their hard work and commitment to my vision allowed our continued growth.

"Cheers to Global, ending another year at the top of our game."

"And to you for closing one of Global's biggest deals to date."

I offered a smile. "Let's not get ahead of ourselves. I don't have the signatures just yet. I have to convince Brighton that we are the best choice he can make—the *only* choice he should make."

"But you will. It's why Global is the number one financial conglomerate on the East Coast and soon to be worldwide."

"I'll let you take that up with the big guy upstairs. For now, I'll humbly accept that affirmation of our company's continued growth and prosperity."

"So modest. I'll try to be you when I grow up, but for now, let's toast to Global taking over the world." Shelby smiled smugly.

"I second that."

"Third."

"Fourth," my team rattled off.

I chuckled, tipping my glass as we all drank to the affirmation. "Okay, guys, the holiday officially begins today . . ."

"For *us*."

"Right. While you're all roasting chestnuts over an open fire with your families and loved ones, I'll be closing the deal with Brighton to ensure you can all afford such luxuries."

"Speaking of luxuries . . ." Gerald lifted his hand, rubbing his fingers together. "When should we expect those Christmas bonuses, boss?"

"Gerald, *really*?" Shelby shot him an evil glare, but I wasn't offended. They were all likely thinking the same thing and had more than earned the very generous gift they'd be receiving.

"Hey, I'm just saying what we're all thinking. Consider me the sacrificial lamb or team advocate. I prefer the latter."

I chuckled. "Accounts payable sent them out already. They should hit your accounts tonight. You're welcome."

"Thanks, boss."

"Yeah, thanks, Kanton."

Shelby tapped her watch, and I nodded. "Enjoy, guys. I've catered breakfast for you, which should be arriving shortly. After that, you're free to head home. I have a flight to catch, and I'll see you after the New Year. Enjoy your holiday."

"With that Christmas bonus, you better believe we will," Gerald stated with a wide grin.

"You're terrible."

"Nope, I'm real."

Shelby and I left the conference room, and she fell in step with me. We stopped by my office to get my packed and waiting bags and then took the elevator down to the lobby, where Shelby filled me in on any last-minute details.

"I sent the final confirmation for the booking. You have the door code to get into the apartment. They have a doorman who works at a station there along with concierges in case you need anything, and I have a cleaning crew on standby, just in case."

I frowned at Shelby, who brushed over my concerns. "I said, *just* in case. You never know with these types of bookings. It's listed in the contract that they'll have the place professionally cleaned before your arrival, but in the event it's not up to your standards, I can have someone there to take care of it within the hour."

I offered a nod.

"I would have had a backup place ready, but—"

"That won't be necessary. I can't imagine the place will be that bad. I can survive for one week."

"Good to know because there isn't an available space anywhere near the city. The closest is about forty minutes away. Atlanta is having the tenth anniversary of the inception of their town's Christmas Festival, so it's a huge deal. Everything's booked."

I groaned at the thought, and Shelby smiled. "Don't worry. I've secured your tickets to all the events for the week. Figured with you missing Christmas with your family, this would be right up your alley."

I narrowed my gaze, and she smiled wider. "Kidding, boss. Lord forbid you actually enjoy the holidays for once in your life."

"I don't know what 'enjoying the holidays' means. Christmas, for me, is a production used to paint my family as the American dream. Perfect, wealthy, and happy. Which, by the way, two out of three we are not."

"Well then, maybe I *should* snag a few tickets. That way, you can experience the real spirit of Christmas. Just might be exactly what you need."

"I'll pass. My focus will be on securing this deal with Brighton. Being in the same building means access. I simply have to figure out how to get to him. If I'm lucky, I can be back home by Thursday evening and I'll be sitting on my sofa, drinking a beer to celebrate closing the deal with Brighton and my newly empty apartment."

After some research, I found out Brighton had a huge Christmas Eve party yearly. The guest list was exclusive, but if I was in the same building, then surely I could crash the party, steal a few minutes of his time to corner Brighton, and convince him that my company was not only unfairly left off his list but we were also the only firm that should have been on the list in the first place.

I knew my shit, and if I could get to him, I could convince him of such. The problem was getting a meeting, which had been impossible; hence, my brilliant idea to fly out and crash his Christmas party.

"Sounds exciting." She sounded anything but. "And I told you, just say the word, and the empty apartment thing is as good as handled."

I smirked and wrapped my hand around the handle of my rolling suitcase when I noticed the Town Car pulling up in front of the building. "Stay away from Jordan. I mean it, and closing deals is all the excitement I need. If I'm right, that's my ride." I glanced at my watch, and she glanced at the vehicle.

"You are, but they're four minutes late."

I chuckled and tipped my head in her direction. "Merry Christmas, Shelby. I'll let you know when I land and reach the apartment."

"Merry Christmas, Kanton."

I started toward the door, pausing just before pushing through the glass roundabout. "And Shelby?"

She looked at me with a raised brow, waiting. "If your perfect proposal isn't so perfect, don't give the guy a hard time. Things happen in their own time."

"Or by way of subtle manipulation." She smiled wickedly, and I shook my head. There was no talking any sense into her, but I believed with all my heart she would find a way to get exactly what she wanted. She always did.

"Enjoy the rest of your day."

"You too, boss. Go do what you do best."

"I plan to."

A moment later, I was meeting my driver, who took my bags and opened the back door for me. On the drive to the airport, I reviewed Brighton's financial statements. I needed to make sure

I had every angle covered because there was no way I was letting this deal slip through my fingers.

I arrived at the building with no issues. It was just after lunch, and I was exhausted from traveling, hungry, and ready to order some food, then dive into my business plans for the evening.

"At least the building is nice," I muttered, stepping into the lobby, where an older gentleman in a tidy black suit smiled and greeted me.

"Good afternoon, sir. Welcome to Grey Plaza Towers. Who are you visiting? I can ring them for you."

"Not visiting anyone. Just here for the week on business."

The guy frowned and nodded. "Staying here?"

"Yes. Shared Space."

"Ahh. Got it. I'm familiar. Many of our residents are getting into that. It's a little weird if you ask me. Letting strangers live in your house while you're not there to supervise. Never know what people are into these days, ya know?"

I raised a brow, and he quickly rolled his shoulders back and smiled. "Not that I think you're into anything weird. Just speaking in general. You look like the normal type." He frowned. "But then again, most of the weird ones do."

I chuckled. "I assure you, I'm the *normal* type and *not* into anything weird. Just here on business. One of my potential clients lives in the building, which is why I opted for Shared Space."

He perked up. "Oh yeah? Who's your client?"

"Richard Brighton."

"Ah, Brighton. Penthouse. Grey suits and a wife who's way too young for him. But I know why he married her."

"Or possibly why she married him?" I smirked, and he offered me a nod of understanding. Brighton was a very wealthy man. "You know him?"

"Sure do. I know all the residents. Been here since they overhauled the place and raised the property value of everything around here ten years ago. What unit are you staying in?"

"Twelve C?"

"Noel Anderson. She's one of my favorites. I didn't know she rented out her place. Just saw her a few days ago, and she was bummed about not being able to spend Christmas with her family. Christmas is kinda her thing."

"Her thing?"

"Yeah, you know what I mean. She's one of those that decorates. Bakes all of us cookies and hands out presents to the staff, and not just socks or ties or smelly candles. She really pays attention and gets us stuff we like. Last year, she got me and the wife tickets to a play. She remembered me mentioning how my wife loves theatre; it wasn't anything fancy. Just something the college put together, but it was still nice, and the wife loved it."

"I see why you like her. Thoughtful."

"Very."

I frowned and nodded, thinking about the fact that he'd just seen her. "Well, maybe something changed with her plans. I have my confirmation for the week."

"Seems that way. Enjoy your stay, and again, welcome. I'm Lewis. I work the front desk Monday through Friday. If you need anything, I'm your guy."

"Thank you, Lewis. It was a pleasure." I extended a hand, which he accepted and shook.

"Elevators are that way."

I offered a nod and followed his instructions, heading to the elevators, getting off on the twelfth floor, and locating my home away from home for the week. Once I had my phone in hand, I went to the email Shelby sent with the security codes to enter. I quickly keyed the four-digit combination and waited for the light to turn green, signaling I could enter.

Immediately, I frowned at the chaos surrounding me. The place was nice and colorful, just as the photos had shown, but there were plastic bins stacked in the living room, one with the lid off filled with tangled Christmas lights and ornaments.

Lewis did say she was a bit of a holiday enthusiast and that she'd had a change of plans. She might have left in a hurry.

Further inspection brought me to the kitchen, where a few dishes were in the sink: mugs, plates, and several food containers. What I'd walked into didn't seem like a space prepared for visitors. I thought about what Lewis had mentioned and got Shelby on the line.

"Please tell me there's not a problem with the apartment. You got in okay, right?" Shelby rushed out.

"I did. I'm here now."

"Your tone sounds cryptic. What's wrong with the place?"

"Nothing is especially *wrong*. It just looks a little . . ." I paused. "Lived in. Not what I was expecting."

"Lived in?"

"There are dishes in the sink and Christmas decorations stacked in the living room. You did confirm my week here, didn't you?"

"Are you *really* asking me that?" I smirked at the annoyance in her tone. "I confirmed and have the email as proof. We had to confirm within twenty-four hours of arrival that you would be there, and they had twenty-four hours before your arrival to cancel. There was no cancellation, Kanton. The place is yours for the week. Hang on. I'll get the cleaning crew on the line and have them there within the hour . . ."

"Let's not go that far yet. Give me a moment before you call in the cavalry. I want to check things out. It's not a huge deal. Just a few dishes which I can handle."

"You sure?"

"Yes, not a big deal. Like I said, the place is nice. Just a minor detail."

"Minor, my ass. I'm noting everything and leaving it in the review."

I chuckled. "I'm sure you will. Let me get settled, and I'll call you back later."

"Will do, boss."

I ended the call and folded one arm across my chest, bending the other at the elbow to brush my fingers over my chin, looking around to decide where to start.

Kitchen.

May as well get those dishes handled. I removed my coat and folded it over a stool positioned at the counter outlining the kitchen. Next to go was my tie, and then I rolled up my sleeves to get to work.

Not a great start to my week. I prayed this wasn't a preview of what was to come.

Noel.

I **AWAKENED, SNUGGLING INTO** my pillow and smiling at the warm, cozy feeling of my bed. I settled into the moment a little more before my eyes shot open at the sound of water running and dishes clattering.

What the heck?

I sat up slowly, pushing my eye mask to my forehead while frowning at the wall separating my bedroom from the kitchen. I stretched my neck and squinted, knowing that I had to be hearing things . . . but there it was again—a dish clashing against something, maybe the counter, and the sound of water running.

Oh no.

I'm being robbed.

Wait, but why would they stop to wash dirty dishes if I'm being robbed?

My mind and body flooded with panic. I threw the covers back and paced beside my bed, trying to decide what to do. Seconds later, I grabbed the first thing I could get my hands on and rushed to the door, hurrying into the hallway and then toward the kitchen . . . just in time to see a body covered in navy slacks and a crisp white shirt, digging through my pantry. He was tall, with broad shoulders, a slim waist, and his clothes were far too neat and *expensive*.

Okay, maybe he's not here to rob and murder me. Just popped in to borrow . . .

"Where the heck are the trash bags?"

Trash bags?

I frowned harder and lifted my arm in the air, prepared to defend myself. "Hey, what are you doing in my apartment?"

My intruder glanced over his shoulder, slowly taking me in from head to toe, and my cheeks warmed because his eyes lingered a little too long in certain places. Okay, maybe I should have grabbed a robe.

Too late for that.

"I said, what are you doing in *my* apartment?"

He turned completely to face me with an amused smile crawling onto his face while his brows lifted slightly.

"Trying to find trash bags. Nothing in there is organized or where it should be."

I tilted my head to the side as he advanced and locked his arms across his chest. His very firm and solid chest that I wouldn't mind a better peek at, nixing the shirt, I might add.

Noel, snap out of it—strange man in your apartment. Focus!

We were still on opposite sides of the kitchen, but still . . .

"Stop moving and answer my question."

His smile expanded, and he tilted his head to the side, mirroring my current position. "And if I don't? Are you going to club me to death with an *elf*?"

My eyes darted to the item I'd mindlessly grabbed before leaving my room. A stuffed elf that my mother had sent in her care package. I quickly drew it into my chest, hating how his eyes followed the motion. His lips twitched in amusement.

"Maybe." I straightened my spine, extending my height as much as I could. Didn't do much good. He still had me by a foot or more. "Now, answer my question, buddy. What are you doing in *my* apartment?"

"I already did. I told you I was looking for trash bags." He tossed his chin, motioning to the pantry behind him. "You really should do better organizing your things, *Ms*. Anderson."

I frowned at him knowing who I was when I had no clue who he was. Well, other than him being a well-dressed stranger who smelled all woodsy and manly with a hint of citrus. Grapefruit . . . no, orange. *Nice.* Definitely a subtle hint of orange. And then there was the inky sheen of well-groomed hair that covered his square jaw, and those eyes . . . Those beautiful dark eyes and God, those lips . . .

Wait! What the heck am I doing? I shook away the lustful haze I'd somehow fallen under and focused on the issue at hand. *Stranger danger!*

"Don't worry about my organizational skills because that's none of your business. Who are you? Why do you know my name, *and* more importantly, what the heck are you doing in my apartment?"

He stepped closer, grinning when I quickly held up the elf defensively. He also didn't stop until that elf and my hand were inches shy of his very solid chest. "It's kind of hard not to worry about your organizational skills when I'm in desperate need of a trash bag to replace the one I removed, *and* I'm here because I rented this apartment for the week. And lastly, my name is Kanton Joseph. Not in the order you demanded, but I've now answered all of your questions, Ms. Anderson. I'd say it's a pleasure to meet you and thank you for the warm welcome, *but . . .*"

He glared down at the elf and then smiled smugly. "I don't quite feel welcomed and wouldn't at the moment categorize you as pleasant." His eyes did that roaming thing again before he added, "Outside of the visual. *That* is quite pleasant."

I'm totally going to ignore the way he's checking me out.

"Well, you shouldn't because you're not welcome. You shouldn't be here. I canceled."

"You did no such thing."

"I most certainly did. I have the email confirmation, *buddy.*"

"Kanton," he corrected, and I rolled my eyes.

"No point in us being familiar. You won't be here much longer."

He smirked and lowered his head so that those alluring dark eyes were fastened with mine. "Would you like to get that confirmation for me? I'll wait."

I frowned hard. "I'm not leaving you alone in here. You might—"

"Wash some dishes and take out the trash?" His thick, dark brow lifted again, and his insanely gorgeous smile was back.

Man, I hate this guy.

Okay, maybe not hate. That was a bit strong. But I really, *really* didn't like him.

Well, beyond looking at him because, let's face it, the guy was easy on the eyes.

"Well, Ms. Anderson?"

"Stop that. Stop using my name like we're acquainted or like you know me because you do not."

He smiled smugly and checked me out again. I groaned, needing to get him out of here.

And for me to put on some clothes.

"Stay here. Right here. Do not move. I need to get my phone."

He smiled arrogantly. "I have no plans on going anywhere . . . for the next week."

I groaned again and stomped off, delivering my warning one last time. "I mean it. Don't you move."

"I won't."

As soon as I entered my room, I grabbed a sweatshirt from the pile of clothes in the corner, which I yanked over my head, then lifted my phone from the nightstand and held it to my face to unlock it. It took me a minute to find the email confirmation, but I smiled widely as soon as I did.

"Aha. Got him," I muttered and turned on my heels to storm back into the kitchen, this time leaving the elf behind. Not that it would do me much good anyway.

"Here. There's your proof. Confirmation email sent a day and a half ago, *which* is actually *thirty-eight* hours before your arrival time. I gave you an entire *fourteen* extra hours to make alternate plans."

He leaned in and studied my phone, which I gladly shoved closer to his face, and after a long pause, he chuckled and extended to his full height.

He shouldn't be laughing.

"What's so funny?"

"You might want to look at that so-called confirmation you're using to argue your case."

"I already did. You need to be the one looking at it, and the sooner you do, the sooner you can get out of my apartment."

"I'm not so sure about that."

"What's that supposed to mean?"

He motioned to my phone, and I turned the device back in my direction and glanced at the screen. Maybe I'd mistakenly moved to another email, but the longer I looked at the one on my phone, the more my stomach twisted uneasily.

No. No. No.

This can't be right.

Thank you, Mr. Joseph, for confirming your stay with Shared Space. You'll find the access code to the unit you've reserved in the email below. We hope you enjoy your stay. Don't forget to leave a review.

I swiped frantically, checking for another email. My cancellation email. It had to be here.

"Wait. I canceled. I know I canceled. I got the email confirmation . . ."

That was when the night came flooding back to me. The hourglass, the medicine I'd taken, and the confirmation email that appeared seconds after I'd gone through the process on the Shared Space site . . . which wasn't *my* cancellation. It was *his* confirmation. I hadn't bothered to double-check.

Shit. Shit. Shit.

"I take it that look on your face means you now realize that this place, *your* place, is *mine* for the week."

"What? No. You're not staying here," I asserted, not willing to admit that he had every right to.

"You sure about that? Because you just showed me proof that I not only paid for the week but confirmed with you within the allotted time requested to do so. And *you*, Ms. Anderson, did *not* cancel within the agreed upon twenty-four hours provided for you to change your mind prior to my arrival." He stepped closer with an accomplished look on his unfairly handsome face. "*Unless* you have *another* email you'd like to show me."

I frowned. "No, I don't, but that doesn't mean I have to let you stay. I'll call security. Lewis will gladly march you right out of here or get the cops to do so."

"Cops? And what will you tell them? That you took my money and refused to uphold *your* end of the contract? Because it is indeed a contract, Ms. Anderson. One you and I willingly entered into the minute you accepted my money through the Shared Space site."

I frowned again. "Are you a lawyer or something?"

Please, God, don't let this man be a lawyer. I mean, he did look like he could be. He had the serious, manipulative, slick-talking thing down.

He seemed amused. "No, I'm a financial strategist. I own a corporate restructuring firm, but I *do* have several lawyers on speed dial who charge extra on weekends and holidays. *Ridiculously* high amounts, I might add. I'd prefer that the two of us work this out independently."

"Of course you would," I mumbled. My hands were officially tied. "Stay here."

"Again, I have no plans on going anywhere, but I'll finish up here while you're gone. Trash bags?"

I growled under my breath and stomped over to the sink, yanking open the cabinet below it. Once I had my hands on the small box of trash bags, I turned and shoved it into his chest, meeting a wall of firm muscle. He grinned, catching them before they dropped to the floor because I kindly released my hold on them and stomped out of the kitchen, again with his voice traveling behind me.

"Take your time, *Noel*."

Oh, now we're on a first-name basis?

As soon as I was in my room, I dialed Simone and began pacing while I waited for her to pick up. Every so often, my eyes drifted to the wall separating me and Kanton.

"Hey, I hope you're—"

"I messed up, and I'm stuck. I don't know what to do."

"Whoa, slow down. What do you mean 'messed up'? What happened?"

"Shared Space is what happened. The guy, he's here."

"What do you mean he's there?"

I threw my free arm up. "*Here*, like in *my* apartment."

"In your apartment? What's he doing there?"

"To my knowledge, washing dishes, taking out the trash, and critiquing my organizational skills."

"Wait, I'm so confused. Why is he there? Didn't you cancel the booking?"

I cursed under my breath and cringed.

"You forgot, didn't you?"

I cringed again and sank onto the foot of my bed, lowering my face into my palm. "No, I didn't forget. I actually canceled when you told me to—"

"Then *why* is he there, Noel?"

"Because the screen timed out. The little hourglass thing came up . . ."

"And you didn't check to make sure it went through?"

"No, but in my defense, while I was waiting, an email popped up from Shared Space with a confirmation, but I didn't read it. I briefly scanned it, noticed the word 'confirmation,' and thought it was from my canceling."

"Then I don't understand."

"It was *his* confirmation that he was keeping the booking—not *my* cancellation. I mean, what are the odds that he was confirming at the exact moment when I was canceling? Anyone could have made the same mistake."

"Yeah, well, it's not *anyone*, Noel. It's you, and now you have a stranger in your home. If you don't let him stay, you'll have to give him back his payment, *and* you'll get a negative rating with Shared Space, which means no more bookings. Then there's the little detail of you having to pay the penalty of 25 percent of the booking's total amount tacked onto the money you must return to him. Neither of which you currently have."

"Right," I mumbled. "What am I supposed to do?"

"Let him stay. You need the money, and he needs a place to sleep for the week."

"I know I need the money, but what good will it do me if I'm not here to spend it?"

"Why would you say that? Does he look dangerous? Oh my goodness. You think he's dangerous, don't you? Where are you? Where is *he*?"

My eyes shot over to my bedroom door, which I'd left open, and I could still hear him moving around in the kitchen. "Calm down, I think he's harmless. A little rude, condescending, kind of stuffy if you ask me. And a little too obsessed with how I organize my pantry, but if I had to guess, his lack of social skills is about the extent of his dangerous persona."

"What's he look like?" Her tone was too smug.

"What does that matter?"

"It matters because you're defending him, which means he's really a nice guy or cute. Which is it?"

"Neither. Again, not the point. What am I supposed to do?"

"Okay, I'll go with cute, and you're supposed to let him stay or refund his money. Maybe he won't mind you being there if you stay out of his way. What other options do you have?"

"No. Absolutely not. I'm not staying here with him. I don't know that man. And what kind of friend are you to suggest I do so?"

"No, you don't, and I'm a very good friend who knows you're broke."

"I'm not broke."

"Okay, okay. Not broke, in between blessings." I smiled, imagining her eyes rolling. "But the fact remains, you can't afford to return his money, nor can you pay the penalty that Shared Space will charge, and even if you could, that's not a good idea. You need the option for future income if it comes to that. You're also surviving off your credit, and a civil judgment won't look good on your reports. What choice do you have? It's only one week. You can handle one week, Noel. *And* if he's cute, heck, who knows? Maybe it *will* be a Merry Christmas after all."

"Are you *serious* right now?"

"I sure am. Now, go, see if he'll agree to you staying. I mean, the site *is* called Shared Space, and if not, you can get a room somewhere."

"Get a room where? It's Christmas, and besides, my cards are just about maxed out—"

"I can . . ."

"No, you cannot." She'd done more than enough helping here and there when she could.

"Then consider using Emmie."

"No, emergencies only." I sighed in defeat and cringed, realizing my hands were indeed tied and that I might possibly have to spend the week with a stranger. A very sexy stranger who was far too opinionated but still sexy. "I'll call you back."

I ended the conversation before she could object and tossed my phone on the mattress, falling back on my bed where I grabbed a pillow and covered my face, then screamed as low as I could.

"This can't be my life," I said with a sigh.

Oh, but it is. And there's not a darn thing I can do about it.

Kanton.

I **SHOULDN'T HAVE BEEN** eavesdropping, and I hadn't meant to do so, but once I heard Noel's end of the call, I froze outside her room. Why was she still here if she'd rented her apartment for the week because she needed the money? Things weren't adding up, but apparently, she was in a bind.

And she was adorably cute and *sexy*, even with her sleep-mussed hair and satin Christmas pajama set with little snowmen printed all over the top and bottoms. Bottoms that didn't leave much to the imagination. I also couldn't leave out her honed determination to prove me wrong when she was, in fact, the wrong one.

Her slipup wouldn't be so terrible if it meant seeing her in more of those satin pajama sets. Either way, I listened to a conversation that I shouldn't have and now better understood the problem. I also had a tough decision to make. Being here in this apartment gave me access to Brighton.

Being here also granted me access to those sexy little pajamas along with the woman who owned them. I managed to make it back to the kitchen before she returned, and I admired how she managed to somewhat pull it together after screaming her head off, likely into a pillow. *Or maybe she used the elf to muffle her agitated vocals.* The stress of the situation was still evident in her deflated shoulders and the enticing way she worried her bottom lip. This was hard for her.

God, she's so incredibly adorable.

"So . . ." she began slowly while I leaned against the counter, hands gripping the edge. I stared at her, expression blank and unreadable.

"I'm listening."

She huffed a sigh. "Maybe I didn't actually cancel the booking."

"*Maybe?*" I taunted.

"Okay, I didn't, *but* I meant to. I tried to, actually, but my computer got hung up. The little hourglass thing popped up, and then there was an email from Shared Space—"

"*My* confirmation?"

She huffed again. "Yes, your confirmation. And I assumed it was my cancellation because, well, what are the odds of you confirming when I was canceling?"

"Slim, but not impossible."

She narrowed her eyes, and I smiled.

So incredibly adorable.

"It seems we have a bit of a dilemma. You can either refund my money, and I can leave . . ." Which I knew she couldn't do based on my eavesdropping.

"*Or you* can stay, and I promise to give you free rein of the apartment while I stay out of your way, with one stipulation," she quickly, yet reluctantly countered.

The determination in her eyes and the struggle in her expression had me willing to bite.

So I did.

"And what might that be?"

"You can have the entire apartment except for my bedroom."

I raised a brow in question. "And where do you propose I sleep?"

She looked past me into the living room. My eyes followed and then rounded back to her. "The sofa? You can't be serious? For the amount of money I paid, you expect me to sleep on the *sofa*?"

"Well, yeah. I mean, it's a fair negotiation. You don't know me, and I don't know you. I'm allowing you to stay—"

"You're not *allowing* me anything. I paid for this place for the week. I'd be willing to bet if I called the *cops* and provided them with our very legal and binding contract, I *wouldn't* be the one they'd escort out of here."

It was a stretch. I wasn't sure how that worked, but she obviously believed me.

"Oh, good Lord, come on, Kanton. It's a fair deal, and I'll even discount the week for you."

Shit, I shouldn't like the way my name sounded on her tongue, but I did. A little too much.

"By how much?"

I wouldn't let her discount the rate, but she didn't have to know that just yet.

She frowned hard.

Again, so adorable.

"Twenty-five percent." She placed her hands on her hips to assert that she meant business and wouldn't budge. I couldn't help but counter her offer.

"Fifty percent."

"*Fifty?* Be reasonable."

I pushed away from the counter and stepped into her personal space. "I'm being more than reasonable, Noel. If I accept your offer, I'm resigned to sleeping on the sofa and sharing the apartment with a stranger, who, by the way, will have access to *me* while she gets the added comfort of locking herself behind closed doors to sleep at night. More than fair."

Her eyes went wide. "Are you *insinuating* that I might be some crazy person who'll like watch you sleep or, heck, I don't know—*do* something to you?"

"I don't know what you may or may not do. Need I remind you about the elf thing." I smiled, and her eyes narrowed.

"You can't be serious? It was a stuffed *elf.* And you're all six-foot-something with the *I spend every free minute I have in the gym* body and you're worried about *me*?" She flicked her wrist in my direction while her eyes roamed freely. "I think it's safe to say I'm in more danger than you are."

Yes, beautiful, you are, but not the kind that will make the evening news. More like the kind you'll invite your girlfriends over to discuss and giggle about over wine.

"I don't know, and if I've learned anything at all in life, it's never to underestimate people."

"Oh, dear Lord, why me?" she groaned shaking her head in frustration, so I decided to put her out of her misery.

"*But* you asked me to be reasonable, so I'll be reasonable. You have a deal."

"I do?" She seemed utterly surprised.

"Yes, and you can keep the money as long as you promise to stay out of my way. You can also have the bedroom if that will make this easier for you. I'll make good use of the sofa and the rest of the apartment. Agreed?"

I extended a hand, and she chewed the corner of her lip before reluctantly offering hers. "Deal."

I smirked, and when she tried to retract her hand, I gripped it firmly, unwilling to let go. Not sure why, but I really didn't want to, so I asked, "But before I fully accept the offer, tell me why you're still here. Why book the place and not leave?"

There had to be a perfectly logical explanation. Not that I cared . . . or maybe I did.

"I was supposed to spend Christmas with my family. I got sick and couldn't. So, here I am."

I stared into those big brown eyes, loving how much I enjoyed the view. I also noticed there was more to the story, but I didn't ask. "Here you are."

She quickly snatched her hand back, and there was something in her expression, but it disappeared before I could decipher it.

"I'm going to . . . I should go back to my room so that you can do whatever it is you're here to do."

I chuckled as she backed away from me. "Yeah, that might be best for both of us."

After Noel left me to my own devices in her apartment, I rolled up my sleeves and got to work, tidying up the space. Washing a few dishes and collecting trash wasn't a huge deal, and it allowed me time to process what I was doing.

Sure, staying here was convenient, but sharing the space with Noel wasn't the wisest option. The woman would be a huge distraction, and I couldn't afford distractions. I needed to prepare for my one shot at convincing Brighton that Global was the best decision for him. Technically, for both of us, but I wouldn't push my agenda. Having Prestige Luxury as a client made a statement.

Glancing around the tiny kitchen that was now void of any reminders that I had a housemate relaxed me just a bit. My next move was to figure out what I was having for dinner.

I settled on the sofa, which would be doubling as my bed for the next week, and retrieved my phone from my pocket. I swiped through several apps and decided on one I knew to be trustworthy, changed the address from my apartment in New York to my current location, and began browsing nearby food choices.

Every so often, my eyes would drift to another corner of the apartment, wondering about the woman who had barricaded herself in her room. I had to fight against the smile that surfaced and my impending urge to see if she had figured out dinner plans for the evening.

She's not your concern, Kanton.

Shaking the thought, I managed to focus on the idea of feeding myself for the evening, and, hopefully, after dinner, I could focus on why I was here.

Noel.

THE DAY HAD gone incredibly smoothly, considering I was shacking up with a stranger. I spent most of the time in my room binge-watching holiday movies, or at least trying to, but every half an hour or so, I would crawl out of bed, tiptoe to my bedroom door, press my ear to the sleek wood, and listen.

My curiosity was running rampant, and I needed to know what my unwanted houseguest was doing for some strange reason. I could hear his voice on calls and then the low hum of the television, but it didn't sound like he was watching anything entertaining. From what I could tell, he was watching the news or something with a lot of commentary.

Figures.

By early evening, I showered and got cozy in another pair of holiday pajamas, a cotton short set with tiny candy canes printed on the shorts and one large one centered in the middle of my oversized matching tee. After a quick glance in my full-length mirror, I cursed myself for purchasing a week's worth of holiday sleepwear. At the moment, my selection felt juvenile.

Who the hell cares?

Everyone should feel like a kid at Christmas . . . right?

I didn't need to impress this guy, *and* I would see very little of him; plus, if he couldn't appreciate my holiday cheer, that was *his* problem, *not* mine. Everyone loves holidays, and Christmas should always be at the top of the list. The thought had me feeling slightly depressed again because I wouldn't be having a very memorable Christmas, and I seriously missed my family.

After a few more minutes of torturing myself by unsuccessfully creeping on my houseguest, I crawled back into bed and pulled up my very extensive list of saved holiday movies. I scrolled mindlessly, noting that most of them I had watched multiple times before landing on one about a city mogul who gets stranded in a small town. It's always a small town.

During his snowed-in weekend, he falls in love with a baker who's at risk of losing her family-owned cookie shop, but, of course, he manages to not only steal her heart but save her business as well.

Totally cheesy but so adorably warm and fuzzy at the same time.

I pressed play to start the movie, releasing a sigh. Why couldn't real life work like it did in these cheesy holiday movies? If they did, I wouldn't miss Christmas with my family, and I wouldn't be confined to my bedroom for the next week while a stranger had free rein of my apartment. My eyes left the TV screen and roamed around my cozy but lived-in bedroom.

My room and current situation definitely reflected my life. Confined and tattered. I released another dramatic sigh, and focused my eyes back on the TV screen just in time to take in the perfectly cooked steak next to a mound of mashed potatoes and gravy.

Within seconds, my stomach growled, reminding me that I hadn't eaten much of anything all day. My eyes drifted to my bedroom door, reminding me that on the other side, I had a refrigerator full of perfectly good groceries that I'd purchased with my last expendable funds to hold me for the week.

Groceries that would go bad if I let them sit. Sure, I'd promised Kanton that he could have full access to my apartment besides my bedroom, but surely he would understand if I slipped into the kitchen long enough to whip up a few meals or make Christmas cookies.

Christmas isn't Christmas without my mom's famous cinnamon and spice gingerbread cookies.

But who was I kidding? Nothing about Kanton Joseph expressed "reasonable." Tyrant, uptight, and all business, but reasonable, he was not.

Well, he did accept the deal you offered.

True, he had. The guy could have easily thrown me out of my own apartment on my ass because he had a legally binding contract that stated he owned the right to occupy my place for the week—without me.

And he didn't.

But that didn't mean he would allow any other concessions. *But* I had to eat. I couldn't very well stay in my room and starve for an entire week. Surely, he didn't expect that.

Or maybe he did.

"*Grrrrrrrrrr . . .*" I growled, kicking my feet beneath my bedding like a petulant child for several seconds before I tossed the covers back and swung my legs over the side. While I pondered what my next move would be, my stomach growled again, very loudly, deciding for me.

Here goes nothing.

I marched to the door, armed with a plan. Say nothing, whip up a quick meal, and then disappear before he can complain. Simple enough, right? Rolling my shoulders back, I turned the knob to exit my room, and the minute I stepped into the hallway, a tantalizing aroma of marinara, veggies, and garlic slammed into me.

As soon as I stepped into the kitchen, I found the source of my torture along with the reason for my elevated stress levels . . . Kanton standing over two boxes of pizza. Romano's Pizza was one of my favorite guilty pleasures, so, of course, my stomach betrayed me, growling so loudly that I was fearful that Lewis would hear the betrayal from the lobby.

"I guess there's my answer right there." Kanton smiled smugly, dropping a second slice onto a plate—my plate—that he'd made himself comfortable with, but instead of diving in, he extended the food to me.

"What's that?"

"Pizza," he rattled off matter-of-factly, and that crater in his cheek and those syrupy-brown eyes complemented every inch of his insanely handsome face.

"I know what that is . . ." I motioned to the pizza that he was still extending in my direction with a nod. "What I meant to say was what '*answer*'? When I walked in, you said there's your answer. What's that about?"

Was he betting I wouldn't hold up my end of the deal by steering clear of what was his temporary territory for the week? And shit, here I was, totally *not* doing what I promised.

"I know we had a deal, but you have to eat. I ordered enough to share. Pizza was a safe choice. Who doesn't love pizza? I would have asked what you liked, but I didn't want to disturb whatever you were doing in there . . ."

"Thanks, but I brought groceries. If you don't mind the intrusion, I can just make something and then be out of your way in no time at all. You can pretend I'm not even here."

He stepped closer, placing the plate on the counter near where I was standing, putting *him* near me, and damn, this man smelled amazing. So did the pizza, and my stomach growled, approving his offering.

"*Or* you can let me do something nice and just eat the pizza. Sounds to me like you could use a *quick* meal."

My cheeks heated, and I locked my arms over my chest. "I'd rather cook. My groceries will go bad if I don't, and—"

"*And* you can cook tomorrow. One day won't matter, and since dinner is on me tonight, you can return the favor tomorrow by making *us* dinner."

"Us?" I frowned. Was he *really* expecting me to cook for him?

"Yes, *us. You* and *I,* unless I should be expecting another guest. I'm not sure where they would sleep because I refuse to share the sofa." He paused and lowered his chin before continuing. "Maybe that's *your* thing, overbooking your place, hoping that the person will get annoyed and leave, leaving you with your apartment and their hard-earned money."

My mouth dropped open, and he grinned but turned his back to me, reaching for another plate which he filled with three slices before facing me again.

"You don't seriously believe I was trying to pull a scam, do you?"

"It's possible."

"I didn't ask you what was possible. I asked if you believed that's what happened."

"No, I don't. I believe it was an honest mistake. I was making a joke to lighten the mood, Noel. You seem a bit tense."

"I *am* a bit tense. You're here, in my apartment, and—"

"*You don't know me.* Right, we've gone over this already. I'm no more of a threat to you than you are to me. I thought I had proved my point by agreeing to this absurd little arrangement. Just take the pizza and say thank you," he muttered dryly, shoving a slice toward his mouth, almost half of which he devoured with one bite. I watched the pizza and then his mouth or rather his lips as he chewed slowly, leaving me in a bit of a lustful daze until I realized what I was doing and snapped out of my trance, only to find I wasn't the only one enjoying the view. His unapologetic gaze was on me, and those damn lips I had just been admiring were slightly curved, offering a cocky grin.

"We don't know each other, and for the record, just so we're clear, forgetting to cancel the reservation *was* an honest mistake. It's probably better if I prove my point by holding up my end of the deal. I'm going back to my room."

I turned to walk away just as my stomach protested again by growling loudly. Against my better judgment, I relented and reached for the plate, taking it with me. I also swiped several bottles of water from the refrigerator and a handful of napkins before making my very dramatic exit.

Just before I bent the corner, I glanced over my shoulder with the weighted feeling that he was still watching me, and, of course, he was, but his eyes were a lot lower than I liked when I mumbled, "Thanks for this."

Those syrupy-browns crawled slowly back to my face, and instead of pretending he hadn't been checking me out because, of course, this guy was too full of himself, he simply tipped his head and smiled once more. I left him there and slipped back into my room, softly closing the door behind me which I leaned against, tossing the bottles of water on the bed.

I wanted to be frustrated, but how could I be when the guy had a face and body like his? Apparently, he wasn't all that bad since he ordered and offered me dinner, but yeah, I knew better than to fall for his wit and charm because men disappoint, life disappoints, and my life was living proof of what was left after the disappointment.

Kanton.

I GLANCED AT MY phone screen, seeing Jordan's name, and I strongly considered not answering. The only reason I did was because I didn't want my not answering to become an excuse for why she hadn't vacated my space once I returned home in a week.

"Hello."

"Oh, thank goodness. I was hoping you would answer," she rushed out, causing me to regret the decision. I sank deeper into the sofa, allowing my head to fall back while I closed my eyes to prepare for whatever headache she was about to lay on me.

"What's wrong?"

"You're already irritated, and you don't have a clue why I'm calling." Whereas I sounded irritated, she sounded amused, so I made an excuse.

"I'm tired. It's been a very long day." My eyes involuntarily moved to the corner of the apartment where Noel was tucked away in her bedroom.

"Oh, that's right. You're traveling for business. Where are you again? I still can't believe your mother agreed to let you skip Christmas."

Jordan didn't know my mother, and my mother had no clue Jordan existed. That would have been a disaster in the making on both ends. Jordan was accomplished in her own right but would never meet my mother's approval.

She didn't have a college degree because the day after she graduated high school, she moved to New York and tried her hand at modeling. That didn't work out, but she did find a way to make a career out of her looks, which also created issues with us.

Her life was a little less structured, and although I supported her entrepreneurial spirit, she had no plans to settle down anytime soon. Her life was centered around late nights at clubs and celebrity events. I had no interest in either, which meant we often disagreed about the structure of our relationship. She was a fantastic woman, just not one who would fit into my world, nor did I fit into hers.

"She didn't have much of a choice. This deal was important."

"All of your deals are important, Kanton," she stated bluntly.

"Did you call to argue, because if so—"

"No, I didn't call to argue. Where business is concerned, we both know that's an argument I won't win. I called to ask for a huge favor. I know that I said I'd be out before you returned—"

"Jordan—" I pinched the bridge of my nose, and she quickly added.

"I'm not trying to prolong this. I get it. We're in two different spaces with our expectations. As much as I hate it, you and I don't fit, and for the record, I do hate it. You're an amazing guy, and the sex is irreplaceable." I smirked, shaking my head. It was. I would miss that the most. "But I'll survive . . . maybe."

"Is there a point?"

"There is. I've just received the opportunity of a lifetime, and it's last minute, which means I need to leave right away. I promised to make this separation seamless and be out by the time you returned home, and I'm keeping my promise, technically, because I won't be there, but my things will. If you can give me an extra week, I'll be completely out when I return from the UK."

"The UK?"

"Yes, I'm going to be there for six weeks. I've exclusively been signed on to a tour with a very exclusive client, so it doesn't make sense to get a new place. I have a break the week of New Year's, so I'll fly in to grab my things, but it would be amazing, and I'll forever be in your debt if you hang onto them until then."

She wasn't asking much, and it wasn't too much of an imposition, so I agreed.

"I can do that."

"Oh, thank God."

Her persistence had me asking, "You already left, haven't you?"

"On the jet as we speak."

"And if I had said no . . ."

"I would have figured something out." She sounded chipper, which made me shake my head again.

"But you knew I wouldn't say no."

"I hoped you wouldn't. Like I said, you're an amazing guy, Kanton. Just not *my* guy. I get that now, and as much as I would have loved for this to work, clearly, it doesn't."

"It doesn't," I confirmed before adding, "but you're pretty amazing yourself, Jordan."

"You're being nice."

I grinned. "I'm being honest. We just don't fit, and that's okay. I am going to miss you—"

"Me or the sex . . ." she teased.

"Both."

My dick jolted in agreement, but no matter how great the sex was, if the emotional connection wasn't there, sex was all we would be, and I wanted more.

Once again, my eyes involuntarily drifted to the corner of the apartment that shouldn't have held my interest. But it did.

"At least I wasn't alone in this."

"You weren't, and Jordan . . ."

"Yeah?"

"Congratulations. That's huge, and I'm very proud of you. I wish you the best with your career."

"Thanks, Kanton. Coming from you, that means a lot. I'll text you the dates when I'll be in town. It should only take me a day or two to get the rest of my things. I'll be in and out. Don't want Shelby coming for me."

I laughed hard. "You're safe. She knows to stay away from this one."

"Yeah, well, I'll still do my best to fly under her radar. The woman is lethal on her own, but she's deadly when it comes to you. If I hadn't seen her actual boyfriend, I'd swear there was something there—"

I frowned and clarified. "I assure you there is not. Our relationship is entirely professional."

"I know. You're not that guy. You have apparent and defined lines about certain things, but I did consider the possibility a few times. Take care, and wish me luck."

"You don't need luck. You've got this."

"I do. Talk soon."

After I ended the call, a weight lifted. When I first had the talk with Jordan, explaining how I felt things weren't working and that she and I weren't a good fit, she opposed ending things. She seemed convinced that we could find a middle ground.

I, on the other hand, did not. As much as I liked her, she and I didn't have that *thing*. Not that I've ever had that thing with anyone before to identify it, but I was sure of what it was not, and Jordan wasn't the person I could see myself with long-term.

When I thought about the two of us, I couldn't see beyond where we were at that present time. Now that she had made peace with ending things, whether because of her new career opportunity or if she realized we didn't work, I was grateful and relieved.

However, the fact that I was slightly relieved because of the woman whose apartment I was in added a new conflict to my life. One that I didn't want to consider because she and I surely didn't fit. Mostly because she loathed my existence. Sure, she found me attractive. Her roaming eyes were proof, but she didn't like me very much.

She also didn't know me. If she did, then maybe she would.

What the hell?

Why was I considering the possibility? Why did I care? I was here for one reason only. To convince Brighton to take on my firm. Exhaling a sigh, I stood up from the sofa and tossed my phone where I'd been seated so I could retrieve some lounge clothes.

The longer I sat there, the more I realized I was truly exhausted and ready to relax for the evening, do a little more research on Brighton, and then call it a night. I wasn't thrilled about sleeping on a sofa for the next few days, but at least it was pretty comfy. She had good taste, quirky and eccentric, but still good taste, nonetheless.

I collected what I would wear after my shower along with my toiletry kit and headed down the hall to the bathroom, immediately frowning once I flipped the light switch. Toilet, sink, no shower.

One bedroom, one-and-a-half baths.

Damn it.

The reminder of the apartment amenities flashed in my head. That meant . . .

My eyes traveled further to my left, where Noel's bedroom was located. The only full bath in the apartment was in her bedroom. Interesting. Unfortunately, she'd have to share because I refused to endure my stay here without washing my ass, and she'd appreciate that consideration as well.

I flipped the switch to kill the light in the hall bathroom and planted myself outside her door, where I knocked and waited.

Nothing.

I knocked again, and a few minutes later, I heard shuffling behind the door before it cracked open.

"Yes?"

This woman.

Hair a mess. Eyes narrowed. Cute little facial expression of hers anything but welcoming to the idea of me being at her door.

"We have to amend our agreement."

Her brows pinched, and she pulled the door protectively close to her body. It took all my willpower not to look down and, instead, keep my eyes trained on her face. It likely wouldn't work in my favor if she caught me checking her out while asking for an amendment to our agreement that gave me access to her bedroom.

She probably assumed I had changed my mind about her keeping rights to the bedroom, although that thought wasn't awful.

"The only full bathroom is in here . . . with *you*."

"And?" Her brows pinched more.

"We're going to have to share."

I noticed the moment when she realized the predicament, and she mumbled, "We have to share?"

"We do, which means you'll have to let me in."

"This is my room."

I grinned. "It is, and I promise not to touch anything in it, but I need access to your bathroom."

A million and one thoughts traveled through her mind. Most of them likely had the word "no" attached, but she decided to do the right thing and stepped out of the way, bringing the door with her. "Fine. Bathroom's right there. Don't use my things, and please, don't make a mess."

"You're really not great with this hosting thing."

"I'm not *your* host," she shot back and stepped into her room, pausing where she stood. She tensed when I leaned in close to her ear, and I smiled internally. I made her nervous, but not in a way that she felt I'd do her any harm. She was nervous because she didn't trust herself around me.

"Is that because you don't want to be *mine* or just because you don't like the host label?" She sucked in a sharp breath, and I pulled back, allowing my eyes to meet hers. They briefly lingered before I walked away so she could release the breath lodged in her throat in peace. As soon as I was inside the bathroom with the door securely separating us, I closed my eyes, growling as I shook my head.

"What the fuck was that?" I mumbled.

Why was I saying things about being mine to this woman?

Because she was incredibly sexy, and I wanted her to be my host. My *personal* host. The swell of my dick was a clear sign of how much I wanted her, period.

I was bombarded with her essence when I opened my eyes and looked around. The light scent of the same notes of fruit that clung to her skin. Her things covered the counter in organized chaos. The bright colors that she used to decorate. The space was clean, and the bathroom was spotless but slightly cluttered with her things.

Skincare products, lotions, perfumes, hair ties, and clips . . . None of these bothered me when I loathed how Jordan kept the same things in my bathroom.

Needing to make this as quick as possible, I pulled the glass door aside, adjusted the water, removed my body wash from my toiletry kit, and placed it on the shelf. I should have adjusted the temperature to ice cold to temper whatever the hell I was currently dealing with, but I allowed the steamy hot spray to flow while I stripped out of my clothes then eased into the stall.

The size was decent, which is another perk for this property. I was impressed with Noel's decision to invest in this specific apartment. Another random thought that once again had me shaking my head.

Why the hell was I keeping score with Noel?

Because you and your dick are very intrigued by her. The thought had me growling internally before my eyes shifted to the tiny shelf with a plastic bottle with bright pink letters and a picture of a grapefruit plastered. Instead of reaching for my own, I lifted hers and held it to my nose after flipping the top and regretted the decision when thoughts of her in here with me and grapefruit-scented suds careening down her body being chased by my hands took over.

"Fuck."

I quickly flipped the lid back, replaced her body wash with mine, and hurried through showering so that I could get out of her space and reset my brain, which had somehow confused the reason why I was here. Me being in Atlanta in her apartment had nothing to do with the very erotic thoughts I was having about Noel.

Noel.

KANTON IS IN *my room.*

In my bathroom.

Naked.

Well, of course, he's naked because he's in the shower. The problem was not him being nude but that I *liked* the idea of *him* being naked in *my* bathroom. I also liked the idea of me being naked in there *with* him.

That is not what I need right now.

My life was in shambles, and Kanton being here was proof of how *shambled* my life truly was. For goodness' sake, I let him share my apartment just to avoid returning money I did not have.

Shambles.

My phone startled me when it notified me of a call. I shifted from the foot of my bed where I'd found refuge since my bathroom door closed, grabbed my phone, settled on the side next to my nightstand, and accepted a call from Simone while my eyes landed on the door that separated me from Kanton.

"Hey."

"What's wrong? Why are you whispering?" she rushed out. I lowered my eyes and then peeked at the door again.

"Nothing's wrong. I don't want *him* to hear me."

"*Him*, as in the sexy houseguest?"

"Don't call him that."

"Then deny it and tell me he's not classified as such."

I can't. I can't. I can't.

56

"Simone . . ." I groaned.

"Okay, fine. Why would he hear you? I thought you were confined to your room while he had full rein of the rest of your apartment."

"I am, but I haphazardly forgot one small detail."

"What?"

"I only have one full bathroom."

"In your room . . . ahhh . . ." she squealed. "Is he in your bathroom? Like right *now*? That's why you're whispering. Shit, Noel. What does he look like naked? Did you peek? Please tell me you peeked. Wait, send me a picture. Can you steal one?"

"Yes, yes, I don't know. No, hell no, and no."

"That was a lot of answers, and I still have no damn clarity."

"You asked a lot of damn questions, but the most important is no, I will *not* be sending any pictures because, what the fuck, Simone?"

"Don't you dare act like that's beneath you because we both know it isn't."

Okay, so maybe I'd snuck photos of men and sent them to her before, but at least I had the right because I was interested and needed her help gauging whether to shoot my shot, or I was involved and wanted to brag about enjoying the time of my life with a man I wasn't planning on making a real connection with, *but* they were never naked.

Okay, another lie. Naked in my bed but covered by bedding, and why the hell am I debating this?

"I'm not acting like it's beneath me because, pending the circumstances, we both know it is not. However, this is very different," I hissed, then cut my eyes toward the bathroom door. "We're not dating, involved, or even a one-night stand. He's a stranger who bullied his way into my apartment."

She was silent. *Too* silent.

"Simone, did you hear me?"

"I heard you."

"Then why aren't you saying anything . . .?"

"Because what I'm going to say, you're going to deny, and I just enjoyed Christmas caroling, and I'm not trying to ruin my holiday cheer by arguing with you, only for you to admit later that I was right, and you were wrong or in denial."

My mouth dropped open, and she followed with, "Just fuck him, get it over with, and then you can pretend it didn't happen after this week is over."

"Why on earth would you say that?"

"Because I know you. I'm your very best friend. You and I are so connected you literally don't have to speak, and I can still feel your thoughts. I know, and what I *know* is that you like this guy, even if only in a physical sense."

"I—"

She quickly cut me off with, "You let him stay."

"I didn't have a choice, and *you* told me to let him."

"Because it's what *you* wanted; again, I know you."

"I couldn't afford not to let him stay. A stranger in my apartment is *not* what I wanted."

"*Emmie.*"

One word had me slamming my mouth shut and swallowing whatever argument I prepared to combat that she would say next. "Emmie" was short for "emergency credit card." I had two thousand dollars on that card and vowed only to use it in case of emergencies. I could have easily refunded his money using Emmie, but I didn't.

"Well?" Simone asked in amusement. The kind of amusement that screamed, "I pulled your card when you refused to pull out your own to solve this issue."

"This technically *isn't* an emergency," I tried, but my argument was weak.

"You allowing—as you keep stating—a *stranger* to share space with you, a man who you don't know shit about, clearly falls under the 'emergency' category. You simply chose not to use Emmie because you didn't feel threatened by this man *and* wanted him there."

"You're exaggerating the details."

"*I'm* being honest when *you* are not. Now, I suggest you take a minute to be real with yourself, even if you don't want to be real with me. I'm going to hang up now and maybe, just maybe, I'll get a photo from you. If not, then even better because that means you like this man enough not to share. I love you, Noel. The past few months have been mentally taxing, your finances are questionable, and your Christmas is not what you hoped it would be, *but* that doesn't mean you can't enjoy the gift that the universe dropped in your lap. Maybe you might even consider sitting on his and sliding south on his North Pole. Either way, I support whatever decision you make because, again, I love you. You need a win, Noel. Think about it. One week of fun, and then the two of you return to your individual lives. No harm, no foul."

"It's not that simple," I pouted.

"It can be. Now, I have to go. Mom's going to have my ass if I'm not downstairs in these ugly-ass onesie pajamas."

I grinned. "You love those ugly-ass onesies."

"I do, but I'm trying to spare your feelings."

Because I love those ugly-ass Christmas onesies too, and if I were home with my family, I'd be wearing matching ones with them.

"Which I love you for, but go. I'll figure this out."

"Ahem, I'm sure you will," she said with a little too much candor in her voice, but I couldn't travel down that road because, at that very moment, a cloud of steam escaped the bathroom, followed by the man in question.

I quickly ended the call and straightened my spine, feeling guilty about the conversation I'd just been having about him. Also, his current state didn't help the situation.

The man was shirtless, in a pair of heather-gray sleep pants that were way too thin and sitting extremely low on his trim waist. I did have the restraint to allow my eyes to travel north instead of south, however, incredibly slow, enjoying every line and contour of the muscles in his abs, chest, broad shoulders, and defined arms. One of those arms was tucked, holding the clothes he'd just come out of, and the other hung loosely at his side, gripping a toiletry kit with his fingers.

It was insanely unfair how perfect this man's body was, and just as my eyes felt greedy, deciding, why not, and traveled low to steal a quick peek of the rest of him, he cleared his throat, and my face blazed with embarrassment for what I was doing.

Regardless, my eyes found his, and the levity dancing in them from having caught me doing what he had done several times today humbled me.

I shifted in place uncomfortably. "All done?"

"Yep."

I straightened my spine a little more. "I hope you didn't leave a mess."

Too late. There was definitely one in my panties.

"Nope. Cleaned up after myself."

He was still staring at me, smiling arrogantly and still standing at the foot of my bed, smelling all masculine and good, assaulting me with a hint of citrus and bergamot, and, oh Lord, this would be a long week.

"You're still here."

"I am."

"Is there something else you need?"

Why did I ask that?

The flicker of longing in his eyes and the way they glided smoothly over my entire body had my nerve endings going haywire.

"Blanket and pillow."

"What?" I shook away the ungodly thoughts that I was having.

"It's late, and unless you've changed your mind about my sleeping arrangements . . ." His eyes lowered to my bed before they rounded back up to me. "I'm going to need a pillow and blanket for the sofa."

"Oh, right." I snatched up a pillow from my bed and shoved it into his chest. He moved quickly enough to cuff it in the arm that wasn't holding his clothes, and I eased around him, heading to the door. "The linen closet is just outside my room to the left. I don't have extra pillows, so that will have to suffice, but you can change the pillowcase, and blankets are in there."

He didn't move right away, those jovial eyes finding me again in a way that heated my skin as he passed. I fought another deep inhale of him.

This is going to be a very, *very* long week.

"Thanks," he muttered, stepping into the hallway. Just before I could close him out, he leaned in, bringing his face close to mine. "Good night, Noel. Sleep tight."

I frowned hard, hurried out of his personal space, and slammed my door, stealing one last look at his unfairly handsome face that I would bet my last dollar would be in my dreams tonight.

Once I collected myself, I leaned my forehead against the door and pointlessly attempted to calm myself by inhaling several deep breaths to slow the erratic pace of my heart. Kanton Joseph was going to test my restraint, and deep down inside, I was somewhat looking forward to the challenge.

Kanton.

I SLEPT LIKE SHIT, and not because of the sofa that was subbing as my bed for the week. It was actually pretty cozy. My issue was the woman who had totally consumed my thoughts. Instead of doing as she suggested and changing the linen on the pillow, I retrieved a blanket and tossed both on the sofa before searching her kitchen for something to calm my nerves and possibly help me sleep.

I lucked up and found a bottle of tequila, which wasn't my favorite but would have to do, so I grabbed a glass, poured a shot, and then tossed it back.

After one more, my shoulders relaxed enough for me to try to get some sleep. I returned to the living room and got situated on the sofa with her pillow beneath my head. I folded an arm and tucked it behind me, allowing my other hand to rest on my chest.

That hand found its way to my abs and inched lower with each breath I inhaled. The light scent of coconut and berries clinging to her pillow had my mind traveling to places it had no business venturing, with my hand moving farther south until I realized where I was.

Needless to say, I didn't get much rest, setting the stage for a grumpy day. Not to mention, I was in dire need of caffeine, and the only thing Noel had that remotely resembled coffee was some French vanilla and caramel macchiato pods, which didn't classify as coffee, in my opinion. At present, I was stepping off the elevator in search of a very strong brew and maybe halfway decent breakfast.

"Good morning, Lewis, right?"

"Good morning, and you got it." He smiled widely after I stepped to the concierge's station. Lewis wore khaki slacks, a navy blazer, and a crisp white shirt as the day before. His salt-and-pepper hair was neatly groomed, giving him a clean-cut and professional look. Lewis was a man after my own heart who apparently took his job seriously.

"I was wondering if you could direct me to a good cup of coffee and breakfast. Any suggestions?"

"Sure, sure . . ." He smiled, nodding. "If you don't feel like battling the cold, there's a restaurant in the building on the second floor. Pretty decent food, but too commercialized if you ask me. A few blocks up that way, there's a place a little less appealing regarding décor, but the food is top-tier. It's called Hanna Mae's, and I suggest the Hero's Breakfast. A big ol' stack, cheese eggs, and sausage. If that's not your thing, you can go the healthy route. They've got that too, but the coffee's strong, and the service is great."

"Sounds like just what I need." I nodded as my stomach approved. "Do they offer carryout service as well?"

He frowned a bit but nodded. "You don't plan on eating there? Food is much better when it's hot off the grill."

"I agree, and no, I plan on dining in, but I figured I might bring something back for Noel. You know if she dines there much?" I tried since he seemed very familiar with her. He might know if she frequented the place because it was close by.

Lewis frowned at me and then inadvertently looked past me toward the elevators. "She's still here?"

"She is."

"Interesting. I thought since you were renting her place, she worked everything out and got home to her family."

"Not exactly. I'm sure that was the intention, but she's still here."

"Interesting," he stated again before rolling his shoulders back. "And you're staying there, in her place, with her, for how long?"

"The weekend and first part of the week."

"She's okay with that? I don't know much about the Shared Space thing, but I didn't assume it meant actually *sharing* space with strangers. Only the place."

I grinned and nodded. "Typically, that's how it works, but there was a bit of a mix-up, and my reservation never got canceled."

"And she offered to let you stay?" The look he gave was accusing and protective, as if trying to gauge how agreeable Noel was to the situation. I wouldn't give him all the details, but I would ease his mind because Lewis was apparently worried. That, however, made sense, considering he had an affinity for Noel based on the warning of his appreciation of her.

"She did. We've found a way to make it work."

"Interesting."

Damn, he really liked that word.

"Lewis, I assure you, I am not a threat to Ms. Anderson . . ."

"You definitely are not." He rolled his shoulders back again, offering me a warning look that screamed there would be consequences if I decided to change my stance on causing Noel harm. I almost laughed at the idea of Lewis launching a vicious attack, but I respected the guy for making sure I knew he would try.

"Understood, but again, I'm here on business. That's my only goal. Noel and I have agreed to coexist while I'm in town. You can rest assured there won't be any issues. I give you my word."

He eyed me skeptically for a long moment before offering his hand. I accepted, and we shook, sealing a gentleman's agreement. "Enjoy your stay then, and I suppose I should be more concerned about you than her?"

"Pardon?"

His smile expanded the expanse of his face before he offered, "Surviving a Noel Christmas. That woman lives and breathes the holidays, and since she's not going home to spend it with her family,

I can imagine she will set up right here in her apartment. Come to think of it, I haven't seen a tree come through yet. Maybe I missed it."

"A tree?"

"Yep, the biggest, fullest tree you could ever imagine. It's her thing. She does that even though she's usually not here."

Interesting.

Now, *I* was the one using the word. That explained the plastic bins of ornaments and lights, but there was no tree . . . which had me thinking.

"You said if I needed anything, you could assist, right?"

"I surely did. What can I do for you?"

"I'd like to get a tree for Noel. Would you be able to handle that?"

Lewis frowned a bit, shaking his head. "The lots are likely all sold out. Not much left to choose since we're so close to the day."

"The stores are usually stocked quite nicely. Cost is not an issue. You can get the biggest they have."

"Artificial?" His eyes went wide before he quickly shook his head. "No can do."

"Why not?" My brows pinched.

"You want to get an artificial tree for Noel Anderson?"

"Considering this is last minute, I think that would work, and she should appreciate the gesture."

Lewis smiled and shrugged. "If that's what you want, then sure, I'll take care of it. I can have one delivered within the hour, I'm sure. There's a place nearby."

"Perfect." I reached into my back pocket and removed my wallet and a business card. "My number's on there. Let me know the cost, and I'll make sure it's covered."

He accepted the card. "I'll get you a tab started with the concierge instead of billing what you need to the apartment. You can leave a card on file or cover the cost when your stay with us is up. They offer carryout service as well."

"Sounds good." We shook on it, and then I pointed toward the door. "A few blocks up that way, correct?"

"You got it. Hanna Mae's. Tell them Lewis sent you, and they'll take good care of you."

I tipped my head. "Appreciate you, Lewis." I paused briefly. "Oh, and don't forget, the *biggest* tree you can find."

One that *won't* fit in her bedroom, so she'll have to enjoy it in the living room . . . with me.

"Will do."

I left him there, but I was unsure why I wanted to give Noel Christmas when Christmas was one of my least favorite holidays. Somehow, knowing she enjoyed it made me open to enjoying it with her. There was no other reason why I was allowing myself to be distracted by a woman when I needed to be laser-focused on finding a way to get to Brighton to close the biggest deal of my life.

However, the thought of making this woman smile was my new motivation. So far, the only emotions I'd experienced with Noel were agitation, defeat, and a tiny hint of lust, which I also shared. The challenge of making her smile simply for my own enjoyment was the reason I was offering up limitless funds to punch a tree and on my way to grab breakfast for a woman I barely knew.

Noel, Noel, what the hell am I getting myself into with you?

Half an hour later, I was back at the apartment, electing to get my food to go as well since I wanted to ensure I was there when the tree arrived. I walked into the unit, placing our breakfast on the counter before I went to offer an invitation for Noel to join me.

Once I approached the door, I heard the light hum of voices and assumed she was awake since the TV was on. After a few light knocks, I was blessed with the visual of those alluring eyes and, much to my dismay, she was covered in red and green plaid pants that were far too slouchy and an oversized crewneck fleece shirt that had me grinning when I read the print. *Dear Santa, before I explain, how much do you know?*

"Yes . . .?"

My eyes shot up to meet hers, and my smile challenged the frown on her face.

"Good morning . . ."

"Questionable," she muttered. "Did you need something?"

"Not much of a morning person, are we?"

"Usually I am, but given the situation . . ." Her eyes narrowed on me, and I chuckled.

"I'd like to offer a truce. I bought us breakfast."

"You didn't have to do that."

"No, I didn't, but I figured it's the least I can do since I've inconvenienced you for the week, albeit not really my fault."

"And there it is. If this is your idea of a truce, you might want to revisit the definition."

"I'm well aware of the definition. I have breakfast from Hanna Mae's. Lewis suggested the Hero, so I got that for both of us. Why don't you come join me?"

"You're friends with Lewis now?" Her eyes narrowed again.

"Maybe not friends but acquaintances. He pretty much threatened me if I did you any harm and then suggested your favorite breakfast spot, so I'd say that counts for something."

Her eyes lit up, and she smiled. "He threatened you?"

"In a matter of speaking, yes. The guy seems to be quite fond of you."

"That's because he and I *are* friends." She shrugged.

"I noticed, so how about it? You joining me, or what?"

"You sure you want me to? If I accept, we're breaking the rules of our agreement."

"We are, but I will make concessions for now."

"Right," she muttered as I walked away. I didn't bother looking behind me but secretly hoped she'd accept the offer. She did. Instead of finding our way to the small table near her kitchen, she hopped on the counter near the carryout bag and removed both containers.

One she extended my way, and the other she opened in her lap after I accepted. I watched her eyes slowly close as she inhaled the aroma of the hearty breakfast. She smiled widely, sending her hand back into the to-go bag to retrieve the two sets of plastic utensils, offering up one to me before she ripped open the other, mumbling a short blessing before diving right into her food.

No shame in this one.

I turned toward the counter, grinning with pleasure at how happy a simple breakfast made her, in turn, weaving happiness into my chest as I ripped open my utensils and then my own container. When I turned back toward Noel, I caught her unabashedly swallowing a mouthful.

"Good?" I questioned, motioning toward the plastic container in her lap.

"See for yourself," she offered, shoving a chunk of fluffy golden pancakes into her mouth.

I did, and good Lord, I see why she was humming approvingly as she enjoyed her meal. The buttery soft pancakes melted against my tongue in a melody of maple syrup and brown sugar.

"This is heaven."

"Sure is. Now, you see why Lewis suggested it. Thanks for this, by the way." She spoke through a mouthful, which, instead of turning me off, had me chuckling at how much she was enjoying her food to the point of not caring that doing so in such an uncouth manner might seem less appealing.

I was curious to the point of desperation of wanting more of Noel, her secrets, the untold stories, hell, anything which had me asking, "He mentioned you usually go home for Christmas?"

She paused briefly but kept her eyes on her food while stabbing at a fluff of scrambled eggs. "I do."

"Yet, you're still here. Why?" Her eyes shot over to mine finally, and I quickly added, "I'm only asking because you rented your place, which means you intended not to be here. What changed?"

"I got sick . . ."

My eyes narrowed, and she rolled hers. "Just a cold. You don't need to contact the CDC. It was pretty average, but I couldn't go home."

"Colds don't usually prevent people from traveling. Especially not *average* colds."

She nodded in agreement. "My dad had cancer." I was about to speak, but she quickly added, "He's in remission, but his system is still recovering. They both said it would be fine for me to be there, but it's my dad, you know? I didn't want to risk his health just because I wanted to be home for Christmas."

My heart clenched with the thought of being in the same position. Sure, I had a conflicted relationship with both my parents, but I loved them dearly and couldn't imagine losing either. The stress of the possibility had to be heavy for anyone.

"I'm glad he's on the mend and hate that you missed the holiday with them."

"Thank you." She smiled softly. "What about you? You're here instead of with your family?"

I nodded. "The deal I'm trying to close could potentially be the best business opportunity I've ever brokered."

"But what about your family? Won't you miss them, and they you for the holiday?"

I stabbed at my pancakes and lifted a forkful, slowly chewing while I decided how to respond. Family was a touchy subject for me. People rarely understood my opposition with mine. Their first thought was you were rich, so how bad could it have been? Noel watched me intently, and for some reason, I wanted to offer her a sliver of truth, even if not the full scope.

"My mother will be too busy with her holiday production to worry about missing me, and my father will be too busy appeasing my mother while she orchestrates her holiday production. They'll survive my not being there."

"That sounds very complicated."

"Because it is. The holidays are overrated, at least when it comes to my family. It's more of a performance for a press release than a family gathering. Working through Christmas is much more favorable than what I'm missing."

Her mouth dropped open before she slowly dragged those luscious lips back together, and I enjoyed the visual far too much. "The holidays are *not* overrated. That's simply blasphemy. Christmas is my favorite time of the year."

"So I've heard." I smirked. She narrowed her eyes, and I added, "Lewis."

"Right. I'm sure he filled you in on how much of a holiday enthusiast I am."

"He did, but he only had great things to say. It seems you're quite the crowd-pleaser here at your building. Your gifts are top-tier and very thoughtful."

She smiled proudly, and it swelled my chest. "He did?"

"Christmas means a lot to you, huh?"

"It does. This will be the first time I won't spend with my family." Her shoulders slumped when reality gut punched her.

Right on cue, there was a knock at the door, and I pointed to the door with my plastic fork. "Maybe that will help." I placed my food on the counter and stepped closer, taking hers from her lap and putting it on the counter. "Come on."

"Where are we going?"

"To the door. I got something for you."

She hadn't moved yet, so I turned to face her again.

"What's at the door?"

"A tree. When Lewis mentioned how much you loved Christmas, I realized you didn't have one. It's like you planned to . . ." I pointed to the plastic bins that still littered the living room. ". . . but something happened. I decided it was the least I could do."

It took a minute for her brain to process and catch up, but when it did, she smiled beautifully, and my dick responded appropriately. "You got me a tree?"

"I did."

"Seriously?" She was beaming like a child as she hopped off the counter and hurried to the door. The minute she swung it open, she found two gentlemen who I assumed worked for the property based on their matching pants and shirts standing there with a massive box between them . . . and that smile disappeared.

She looked at them, the box, and then swung her eyes back to me, pointing toward the hallway.

"What's that?"

"A tree."

"That's *not* a tree."

I approached, lowering my eyes to the tree box that clearly was a tree based on the stock photos displayed on both sides. "Yes, it is. See?" Confused, I pointed to the side of the box after catching the smug grins the men were sporting.

"I mean, it is a tree, but not a *real* one."

Ahhh, now, that made sense. My mother made sure the main tree in our house, which was positioned in the foyer, was live. However, she still had several more strategically placed throughout our home, similar to this one.

"It's a tree, Noel . . ."

"Is not. That's . . ." She frowned and dramatically threw an arm out to the side. ". . . plastic and metal, which is unacceptable. A tree has a spirit, a soul, smells like pine, and it just feels good. *That* . . ." she offered even more dramatically again, pausing, "is *not* the same."

"You don't want it?" I asked in frustration. I was trying to do something nice, and here she was being unappreciative. This was *precisely* why I didn't like Christmas. There was no real holiday cheer, even though people claimed to be all loving and ardent toward others.

Noel's eyes slowly danced over my face, like she was attempting to soften the blow of what was coming. "I . . . it's great . . . and I really appreciate you doing this for me, but that's . . ."

". . . not a real tree," I murmured.

One of the men said, "We bringing it in or what? Lewis said she wasn't going to want this thing. We should have listened."

He warned me. I should have listened.

He knew that she had an affinity for real trees.

She carefully lifted her eyes to me because she didn't want to be rude, but she also didn't want the damn tree. I wanted her smile back, so I quickly shook my head. "No, you can take it back. Please apologize to Lewis and tell him to bill me for any inconvenience caused by returning that."

"We got you covered, and, Noel," one of them spoke, turning his attention to her. When she was focused on him, he continued. "Lewis said he called over to a tree lot. Their stock was limited, but they promised to hold the best of what they had for you as long as you can get there before they close tonight."

"Aw, that's perfect. Tell him I said thank you."

What the fuck?

"Why didn't he just tell me that in the first place?" I stated roughly through my annoyance.

The other guy shrugged as he leaned to lift the box upright to place it on the dolly off to the side. I hadn't noticed it until now. Once they had it secured, he offered, "Said you were determined for him to order one instead. The biggest, most expensive they had. He was doing what you asked."

What he knew she would hate. Maybe Lewis and I weren't friends after all.

"Right."

Once they were gone, I returned to the kitchen, grabbed what was left of my food, and settled on the sofa. I retrieved my laptop so that I could finish researching Brighton's companies. I needed every single detail I could devour, not only about him but about the three competing firms that had found their way to the top of his list—a list I wasn't blessed enough to be considered for. I decided it was best to shift my focus back to the reason why I was here.

"What are you doing?"

"Working."

"Oh, well, thanks again for trying. I really appreciate it."

"Did you now?" I lifted my eyes to hers and instantly regretted my foul mood. Yes, I was being every bit of an ass, but I was annoyed that I allowed this woman to affect me enough to have me purchasing trees instead of dumping my energy into closing the deal with Brighton. That wasn't Noel's fault; it was mine.

"I did. Regardless of whether you believe it . . ." She stood there staring, and when she realized I wasn't going to cave, she retreated. "I, um, I guess I'll leave you alone. Thanks again for breakfast too. I really appreciate it."

I should have said something, but instead, I let her walk away, and as soon as I heard the soft click of her bedroom door, I threw my head back and closed my eyes.

What the fuck are you doing, Kanton?

Noel.

I **FELT TERRIBLE. KANTON** bought me a tree. And breakfast. And I basically shitted on the effort like a spoiled brat. So, yeah, I felt awful. It wasn't that I wasn't grateful because I was. That was the sweetest thing that anyone had done for me in . . .

Hell, since I couldn't remember when, which was the problem.

Evan started off just like Kanton. Saying and doing all the right things, and then the *real* him showed up. He was a selfish asshole who didn't give a damn about me or what I wanted.

Now, I felt like my life was circling the block again because this infuriating man I was insanely attracted to was slowly crawling beneath my skin. It was no longer just about how sexy the guy was, and he was, indeed, romantic porn in the flesh, but it was now about me actually liking the guy. I'd misjudged him, even if just a little, and now, I felt terrible.

He bought me a tree.

My stomach twisted in disgust as I stared blankly at nothing in particular. After a long moment, my shoulders deflated even more, and I knew I had to fix this. I needed to apologize and properly thank him. Maybe if I wasn't too late, I could call down to Lewis and have him bring the tree back.

I'm awful.

An awful, ungrateful human.

Closing my eyes briefly, I regrouped and then turned to face my door, gathering the courage to go do the right thing. When I passed the kitchen, I peeked into the living room and found Kanton with a scowl beneath a pair of square-framed glasses that gave him a distinguished look. The computer propped on his thighs and the laser focus added to the appeal, which made me feel even worse. Here I am, lusting after the man to whom I was unnecessarily rude.

Yep, you're a terrible human, Noel.

Where the hell is your Christmas cheer?

I hesitantly moved to the living room and stopped at the edge of the sofa, but Kanton didn't acknowledge me immediately. When he did, his expression schooled, and damn if that stoic look didn't make him that much more attractive.

"Did you need something?"

"Yes, actually, I did. I know I'm breaking the 'stay in my room' part of the deal again, but maybe you'll offer me a pass after I say what I have to say."

"I didn't expect you would actually spend the entire time I was here cooped up in your room. I'm not that much of an asshole. This is your space, and you're free to move about however you like."

"Right . . ." I huffed a sigh, feeling even worse. "Which confirms that you're not the asshole in this particular situation— however, I reserve the right to adjust my opinion as we navigate the rest of your time here."

He smiled. Thank goodness.

"You wouldn't be *you* if you didn't leave a little wiggle room to be on the right side of things, now would you?"

"Nope, *but* I owe you an apology." He scowled at me, and I added, "About the tree."

"You don't owe me anything." He placed his laptop on the sofa beside him and tugged off the glasses. I took that as a sign of him welcoming the conversation, so I eased onto the massive leather trunk, which doubled as storage and my coffee table, and placed my hands in my lap.

"I do. You got me a tree . . ."

"Made of plastic and metal," he stated with amusement in his tone that traveled up to his eyes.

"Well, yeah, that part, but it was still very sweet, and considering how I inconvenienced you by being here when I shouldn't, you really didn't have to, so thank you."

"You're welcome."

"I also want you to know I'm usually not this much of a Grinch. I'm typically pretty happy-spirited 90 percent of the time, but the past few months have been a bit taxing on me mentally and emotionally. Then I got stuck here for the holidays, and, well, it's not an excuse, but it's the truth."

"Stuck here with *me* for the holidays."

My eyes widened, and I smiled softly, shrugging a little. "That part isn't so bad. You're kind of nice to look at."

Being stuck here with Kanton wasn't bad at all. He was broody and uptight but very easy on the eyes.

"Good to know I'm aesthetically pleasing enough to place a check in the positive column of your pros and cons for this disastrous holiday week."

I grinned and shrugged again. "I mean, you are all this . . ." I flicked my wrist in his direction. "Which again is easier to ignore than the asshole."

"I'm back to being an asshole." He arched a brow, and, well, damn, this man's face was praiseworthy.

"For now, we share the title, so, yes, but I was thinking I should call the concierge to see if Lewis can send the tree back up."

"*Or* . . ." he added, scooting to the edge of the sofa where he placed his hands on my knees. The warmth of his palms and the gentle squeeze from his very long and nimble fingers through the thin material of my pajama pants had something dangerous swarming in the pit of my stomach.

Had me thinking about how nimble those fingers were.

"We could go check out the tree they're holding for you."

I was not expecting that response, and, well, shit, I quickly shook my head. "No, we don't have to do that. The one you purchased is just fine, and you have work to do. You didn't come here to tree shop with your forced roommate."

He smiled sinfully sweetly. "Is it just fine?"

The tree?

It wasn't, but . . .

It took me a beat too long to respond, and he apparently read my mind.

"That's what I thought."

"I didn't say anything."

"You, no, but your face did, and it screamed that the plastic and metal tree would totally ruin your Christmas."

"My Christmas is already ruined."

"And here I was thinking we were making progress. We're back to you being stuck here with me instead of enjoying a perfect Christmas with your family?" he murmured, and I grinned.

"I thought we agreed being here with you, albeit not expected or my preference, was in the bonus column."

"For now . . ." he countered.

"Well, yeah, but it's still a bonus."

"Listen, you're right about one thing. I didn't come here to tree shop, and I do have work I need to get done, *but* if you can give me a few hours to power through a few things, we can go out later and get you a tree. They close at eight, right?"

My face lit up with the possibility. Not just with the prospect of getting a tree but also with Kanton being a part of the experience. "Eight, yes."

"Give me a few hours to tackle this, and I'm all yours for the evening."

The way my stomach flipped with that decree—a promise of spending time with Kanton while he was all mine, surely wasn't what he meant, but my body still received it as such.

"Oh, okay, perfect. I'll get out of your way."

His hands fell from my thighs, and I immediately missed the connection. His hands on me weren't the explosive sparks and electric jolts that love spoke of. It was more of a naturally organic connection, which also had my stomach in knots.

I was walking back to my room when he called out behind me. "And, Noel?"

"Yeah . . .?" I turned to face him, and those glasses were back on his face, with the computer in his lap. There was something about that bossy, sexy look that really worked for him.

Dear Lord, save me.

"I meant what I said about you being confined to your room. I'm sure we can coexist without you being exiled from your own living space."

I smiled. "We can, but I think I will binge-watch some Christmas movies until you're done. I feel a little more *Christmassy* now, so thanks."

He nodded his approval and lowered his eyes to the laptop. I almost skipped back to my room, grinning, as I closed the door and leaned against it for a minute to fully absorb what had just happened.

Maybe Simone was right. Perhaps the universe was doing its best to offer me a very Merry Christmas after all.

"You're wearing *that*?"

I looked down at my jeans, duck boots, and bright red sweatshirt that read "*Son of a Nutcracker*".

"Yes, why? You don't like it?" I said teasingly. Kanton was not a Christmas guy. I could tell from his demeanor when discussing the topic. He was also very conservative. The guy had style, even now, dressed in jeans, a cable knit sweater, and a stylish army green field jacket, so it wasn't that. He looked like a winter ad for tall, dark, and sexy, but there was nothing Christmas about him at all.

"It's . . . *interesting.*"

I rolled my eyes, turned to the coatrack near the door, and grabbed the bright green scarf that I intended to wear, but instead, I lifted onto my toes and draped it around his neck.

With a displeased expression, Kanton lifted the end, reading the printed letters that were weaved into the soft, fuzzy fabric. "*This is as Jolly as I get.*" His eyes found mine. "Seriously?"

"It's fitting, don't you think?"

"No, I don't, and I'm not wearing this."

"Yes, you are. You have to embrace the spirit of Christmas to pick the perfect tree, and that will help. As much as I love the sexy, GQ resort look you have going on, you need something Christmassy, or this won't work."

He stepped closer and smiled smugly. "You think I'm sexy?"

Yes, yes, I do.

"Your look, not *you.*"

He chuckled in a way that let me know he read between the lines, and I stepped around him, reaching for the door. Kanton walked up close behind me so that his chest brushed my back. "And for the record, *I'm* not picking the perfect tree. *You* are. I don't know a damn thing about tree selection and have no plans on learning."

I threw my head back so that I could grab a peek at his face, and it landed with a thud against his chest. "Nope. Not an option. If you're doing this, then it will be as a *participant.* Not a *bystander.*"

He groaned. "You're really making me regret my decision to be a part of this."

"Don't be a Debbie Downer. You can't possibly be that much of a Scrooge."

We stepped out into the hall, and Kanton pressed the code to lock my door. I watched, enjoying the idea of this being a regular thing, and I had to shake away the thought, which I did when he fell in with me, heading toward the elevators.

"I'm not a Scrooge. Christmas just really isn't my thing."

"Care to explain why?"

"Not particularly." His tone was muted, so I assumed there was something he wasn't willing to discuss, so I left it alone. Instead, I turned to him and changed the subject.

"What's this big business deal that you have to close while you're here, and why during Christmas? I thought you corporate types took off the entire month during the holidays." I smiled teasingly.

"Possibly *some* corporate types, but as the owner of my company and a minority in the field I'm in, I have to work harder than anyone else, which means me being here during the holdings. My team is off enjoying their families."

"You actually are a good guy. You're doing all the heavy lifting while your employees get to spend the holiday with their loved ones. Admirable."

He leveled his eyes to mine. "Did you assume I *wasn't* a good guy?" I smiled inconspicuously before he murmured, "Of course you did."

"What's the big business deal, or is it top secret?"

We stepped off the elevator and fell in step again. "It's not top secret, but also not something I choose to broadcast."

"You don't have to tell me then." I pouted slightly, feeling disappointed.

"I don't mind. It's rather boring, though, for most."

"I love boring," I said, perking up, and he shot me a "whatever" look before explaining.

"The deal is with Prestige Luxury Brands. They're family-owned but publicly traded, meaning they have access to a lot of capital. Unfortunately, they're not doing the best with their brand. The company is hemorrhaging money because of poor management decisions, and I want them to take me on to help restructure how they're spending to keep them from going bankrupt and to revamp how they're marketing their brand."

"That wasn't so boring."

He gave me another look that had me smiling wider. "I mean, it wasn't hang-on-the-edge-of-your-seat excitement, but not exactly *boring*. When's your meeting?"

"I don't have one."

I paused. "Wait. You don't have a meeting? How is that going to work?"

"I haven't figured that part out yet. Not only do I *not* have a meeting, but he's already selected the three firms he wants to work with. I'm not one of the three on the list, but he lives in this building, and I've never been one to shy away from a challenge."

"That's why you booked my place and accepted my deal."

He nodded. "Pretty much."

"Technically, you need to be here. Maybe I should renegotiate that 25 percent discount."

He gave me a warning look, and I shrugged. "You can't blame a girl for trying."

"Yes, I can."

"Who's the guy?" I asked, feeling a need to help if I could. I was familiar with many of the residents who lived here. His determination was impressive and relatable.

"What guy?"

"You said the guy you want to work with lives in this building."

"Oh, Richard Brighton. I was hoping that maybe Lewis could help me access him."

I smiled knowingly, stopping to inform him, "Although he would gladly help because that's just who he is, you don't need Lewis. I can't get you a meeting with Brighton, but I can get you in the same room with him."

"You know Brighton?"

"I do, and I know his wife even better. She invites me to their annual Christmas Eve party every year, but I usually decline because I go home for the holidays. She really loves the gingerbread cookies I bake for her every Christmas, and since I'm here, maybe I'll go, and you can be my plus-one."

The way his face did that happy thing had my stomach in knots again.

"You'd do that for me?"

"Sure, why not? You bought me a tree, albeit metal and plastic, but you're totally making up for that terrible lapse in judgment by agreeing to shop for a real one with me."

He chuckled and nodded, leaning into me when his lips brushed my ear, and when I felt the warmth of his breath, I froze. "Looks like you might be in the position to renegotiate that 25 percent, after all, Ms. Anderson."

Before I could fully enjoy the proximity, he was gone, but he extended a hand to me, which I accepted.

"Looks like I've got some tree shopping to do."

He tugged me into his side as we walked through the garage toward my car. It was beginning to feel *a lot* like Christmas.

Kanton.

"How's it going?" When Shelby asked the question, I glanced at Noel, who was giddy and overjoyed at being in her happy place.

I had stepped away to accept a call from Shelby while Noel chatted it up with the tree lot owner like they were old friends when, in reality, she'd never met the guy before. I couldn't help the smile that eased onto my face watching how happy and carefree she was.

"You're supposed to be enjoying your trip. Not checking in on me."

"I *am* enjoying my trip. We have a private chef cooking for us as we speak. I haven't heard from you and wanted to ensure I still had a job to return to. So again, how's it going?"

"Great, actually. I think I have a way to get to Brighton."

"Oh yeah? Great, how?"

"Noel."

"Noel? Who the hell is Noel? And please don't say some Christmas angel because I might have to catch a flight to Atlanta to make sure you haven't lost your mind."

I smirked at her curt tone. "Noel *isn't* a Christmas angel." *Or maybe she is.* "You know I don't believe in all that. She's actually the owner of the place you rented for the week."

"Wait! What am I missing? You've been talking to the owner? Was there an issue? You had to reach out to her?"

I cringed, knowing I'd have to fess up about my current situation with Noel.

"Not an *issue*, but her plans changed, and we arranged to share the space for the week."

Shared Space took on an entirely new meaning with this situation, but I wasn't complaining. My eyes again drifted to Noel until Shelby's voice belted through the phone.

"What the fuck, Kanton? Why didn't you call? I could have—"

"I'm more than capable of handling the situation, and I did. You're on vacation."

"I am, but—"

"No buts. We worked it out, and I'm grateful that this hiccup happened. She's close to Brighton's wife and gets invited to their Christmas Eve party yearly. Normally, she declines because she usually visits family, but this year, she's going, and I'm her plus-one."

Shelby was quiet, which meant I wasn't going to like what she had to say, and sure enough . . .

"That's a one-bedroom apartment, Kanton." Her tone was light.

"I'm sleeping on the sofa."

"Oh, wow. It's worse than I thought. What did you say her name was again?"

"Noel, why?"

"I need to look her up. If you're sharing her apartment and sleeping on the sofa, she must be something. You like her, don't you?"

"Shelby . . ."

"What? This deal with Brighton is important, but I can't imagine it's important enough that you'd spend the week with a stranger, sleeping on her sofa, unless there was something about her that sweetened the pot. I will do a little digging to find out what you're *not* telling me."

I glanced at Noel, who had just happened to look at me at the same time. I held up my finger to signal that I was almost done, and she nodded and smiled.

That damn smile.

Hair piled on her head in a curly mess, and those tight jeans that hugged her long legs were also nice to look at.

All the reasons why I was sleeping on her sofa. Shelby was right, but I damn sure wasn't about to admit she was.

"You absolutely will *not* do any digging. It's not what you think, so leave it alone."

"You're defensive. It's *exactly* what I think. Considering your last choice of partners, I might just need to do the digging."

"Shelby, I mean it. Leave it alone."

"Sure thing, boss." She laughed, and I groaned. Shelby would likely have this woman's entire life in a portfolio within the hour.

"I have to go. We're tree shopping."

"*Tree* shopping. What the fuck, Kanton? What has this woman done to you? You *hate* Christmas."

I didn't hate it. Just didn't like what it represented in my life. My eyes landed on Noel again, who was tugging at the branches of a tree while she had a determined look on her face as if she was thoroughly inspecting it. Or maybe I hated what Christmas *used* to represent in my life. The thought of adopting a new version with her wasn't so bad.

"Goodbye, Shelby," I rattled off and ended the call to her laughing.

When I joined Noel again, she peeked at me from the side and then pointed to the tree. "What do you think of this one?"

"I think it's a tree."

She rolled her eyes and pointed to the branches. "It's not *just* a tree. It's green, which means it's healthy. The branches are full, which means it will look amazing once we decorate it, and, oh my God, the smell. It smells amazing. Try it."

"No thanks."

"Kanton . . ." She shot me a warning look, and Carl chuckled.

He passed by and then mumbled, "Just smell the damn tree, Kanton. You won't win this argument with her. It's better to play nice."

She smiled wildly. "Thank you, Carl. See? He gets it."

"Oh, I get it all right. Been married for fifteen years. My lady is *always* right, and I never argue with her when she has that look on her face."

"What look?"

I pointed to hers. "*That* look. The 'fall in line because I'm not changing my mind look,' which you have right now."

"Good, then smell the damn tree, Kanton." She repeated Carl's words, and I did as I was told and leaned into the tree, inhaling deeply. The pine scent reminded me of what my parents' foyer smelled like, but the feelings that settled in me when I turned to find that goofy grin on Noel's face contradicted what I usually felt about trees and Christmas.

"Still a tree," I teased, and she shoved my shoulder, attempting to move me, but my weight was no match for hers.

She turned to Carl and pointed. "We'll take this one."

"Sure thing, pretty lady. You want it delivered? That's an additional twenty-five, but I'll waive that for you." He winked at Noel, and I felt territorial. Carl was at least fifty and competing with Santa in the midsection, but the way Noel's face lit up had me removing my wallet and handing over a card.

"Keep the fee and bump it up some if you can get it delivered as soon as possible."

Her head whipped around to me. "You don't have to do that. You already bought me a tree."

"That you don't like. Consider it a thank-you for getting me in with Brighton."

"You don't have to thank me. It's the least I can do."

"As is this. Take it," I said to Carl, who glanced between us, smiled, and accepted my card.

Good man. Never turn down a sale.

"I can have it delivered this evening between eight and nine after we shut down out here. How's that?"

I glanced down at Noel, who turned to Carl and responded. "Perfect, thank you."

"Don't thank me. Thank the guy beside you. Be right back with your receipt." Carl walked away, and Noel turned to face me.

"Thank you." She lifted onto her toes and kissed my cheek, and I'd swear her lips lingered for a moment longer than necessary, or maybe that was just me wanting her to. When her face was in full view again, I swear her cheeks blushed.

"You're welcome. Now, can we discuss this decorating thing? I don't think I signed on for that. I've done my part," I teased, remembering how she'd mentioned *we* when she noted how great the tree would look decorated.

She stepped closer to me and tugged at the scarf around my neck. "I'm thinking your gracious participation can be accredited to this, so maybe when we get home, I can loan you one of my sweatshirts, and you'll change your mind about the decorating part. Mine are two sizes too big, so I think they might work."

"Hell no. I'm *not* wearing one of those." I motioned to her sweatshirt and eased politely to the side. Her smile grew.

"Never say never, Scrooge."

I chuckled and stepped away to accept my card from Carl, who returned with it and a notepad, which he handed to Noel.

"You're all set. Just jot down your address and phone number, and we'll get that tree to you."

She giggled and accepted the notepad and pen, scribbling on it before she handed it back to Carl, who thanked us for our business, and then we were gone.

Noel.

"TELL ME THIS is not perfect."

I beamed at the visual of the Fraser fir tree positioned in the corner of the apartment. It was an eight-footer. The beauty was a little on the scrawny side, but it smelled amazing. The scent already filled my apartment and had me humming Christmas songs since Carl and his two nephews arrived with it an hour ago.

"It's a tree." Kanton stood next to me, staring impartially at the tree. I peeked at him, getting a quick rush from the fitted T-shirt he was wearing. The way the material clung to his broad shoulders and biceps created a nice visual, and the spicy scent tickling my senses since he showered and changed after setting up the tree for me was an added bonus.

"How can you say it's just a tree?" I turned my head, staring at his profile, but he turned his seconds later, meeting my stare with a smug grin in place.

"Because it is just a tree."

"It is not *just* a tree. This is a Fraser fir, the Range Rover of trees. Autobiography edition."

"I've owned an autobiography, and they're nice, but if you've seen one luxury car, you've seen them all." The smugness of his tone proved he only stated the obvious to annoy me. I returned a glare, which had him grinning and further pressing his point.

"I never understood the excitement of this whole aspect of Christmas. You buy a tree, spend hours digging through an assortment of ornament collections that you've spent years packing and unpacking, wrestling with clusters of tangled lights and other stuff, only to turn around and spend more countless hours *un*doing it. I don't see the appeal."

I slipped in front of him, searching his face for a moment. His eyes remained on me, and his expression remained stoic until I asked, "Who hurt you? Because someone has truly destroyed your Christmas cheer for you to think so little of how amazing and satisfying it is to decorate a Christmas tree."

He threw his head back, and the deep rasp of his voice when he laughed vibrated through me, traveling right down below my waist. "No one hurt me, Noel."

I quickly shook my head. "No. Someone definitely hurt you. You've got some deeply rooted traumas associated with Christmas, buddy, but don't fret. I plan on giving you the most amazing Christmas experience ever, and maybe, just maybe, you'll lighten up a little and encompass some Christmas cheer."

As I spoke, I poked my finger into the wall of muscle that was his chest, not realizing what I was doing until *his* fingers wrapped around my hand, halting my motion.

"There are no deeply rooted traumas, and I assure you, no one hurt me. Christmas means different things to different people, and for me, it's more or less an opportunity for my mother to highlight just how perfect her life is. My father and I were just props in her production, so there's nothing warm and fuzzy about the holidays for me. Don't waste your time trying to repair me, Noel. I'm not broken. I just don't give a damn about Christmas."

He lifted my hand to his mouth, kissed the inside of my wrist, and then released me. "I do, however, promise not to ruin your Christmas. Let's just agree to disagree on the matter to keep the peace." His eyes bounced over my head to where the tree was, and I exhaled a calming breath. My body was still reeling from that kiss. Something as simple as his lips on my wrist had my insides liquifying and my mind eager to explore what else he could kiss with that mouth of his.

"Agree to disagree, I will not. Sorry, Kanton. You picked the wrong rental for that. You're going to change your mind about Christmas. That's my sole mission for the next couple of days."

"You're that determined?"

"I am, and since it's late, and I see that I have to ease you into this gently, we'll leave the tree decorating for tomorrow. Tonight, I have other plans for us."

The look he gave was one of sheer pain and maybe a touch of intrigue, which had me saying, "Don't worry. I'm not going to have you writing letters to Santa or making reindeer food . . ."

"There is a God."

"Maybe not. The reindeer food is more of a Christmas Eve activity. Tonight, we're watching movies." I winked and walked toward the kitchen to the sound of him groaning his displeasure.

"And if I disagree?"

"You won't, so let's not waste time traveling down that road. You need me to get into Brighton's Christmas party."

"That sounds a bit like emotional blackmail."

"Because it is. Seems to me like the power has shifted, Mr. Joseph, and I'm taking full advantage."

"You do realize I could still call the authorities to present our very legal and binding contract to have you vacated from the premises until the 27th."

"You could, but how would you get to Brighton?"

"Lewis."

"He won't help you if I ask him not to."

"Are you sure about that?" He lifted a brow in a challenge, and I shrugged.

"You could take your chances and try."

"I could—"

"*But* you won't," I countered, smiling as I yanked open a cabinet and removed two bags of flavored popcorn. "Caramel with white chocolate or toffee with candy cane?"

"Neither," he murmured.

"Okay then, lady's choice. Both."

He groaned again and flopped down on the sofa while I prepared our movie snack and snagged two glasses and a bottle of chocolate peppermint wine.

When I set everything up and settled next to Kanton on the sofa, pulling my legs onto the cushion and crossing them at the ankles, I found myself shoulder to shoulder with him. He glanced at my holiday treats and then at me. "Is all this necessary?"

"*Very* necessary. Now, where do you want to start? Small-town romance where the man single-handedly saves the entire town while winning over the one that got away when she offers him a second chance at love or my personal favorite? Corporate asshole comes to town to ruin everyone's Christmas by bulldozing the lovely novelty holiday town but falls in love with the local favorite after he realizes the error of his ways. Spoiler alert: he chooses the girl over bulldozing the town."

He shot me a deadpan look, and I grinned. "Again, lady's choice. Corporate asshole it is, then."

I scrolled through my saved movies and selected the one I wanted, pressing play and then leaning forward to grab both bowls of popcorn. I placed one in the fold of my legs and the other in his lap, inadvertently brushing my hand over something that had me quickly pulling my hand back while fighting the urge to keep it there. When his eyes remained on the TV instead of flicking over to me, I relaxed, attempting to slow my erratic heart.

Hours later, we were three movies in. After selecting one that was showing live as my second choice, I allowed them to run consecutively, which meant we watched three varying plots, all of which were overly cheesy. Still, the girl got the guy of her dreams, and the guy realized he had been in love with the girl the entire time. I was in holiday overload because, sitting next to Kanton, watching his expression shift from intense to humorous while he ripped apart every cheesy plot and theme, complaining the entire time while smiling through insults, I realized that, ultimately, he enjoyed himself.

His usual demeanor, which screamed tense and uptight, relaxed. He engaged me in friendly banter while devouring popcorn from both my bowl and his. His hands mindlessly made their way to the bowl in my lap, grabbing handfuls while mine did the same to his.

We drank, ate, and engaged in friendly arguments about the realism of the movies, and I understood exactly how each and every one of those women felt. I wanted that cheesy, unadulterated experience with the man whose body heat was flush against my arm and whose voice was a melody in my head. He was comfy and had me forgetting the troubles of the very complicated world that awaited me beyond the doors of my apartment.

At some point during the fourth movie, Kanton dozed, leaving me to my wits. Watching him sleep felt like I was being a creep, and enjoying the movie without him felt like I was breaking some unspoken agreement that we would do this together.

After an internal war, I carefully leaned forward, placing my half-empty bowl on the trunk, and unlocked my legs, feeling a wave of relief from the tension of them being crossed all evening. Slowly, I eased away from the comfort of Kanton's body to stand.

Once I shut off the TV, I reached for his bowl and placed it on the trunk next to mine, intending to walk away, when I felt his warmth again. His hand latched onto my wrist, and when I lowered my eyes, his were hooded and demanding. They slowly pulled away from my face, lowering to the Christmas hoodie I was in, down to my midthigh spandex shorts.

I would swear to feeling the heat of his gaze as it moved lower and then back up my body, landing on my lips. His pressed into a firm line, and his brows pinched like he was annoyed or at war, and I knew why seconds later when I landed on his lap with a yank of my arm.

His hand was at the base of my neck, and his lips met mine. I sighed into the kiss, leaning deeper into his chest as I adjusted my position so that my knees pressed into the sofa, encasing his thighs while I straddled his lap.

The minute I settled into the kiss, he pulled back, and his eyes were on my lips again. "You taste like peppermint and chocolate."

"So do you."

"I'm partial to both but can't decide which I like more."

"Neither can I."

"Then maybe we need a tiebreaker." His voice was low and sultry.

Those sinful lips of his curled. His mouth was on mine again. The kiss was slow and greedy, just like his hands, which found their way beneath my sweatshirt. The swipe of his tongue and the pressure of his fingers digging into my skin, dancing up and down my spine, and the swell of him beneath me had my core optimistic and pulsing uncontrollably.

When we separated again, his tongue glided across his bottom lip. "I'm going to have to stick with my original answer. Still partial to both."

My smile was slow when I nodded. "Me too, but . . ."

I couldn't believe I was doing this; however, I was.

"It's late. I should probably . . ." I glanced at my room, and his brows pinched again.

"Yeah, you probably should."

Neither of us moved for a moment, but after an internal struggle about doing what was right, I eased off his lap and lifted our empty glasses, the wine bottle, and stacked the bowls.

"Good night, Kanton."

"Good night, Noel."

I placed everything on the counter and then headed to my room. My head was spinning, and my body was on fire, but my heart was at war because I realized I wanted the guy just like those movies. This, however, wasn't a holiday movie where I was guaranteed a happily ever after, and then I felt the sting of knowing my world didn't include the man on the other side of my bedroom door.

Kanton.

MY EYES TRAVELED down my chest and landed on a head full of chocolate spirals that brushed against my skin each time Noel's head lowered enough for my dick to reach the back of her throat.

I was close, so close, and she could feel it based on the teasing look she delivered when she lifted her eyes and circled her tongue around my head.

Oh, fuck.

She was purposely teasing me. Her eyes, her tongue, and her lips were sensation overload. I lifted my hips, meeting her each time she dropped her head. I needed more of this.

Of her.

"I'm gonna come . . ." I murmured in a low growl, squeezing my fists tightly. My nails dug into my palms somewhat, grounding me, but nothing would stop this descent.

"What?"

"I'm gonna come . . ." I hissed with a little more aggression behind it.

"Yes, you are. Now, hurry up and get dressed. I'm done in the bathroom, so it's all yours."

My brows pinched, and I realized a horrifying detail. The voice I heard wasn't traveling from below my waist. It was somewhere over my head.

"Shit."

My eyes popped open to find Noel standing over me in another one of those god-awful holiday shirts, and her hair cascading around her face. The same hair that I had only moments ago enjoyed crowning her face while she swallowed my dick.

I had been dreaming.

But Noel standing over me now wasn't all in my head. Neither was the thickness of my dick, tenting the blanket that covered my lower half. Thank goodness it was still in place.

"Sorry. I was still asleep. What did you say?" I quickly sat up, making sure to keep the quilted material pooled around my waist bunched enough to hide my erection prayerfully.

"I said we have some shopping to do, and you said you're coming."

I was . . . until you interrupted.

I raked a hand over my face. "Shopping for what?"

"Christmas presents. I've already delivered mine to those I care about in the building, and though my funds were a little tight, I managed to get it done. You, on the other hand, have not, and you never show up to someone's house empty-handed. We're going Christmas shopping so that you can get presents for Brighton and his wife. It's the least you can do since you're crashing their party. And it might improve your chances of winning them over."

"I'm not crashing. *You* invited me," I murmured, not feeling this idea but knowing she wouldn't accept no as an answer so I could return to the dream she so rudely interrupted.

"Technically, you are crashing because it's unclear whether I can bring a plus-one. Since his wife, Kristian, knows I'm not actively dating, she likely wouldn't expect me to have a plus-one."

"You're not actively dating?"

Her expression shifted when she realized her slip, but she rolled her shoulders back and narrowed her eyes. "No, are you?"

I smirked and shook my head. "No, but it might have been responsible of you to ask that before you allowed my tongue down your throat last night." She didn't appreciate the smugness of my accusation or my tone, which she proved by countering with, "Shouldn't you have been the one questioning me about *my* relationship status since *you* were the one doing the tongue shoving? *You* kissed *me*, Kanton."

"I did, and *you* kissed me back."

"And welcome back, asshole," she muttered.

I chuckled after standing now that my situation below the waist was somewhat under control. I towered over Noel when I asked, "I thought you liked assholes. Something about the humbling he experiences after being put in his place by a savvy yet loving heroine who checks all the right boxes."

I repeated her words from last night when I questioned why women were so head over heels for enemies-to-lovers-type plots.

"Not all assholes are redeemable." She shrugged and then rattled off, "Now, get dressed. We have a schedule, and I like to stick to my schedules as closely as possible."

"A schedule for shopping? How much planning can that take?"

"We're not *just* shopping. I promised you a real Christmas experience, and that's what you're getting."

"And I'm assuming the option of me sending you with my card to get whatever gifts you think will get me into Brighton's party is out of the question?"

The look she gave me answered my question, and with a groan under my breath as she walked off toward her room, I said, "And, Noel . . .?"

"Yes?"

"I didn't ask about your relationship status before I kissed you because I didn't care. If you recall, I told you I'm a man who never shies away from a challenge, and had you been dating someone, I would have considered that a challenge."

Her mouth dropped open and then slammed shut. She was at a loss for words, which worked in my favor because had she said anything at all, I would have had to address the fact that not only did I *want* to kiss her, but I wanted to do it again. Based on the dream she inadvertently interrupted, there were a few other things I wouldn't mind experiencing with Noel.

"Don't they sell these things in regular stores?"

I peered at the massive banner that welcomed us to the 10th Annual Christmas Extravaganza. After I was dressed, Noel and I made the ten-minute walk downtown after sharing coffee and bagels at a place near her building.

Now, we were entering a space I could only describe as an explosion of all things Christmas. Said explosion created the appearance of well-organized chaos. The decorations, holiday-themed attire, and locals willing to peddle their Christmas cheer through specialty items and treats were a bit overwhelming.

"They do, but being here gives us a one-stop shop. You can buy gifts for Brighton and his wife, and I can expose you to the finer side of holiday cheer."

"The only reason I'm willingly going to suffer through this is because your enthusiasm is too adorably pathetic for me to rain on your holiday parade."

"Good, because that would make you very Scrooge-*ish*, which is far more pathetic than adorably enthused."

"According to you, I am Scrooge."

She leaned into me, bumping her hip into my thigh, but then looped our arms together while we navigated to the twenty-one-or-above side of the shops. Our first stop was Flavor, where I secured a case of Cohiba Behike 56 for Brighton, along with a bottle of Black Exclusive Barrel Bourbon from Black Ops. Noel informed me it was his favorite, and the sales associate told me it was their top-of-the-line aged twenty-one years, explaining its exorbitant price.

I also got a bottle for myself based on the sample I had. I loved a good bourbon.

We were now at the specialty pop-up for Harmonious Blaze, which was one of Brighton's wife's favorites, and Noel's as well, considering she had been oohing and aahing over their entire line since our arrival, which made it impossible to select something for Kristian Brighton. Noel would lock down what she considered the perfect scent and then change her mind by sampling another.

"How about the Tempt Me collection?" the sales associate, who had been graciously assisting and not once annoyed by Noel's indecisiveness, suggested, registering that we weren't any closer to deciding than we had been when we arrived.

"Ooooh, what's that?" The way Noel's face lit up with intrigue made me smile as I watched them interact, something I'd grown very fond of since this shopping excursion began.

Watching Noel.

She had such a carefree and pleasant spirit. Her quirky, weird ways resonated well with everyone she encountered. They loved her, and she loved them back. This woman had never met a stranger because I assumed she knew these people. She was familiar with a few, but most she'd never met in her life. However, the way she engaged, with kindness and acute interest in their ramblings about one thing or another, was infectious.

Noel intruded on their personal space, offering help and suggestions, which they welcomed with open arms. I had to attribute that to her nurturing spirit. Everything about this woman was impossible to deny or ignore.

I personally was having a tough time ignoring her presence, spirit, and unintended sexiness, which meant I was *hard*. Not a great feeling when surfing by families who were radiating Christmas cheer while I was thinking about cheerfully fucking Noel in one of those ugly-ass Christmas shirts.

"It's a collection of our top scents, but they're our regular thirteen ounces instead of the smaller four to six. Tempt Me has been selling well but is a bit pricey."

Of course, it is.

"That sounds like exactly what we need. We'll take one of those. Can I have it delivered? I don't live far from here."

"Absolutely. There's an additional charge if that's okay."

The associate looked at Noel, who looked at me.

"Now you want my input?" I teased, and Noel shrugged.

"You told me to handle this, so I handled it."

I chuckled and nodded, turning to the associate. "The additional fee is fine, and make it two of those."

"Yes, sir." She smiled, likely running the total in her head, but Noel glared at me.

"Two is a bit of an overkill. One would be good enough."

"Kristian's only getting one. The other is for you."

"You don't have to buy me candles."

"After watching you in here, I most certainly do."

"And what did you learn after *watching* me?"

"That Brighton's wife isn't the only one who loves these candles."

She smiled slowly but quickly added, "I do; however, this isn't about me."

"It's not, but weren't you the one who said you never show up to someone's house empty-handed?" I challenged.

"I did, but our situation doesn't apply."

"Maybe not, but the deal's already done." I noticed the woman assisting us approaching with a handheld card reader. I gave her mine, and Noel provided her address. Once the sale was complete, we were on our way out, but once again, Noel saved the day for an indecisive couple arguing over scents.

She stepped right in between them and pointed to the shelf of candles. "Good Gracious is my absolute favorite, with Blueberry Bliss as a close second, but if you want to try a little of everything, ask about the Tempt Me Collection. It has a few of their top sellers. Trust me, you'll thank me later." She offered a huge smile before walking toward me.

"You can't help yourself, can you?"

"What?"

"That thing you do with people. They didn't ask for your help."

"No, they didn't, but what does it hurt to be of service to people in need?"

I grinned. "I wouldn't consider a couple who couldn't agree on candle scents 'in need.'"

"I do. What if they don't decide, and it causes a pointless argument that ruins their day? I might have just saved Christmas for them."

"Or prevented some amazing makeup sex."

Her eyes shot up to mine, and they were waiting. Instead of shying away, I stood firm in my stance, which had her countering my argument.

"Who's to say that appreciation sex won't be just as amazing?"

"That's not a thing."

She paused, stopping in front of me, pausing my steps as well, or we would have collided.

"It's *definitely* a thing. You spend the day with someone you care about, enjoying the vibe, getting all the feels, and the tension is so over the top that before you can make it in the door, you're ripping each other's clothes off and experiencing the best orgasms of your life."

Her eyes met mine, communicating something I didn't want to overthink. Is that how she wanted or expected our day to end? I would totally be on board with that.

"Are you speaking from personal experience, or did you just reenact a scene from one of your cheesy holiday movies?"

"Wouldn't you like to know?"

Yes, the fuck I would.

She smiled smugly and stepped out of my way, pointing to another section near us where a man dressed in a Santa suit was smiling bigger than necessary while a line of parents and children stood fidgeting, waiting their turn to see him.

"We have to take Christmas pictures, and then we can head back."

"Not happening."

She turned to me, pouting, and fuck me, her lips lightly puffed, reminding me of the dream she interrupted this morning.

"Why not?"

"Because there's no way in hell I'm sitting on another man's lap . . ." I moved closer. "And neither are you."

She grinned smugly. "Fine, then let me offer an alternative."

"Which is?"

"Photo booth." She pointed again to a spot next to the Santa line. "They have that too. The booth might be even better because they have props, and before you say no, you're using the props, Kanton."

I wasn't allowed time to object before she was dragging me toward the booth. We waited in line, and when it was our turn, she took the bags from my hand and set them on the floor of the booth before pointing to the clear pocket affixed to the side.

I groaned at the assortment of Christmas props on sticks. She snagged a few and shoved them into my chest while carefully selecting hers and then dragging me into the tiny booth, closing the curtain.

Noel gently nudged me until I was seated and then stood next to me, shifting through her props, only to squeal when I hooked my arm around her waist and yanked her down onto my lap.

"I thought we weren't sitting in other men's laps," she teased.

"I'm not; you are, but only mine."

"That seems wildly unfair. Shouldn't I get to choose?"

"Fair enough. You want to choose, then choose. Him . . ." I turned my head to the left, motioning in the direction of the Santa station beside us. " . . . or me."

When she shifted as if she were going to stand, I locked my arm around her waist, and Noel glared over her shoulder when she landed back in my lap. "What happened to me getting to choose?"

"I assumed you would choose responsibly. You didn't. Now, are we doing this or not?"

A triumphant smile expanded, and she removed the deer antler prop from my hand and waved it in front of my face.

"We'll do it, but you have to use this."

When I frowned, she smiled wider. "Your decision. Either *you* be my holiday cheer, or I'll let *Santa* do it."

"Noel . . ." I warned. She had no clue what I was already thinking, and poking the bear was not going to do either of us any good.

"I'm serious, Kanton. The choice is yours."

I snatched the antler prop from her hand, and she smiled, feeling accomplished, turning toward the side of the booth where the screen that held the camera was. They had multiple options, so she tapped her finger on the glass to select and, in the process, managed to wiggle her very cute ass that I had been enjoying all day in those very tight jeans against my lap, resurrecting my dick to life. Not a good idea, but technically, I couldn't blame him. The contact was quite nice.

And when she finalized the selection, I was even more grateful because she snuggled next to me to align our faces side by side while the screen counted down.

During the first round, I watched her make funny faces, and when she brought the playback up and fussed at me for not doing my part, I joined in on the next set.

Noel laughed and smiled freely, mostly from teasing me. By the fourth round of photos, we had a little thing going, which ended with us staring at each other for the last one, her mouth a hair away from mine, but before I could kiss her, and I really fucking wanted to kiss her again, a voice outside interrupted the moment.

"You guys about done in there? The line's building."

"Uh, yeah. Finishing up now." Noel hopped up and turned away from me, stepping to the screen to enter her cell number to send the last set to her phone, and then rushed out of the booth. I lifted our bags and followed, dumping our props on a stick in the clear cubby extending from the side.

After a minute, we fell in step, walking silently through the crowd until Noel spoke up. "I was thinking about dinner; I could cook something."

I grinned at her as she peeked at me. "You want to cook for me?"

"I'm offering to feed you since you've been so graciously feeding me, and besides, I have the groceries, remember? Don't want them to go bad."

Once I recovered from the thought of her *feeding* me, which had nothing to do with groceries going to waste, I managed a comeback.

"You don't have to cook for me, but I won't reject the offer if it will make you happy."

"I had a feeling you wouldn't, and besides, I figured if I'm going to convince you to help me decorate the tree later, it might help to use a home-cooked meal as a bargaining tool."

"Wait. Before I agree, that home-cooked meal doesn't have anything to do with reindeer food, elf stew, or Santa porridge, does it?"

She threw her head back and laughed, and damn, if it didn't have my dick reacting again just as quickly as thoughts of her lips wrapped around it did. How was I so turned on by everything about this woman?

"You better be glad I'm not easily offended, and no, none of the above. At least, not for tonight. We're still making reindeer food on Christmas Eve if we have time."

"We'll hopefully be at a party Christmas Eve with me closing the deal with Brighton."

"Only for a few hours. That leaves us plenty of time to get home and make our reindeer food and cookies while we wait for Santa."

She winked before tugging my arm so we could cross the street to her building, but I was stuck on how natural the idea of her apartment being *home* sounded.

"You will not make me a fan of Christmas, so please don't waste your time."

"Don't be so sure, and maybe it's not about you. Maybe I'm just really enjoying Christmas for the first time without my family, something I didn't believe possible."

As soon as we entered the building, Noel dug into one of the bags I held, removing tiny kraft paper pouches that she passed out to Lewis and the two other staffers on the clock. She purchased roasted chestnuts for them. Another Noel thing—always thinking of others.

"I have some candles that will be delivered. If you don't mind, can you send someone up with them when they arrive?"

"I sure can, and thanks for these. You're right on time. I was just about to hit up a vending machine and didn't need that. Been trying to do better with my diet." Lewis rubbed the cushion of his stomach.

"You've been trying not to piss off your wife is more like it."

He smiled wide. "That too, so it's a good thing you always come through with healthy snacks for me so I can stay in her good graces." He held up the small chestnuts, and she grinned, nodding.

"What can I say? I'm in love with love, and since I'm living vicariously through your happy marriage, I'll do my part to keep you lovebirds singing a harmonious tune."

Lewis laughed lightly before kissing Noel on the cheek. "Your day's coming, Noel. Just you wait. You're a sweetheart. The right man will realize it and marry you in the blink of an eye."

His words had me internally frowning at the idea of there being a *right man* for her if that man wasn't *me*.

"From your lips to God's ears, Lewis. I'm counting on you."

"I got you covered."

Lewis nodded and turned to answer the phone. Noel and I moved to the elevators and stepped inside when a car arrived.

"In love with love?" I asked, and Noel's eyes lifted to me.

"My parents have been married for thirty-two years. It's hard not to be. They're best friends and the real deal. Not like many couples who stay together out of familiarity or because it just makes sense to stick it out because years have passed them by."

"Makes sense."

"What's that?"

"Why you're so disappointed about missing Christmas with them."

"I was disappointed, but truthfully, this week hasn't been so bad," she said and then quickly stepped off the elevator after we made it to her floor. When we reached the door, both of us attempted to key the code and then she awkwardly looked up at me. I was far too comfortable with her and this situation, so I pulled my hand back, allowed her to do it, and followed Noel inside.

"I'm going to change. You should probably get comfy too. We've got work to do." She glanced at the tree and then went left toward her room while I went right to the living room.

I dug through my luggage and found a pair of sweats and a T-shirt so I could get out of my jeans and sweater, and while I changed in the bathroom, I couldn't help but consider the possibility of crossing lines with Noel.

She's beautiful, smart, funny, quirky, weird, selfless, and everything I didn't need to be intrigued by, considering she lived in Atlanta and I lived in New York. My business was there, as well as my home. Long-distance relationships didn't work, and if I were being honest, I couldn't see myself agreeing to one. Most certainly not with Noel. I'd want her in my life daily.

Relationship?

What the hell is wrong with me?

I quickly shook the thought and changed, gathering my things and then staring at my image in the mirror.

"Get the deal with Brighton and then return to your life."

I needed to focus on that, but I felt it would be much more complicated than I could ever imagine.

Noel.

WHAT THE HELL *is wrong with me?*

I spent the day with a man challenging my ability to use common sense. Absolutely nothing I was doing made any sense.

Kanton kissed me, and I kissed him back. I spent the day with him holiday shopping, thoroughly enjoyed myself. I also planned on spending the evening with this man, decorating a Christmas tree, and then, hopefully, snuggling up on the sofa for the second evening to watch holiday movies.

I wanted all of this so badly—*needed* it. I even found myself wishing that Kanton being here wasn't temporary. That at the end of this week, he wasn't catching a flight out of my life to land back in his.

I was sure the guy had plenty to look forward to after this week. He would secure the deal with Brighton and then travel home to celebrate the victory while settling back into his picturesque existence in New York.

On the other hand, I had to prepare myself for the potential rejection that was coming if the Coleman Group decided that I wasn't the best fit for their design team, and if that rejection came, what the hell was I going to do?

Sure, I had sent proposals to several other businesses, hoping they could see my vision. I prayed they took a chance on a woman who blindly allowed her impatience and ego to lead her into entrepreneurial hell simply because I believed in myself.

Evan called my dream a hobby, but I knew it could work. I believed I would win if I took a chance on myself. The inspiration, sheer will, and *belief* in my dream wouldn't, however, pay the bills.

My eyes darted around my bedroom. I loved this place. I couldn't imagine having to sell it because I couldn't afford the mortgage any longer. My chest constricted at the thought, and as much as I loved spending the holidays with my family, I most certainly didn't want to pack my things and go crawling back home. They would be so disappointed in me. *I* would be so disappointed in myself.

I'd have to get another job. One where I would be overlooked and undervalued, and my creative talents wouldn't be respected because I would be an employee, not the boss. I honestly didn't want to spend the next twenty years punching someone else's clock.

I didn't want to think about tomorrow, the next day, or the one after that because *today* had been wonderful. I was happy, living in the moment, and even if it would all come crashing down around me the minute this week ended, I was going to live in the moment.

I glanced at my door and then briefly at my phone, which was in my hand, before I found the nerve to make the call.

"Noel, hey. I was just about to dial you. How's everything going?" Simone rushed out like I caught her in the middle of running a marathon.

"Good, what's wrong? You sound out of breath."

"I am. I was running up the stairs."

I relaxed a bit before I huffed and rushed out, "I deserve a win, right?"

"Of course you do."

"No matter how insignificant or *temporary* that win might be?"

"Noel, you're scaring me. What's going on?"

"Nothing major. I just had a really good day. The most amazing day I've had in a *really* long time."

"Oh, thank God. I was worried that the reality of your ruined Christmas had finally gotten to you, and I needed to call Lewis to make sure you didn't do anything crazy."

I frowned into the phone. "Crazy like what?"

"I don't know, like overdosing on gingerbread cookies or shorting-out-the-entrance-to-the-building-from-excessive-use-of-twinkly-lights kind of crazy. Who the hell knows?"

"That would be a lot of damn lights."

"You own a lot of damn lights, Noel, and there was a small possibility you might have used all of them to bring Christmas to you since you couldn't go to Christmas. I wouldn't put it past you. You'd try."

I smiled widely. "You're not wrong, but I promise I have no intentions of shorting out the building's electrical system. That's not why I'm calling."

"Then why are you calling?"

"Because I need you to tell me no. If you don't, I'm possibly going to have the most amazing Christmas ever and then be ruined afterward because when it's all said and done, the memories of that amazing Christmas will be all I have."

"Okay, you're scaring me again. Stop with this cryptic shit and just tell me what's going on. How did you go from best day ever to *this*, whatever *this* is?"

"I spent the day with Kanton. We had breakfast and went shopping, and now, I'm supposed to be in there making us dinner so that we can decorate the Christmas tree *he* purchased for me."

"Who the hell is Kanton?"

"Shared Space guy. Keep up, Simone."

"Wait. So you've been hanging out with him?"

"Not hanging out per se. We watched movies last night and went shopping today, but only because he needed gifts to bring to the Brightons' Christmas Eve party. It would be rude to show up empty-handed, and it might help him close the deal, which would be great. It's the biggest deal of his career and could really—"

"Noel . . ." her voice was eerily calm.

"What?"

"Are you falling for this guy? Is *that* what this very dramatic call is about?"

"What? No. I'm not falling for him."

"You are. Shit, I knew it. Am I good or what? I should start a matchmaking business. I can read people like a book, and based on your first reaction to the man, I saw *this* happening. You're living one of those stupid-ass movies you love."

"Don't call my movies stupid. They're feel-good holiday classics."

"Don't deflect."

"I'm not."

"Yes, the hell you are. You like this guy."

"I do." My shoulders slumped slightly.

"Then, hell yes, you deserve a win. Whatever you want my confirmation for, you have it. You want to jump his holly jolly boner, then do it. You want to tongue him down under the mistletoe, do that too. You want him to be your *lay* in a manger? My vote is yes. Yes, to all of it!"

"First of all, what in the horny holiday is all that? Your analogies are terrible, and you're missing the point. I *like* him. A lot, but he's temporary. He leaves after Christmas to return to his life, and I have no idea what that life is, but I know for certain it doesn't include a failed businesswoman with commitment issues and an empty bank account."

"Noel, you're top-tier."

"I know that. I'm not saying I'm not good enough."

"Then what are you saying because I'm utterly confused right now?"

"I'm not good enough *right now*. My life is a mess; it will take a miracle to pull it all together. We live in two different cities and—"

"*And* stop overthinking this. You have a lot of amazing qualities, but one of your worst flaws is the ability to get in your own way. You like him, right?"

"Yes."

"And I assume he's feeling you too, or we wouldn't be having this conversation right now."

"He kissed me, and I'm pretty sure he had a very naughty dream about me last night." I smiled, remembering our interaction from this morning. "But to your point, I think he does."

"Then that's all that matters. You asked if you deserve a win, and my answer is yes. No matter what that win looks like and whether it's nothing more than the best Christmas ever, then so be it. Do what makes you happy. Worry about the rest later. If that man is giving you the 'cum all ye faithful' eyes, you better jingle his bells properly."

I burst out laughing and rolled my eyes. "You need therapy."

"No, I need to write for Christmas After Dark."

"You absolutely do not, and I pray that's not a thing."

"Oh, it's a thing, Noel. Naughty or Nice, She's Getting It Twice. Christmas Cums Early, Little Cummer Toy, Jingle Bell Cock . . ."

"Please stop," I choked out through a laugh.

"I'm telling you, you're missing out. *Those* are some Christmas movies worth watching. Far better than Holiday Disaster in Boring Valley Falls."

"The disrespect." I feigned offense.

"I'm being honest, and you know I am. My selections are way better."

"I'll take your word for it, and thank you."

"You're welcome. So does that mean after you finish hanging all your *pornaments*, you'll be fucking around the Christmas tree having a happy holiday? Everyone's screwing merrily—" she sang, and I cringed, cutting her off before the lyrics were progressively worse.

"I'm not going to answer that. I love you. Goodbye."

"Love you too. Make me proud."

"*Goodbye, Simone . . .*" I asserted, ending the call before being gifted another naughty Christmas pun.

I was already dressed in a satin short pajama set. The shirt was long sleeved, buttoned up the front, and the shorts matched. I purchased it a size larger than I needed to offer a comfier fit, but as I raked my fingers through my coiled mane, staring at my reflection in the mirror, I almost considered selecting one of my more revealing sets. I had a few with camisoles and shorter shorts that would be a lot more enticing, but after a long pause of consideration, I released the thought.

"Am I *really* considering the option of seducing a man with skimpy holiday pajamas?"

Yes, you are.

Deserving of a win or not, Kanton would have to love me as I am, and right now, I am embracing all things Christmas.

Then why are you using the word "love" in reference to how he feels about you?

"Get it together, Noel." I threatened the image staring back at me in the full-length mirror in her winter-green satin covered in tiny white Christmas trees and matching fuzzy socks.

Inhaling slowly and releasing it in a huff, I headed to the door, pausing in the hallway, when I heard the low, raspy sound of Kanton's voice. When I inched closer, my vantage point offered me a view of his broad shoulders and muscular back, which was covered with a navy T-shirt that made me insanely jealous of how it hugged his body. He was standing in the kitchen with his back to me, one arm folded, holding the phone to his ear and the other hanging loosely at his side.

I could easily get used to that scrumptious visual as a breakfast treat every morning.

"No, Mother, I have not changed my mind. I will not be surprising you for Christmas, and if the plan had been to surprise you, why would I tell you now instead of just showing up?"

His tone wasn't kind. Not the same as he'd been using with me all day, but it wasn't exactly mean either. More agitated if I had to label it.

"I know you don't like surprises. Surprise deviates from your well laid plans, which would be disastrous, so I had no intention of surprising you. As I've told you multiple times, I'm working through the holiday."

Not the warm and fuzzy feelings you would expect from mother and son during the holiday.

"You're impossible. You hand select women to line up and interview for the position of my girlfriend—"

"I'm quite aware that I'm getting older, but I also don't have one foot in the grave."

"Lover, girlfriend, wife—all one and the same at the moment, considering I'm not in the market for any, so me being home for Christmas doesn't change a thing. Cancel the brothel you set up and let them know I won't be sitting in while they pitch their hows and whys on the ways they can be my perfect match."

Oh my, that's interesting.

And I shouldn't be listening to this.

"I do love you, Mother, but loving you should not be marginalized by my willingness to be a part of your annual

Christmas production or by being subjected to watching you parade women in front of me like Shetland ponies. I don't know how many other ways to make you understand this."

"Yes, I know, and I assure you, you'll have grandchildren before your face wrinkles beyond your surgeons' ability to make you look less than a glam-mom in family portraits or while you vacation with my children in the Hamptons for the summer."

His voice lifted to the point of delivering as teasing, and I smiled, knowing that their conversation was taking a turn in a positive direction.

"Because I know that's one of your biggest fears, being immortalized in photos with frown or laugh lines."

"Okay, okay, I apologize, and yes, I do love you. You'll survive a holiday without me."

"I will. Okay, goodbye."

The minute he ended the call, Kanton turned his head, those intense brown eyes of his boring into me. His were unreadable.

Shit.

Okay, so he's not a fan of my eavesdropping.

"Sorry, I was about to head back to my room . . ."

"Were you?" He lifted a brow in a challenge, and his beautiful lips tilted at the corners just enough to make my heart flutter.

"I was . . ."

"But the call with my mother was far more appealing than snuggling with your favorite stuffed elf."

"Don't be mean." I narrowed my eyes, marching into the kitchen. When I was within reach, he tugged the hem of my shirt before I could completely pass him.

"I might need to buy stock in whatever company makes these. Seems like a great investment considering how many you own."

"Cute, but don't try to dim my light because you prefer this . . ." I flicked my wrist in his direction, and damn, why the hell did I do that? It was impossible to ignore the inanely sexy body making a boring pair of sweat bottoms and pocket tee look like a cover feature for Sexiest Man of the Year.

"What's wrong with this?" He smirked and pinched the tee shirt slightly, pulling it away from his solid chest, and I shamelessly watched that too.

"Nothing's wrong. It's just very . . . Scrooge-ish."

"In comparison to your Christmas explosion?"

"For a man depending on me for his dinner, you might want to be careful with the insults."

He chuckled, and it vibrated through me like a tempting tease. "It's not an insult. I've leaned on the favorable side of you in those." When I glanced over my shoulder from the refrigerator, I was blessed or cursed enough to catch the heated blaze of his gaze traveling down and then back up my body. His eyes slowly fastened on mine, and that arrogant smile nearly sent me over the edge. "Those pajamas are very . . . *you*."

"That sounds dangerously close to an insult," I stated into the refrigerator while removing what I needed for dinner.

"You won't receive any insults from me unless you renege on your promise to bypass Santa porridge for dinner."

I whipped my head over my shoulder and narrowed my eyes on Kanton, and to my dismay and pleasure, he was still watching me in a way that had me wondering if he'd rather have me for his dinner.

Noel, stop that.

"Since you're painfully aware I overheard your conversation with your mother, can I ask a question?"

"You can ask whatever you want. The question is whether I will answer." I heard the smugness in his tone but didn't bother looking at him. I wasn't sure I could handle another dose of those brown eyes on me again.

"Is she really lining up women to parade in front of you like Shetland ponies?"

That time, I did chance a look as I crossed the tiny space to grab a bell pepper from the counter beside him.

"Unfortunately, yes, or at least that's what it feels like. Christmas is her chance to force my hand into getting married. During each scheduled event, she always invites some very single and willing women with impressive résumés, hoping I'll be interested."

"Why aren't you if their *résumés* are so impressive?"

He smirked at my emphasis on the word résumé, and I assumed he understood what I meant because he clarified. "Most of them have been raised to be the perfect partner and wife, which means they've gone to the best colleges and have mile-long lists of their charity involvements and partnerships with local foundations. They spend a lot of time in yoga classes and spas to ensure their physical *résumés* are pleasing to the eye, but that's not what I want."

"Hell, sounds good to me. I might even be interested."

He frowned and then said, "All those things are nice. They look good on paper and are great coffee table talk, but they speak more to who they've been groomed to be, not who they are . . ." I was near him again, reaching for an onion. Kanton placed his hand at my waist, barely there, but enough of a presence for me to feel the warmth of his fingers through my shorts. He leaned in closer when he added. "Perfection is overrated. I prefer my women to be real. You could say that I'm a man who likes to expect the unexpected."

When he released me, I released the tension that crawled into my muscles and hurried back to my side of the kitchen.

"You're not the type who wants a wife catering to your every whim with no ambitions, standing at the door with a bourbon and cigar for you after a long day's work?"

He laughed, those eyes of his dancing with amusement. "I never said they don't have a brain. Many of them have great jobs as CEOs of multimillion-dollar companies. Some are doctors and lawyers, while some own their businesses. I can't imagine any of them waiting at the door with a bourbon or cigar. Hell, they would probably expect that from me."

"Oh, now, *that's* a visual *I* can get on board with," I teased, and he smiled in the most insanely handsome way.

"I suspect you could, but considering you're the entrepreneur with flexibility, I'm sure you'd be the one waiting on *me*."

My heart shuddered, and my stomach flipped at the idea, but then my walls came up. "I'm nothing like those women. The only successful thing about my business is how successfully it's failing."

I froze and slammed my eyes shut.

Why the hell did I just say that?

"Why is your business failing?"

I scoffed a laugh, turning to face Kanton, leaning against the counter like he was across from me. "Because I'm a visionary."

His eyes narrowed some, and I added, "Visionaries are often misunderstood, and the masses aren't willing to risk their tried and true for something they haven't seen success in, which is a catch-22 because how can an idea *be* successful if no one supports it enough to prove the idea is good?"

"Then what you're saying is that your business isn't failing or unsuccessful. Only that the idea hasn't landed in the right hands of someone willing to take a chance on something new?"

"That's a very pretty way of saying *failure*."

"You only fail if you don't try. You're trying, Noel."

"Great advice from the man here to broker a gazillion-dollar deal and then ride off into the sunset."

"I don't like horses, so riding is a bit of a stretch, and riding from Atlanta to New York is out of the question," he teased. I sensed that he was simply trying to lighten the mood, so I gave in.

"Okay, then let's go with a private jet to New York and bypass the sunset."

He smirked and nodded, locking his arms over his chest. "Let me help you."

"With dinner?"

"No. Sad to say, I'm not much of a cook either." The look I gave had him grinning. "No, I don't have a personal chef. I'm just extremely busy and *very* single, so I often eat out. With your business, let me help."

"You can't help."

"I'm pretty sure I can. It's what I do."

"You're a restructuring firm that works with Fortune 500 companies. You can't help me. My issue isn't finances. That's an easy one. I don't have any finances for you to strategize or restructure."

I smiled even though my chest felt tight with the reality of what I was saying.

"I'll overlook your very colorful yet far-from-realistic impression of me for now so we can stay on topic."

"Which is?"

"Me offering to help you with your business."

"You're not a good listener, Kanton. You can't help me."

"Humor me. What exactly is it that you do?"

I narrowed my eyes at him but gave in. "Virtual interior decorating and staging."

"Virtual staging . . ."

"Please don't be like them. Think outside the box."

He smiled. "There you go, judging me again. I know what virtual staging is, Noel."

"Sorry. Habit."

"No offense taken. Since you have no finances, I assume you have little to no business. Virtual interior design and staging is, well, *virtual*, which means you can do that from anywhere. No office is required; the only investment is a computer and software unless you build your own."

I peered at him, and he grinned. "I told you this is what I do. No business then."

"I've had a few contracts here and there, but mostly from individuals. I did a few new construction projects where they needed virtual staging and setup for potential residents to see the various models they intended to build. I've also done a few local businesses that were remodeling, but I haven't been able to lock down any major contracts."

"Who have you reached out to."

"Just about everybody, but mostly hotels, business suites, and anyone with a huge need for design that changes regularly."

"All valued choices who could benefit from virtual staging."

"The problem is not my drive. The issue is others' reluctance to see my—"

"*Vision.*"

"Yes."

"Let me see what I can do to help. You're helping me by getting me access to Brighton."

"You bought me very expensive candles *and* a tree." I pointed to the table where the candles were still sitting after delivery.

"I did, and I'd prefer you not keep a running tab of what I've done for you, Noel. I'm not expecting anything in return. I'd also like to help with this, but I won't if you prefer I don't."

"Fine. Knock yourself out because I have a feeling you're going to do what you want regardless of what I say."

"Then you'd be right. It's a side effect of my asshole behavior. We tend to have an issue when it comes to minding our own business." He winked. "How long before dinner's ready?"

"Forty-five minutes, an hour tops."

"Okay, well, since I'll be of no service to you in here, I'll start working on untangling those lights."

Regardless of the agitation in his voice about untangling lights, my heart seized because Kanton, who hated all things Christmas, was volunteering to be a part of mine. And like a cruel joke from the universe, I had to experience this man, knowing that all this was temporary.

"It's perfect, right?"

"It's Christmassy."

I glanced over my shoulder after imagining the face that Kanton had, and I was spot-on when I caught him with his eyes slightly narrowed, lips tugged down at the corners, and head tilted to the side. He was not impressed, but he was, by default, enjoying the moment for me.

"Then it's exactly what it should be. A thoroughly decorated Christmas tree." I turned to find Kanton watching me and not the tree. And I liked how it felt to be the focus of his attention, but the intensity of his deep brown eyes on me had me rambling. "You can't tell me that seeing this tree doesn't make you feel something."

Kanton's eyes darkened with lust while a salacious smile eased onto his face. "I feel a lot of things, and although they're indirectly related to that tree, I can't give full credit to your decorating skills."

"Skills—" I gasped when I felt the warmth of his hand at my hip. "You've been complaining the entire time, and now you believe I have skills."

The warmth of his breath fanned across the side of my face when he leaned in closer. "I don't *believe* you have skills, Noel. I *know*, and I've been obsessing over those skills all day, but again, they're indirectly connected to that tree."

When he pulled back, and his eyes darkened a little more, that dark stare lowered and focused on my lips.

Oh . . .

Those skills.

"Would now be an appropriate time for me to kiss you again?" The low rumble of his voice caused a succession of pulses in my core. My brain scrambled, but not so much that I couldn't think of a comeback.

"We don't have mistletoe."

"We don't need it . . ." The warmth of his palm met the back of my neck. His fingers slipped into my hair and his mouth brushed against mine . . . gently at first, but then he was kissing me, and I was kissing him.

Our tongues moved in sync, mine feeling as if it had returned home, his coaxing me into the perfect bliss while his fingers dug into my hip. I wasn't sure if he was moving me closer or if I was advancing on my own, but I felt him. The lines and planes of his muscles, the bulge, and his length, hard and long, were digging into the softness of my stomach.

Everything about the moment was perfect, and my mind was clouded with thoughts of how much more of him I wanted to consume. *Needed* to consume, and he must have read my mind because that hand left my neck and leveled with the other at my waist. When my feet left the ground, I instinctively locked my legs around his waist and smiled when his hands slipped beneath me for extra leverage to hold me in place.

Our eyes met once more, but this time, his held questions. I slowly nodded because I wanted this too. It wasn't the smartest thing, but who the hell cared? I was living in the moment, and apparently, so was he because we were moving with long, intentional strides.

My back landed against the wall next to the door when we entered my bedroom, and his mouth met mine again. His tongue swiped greedily while the pads of his fingers dug into my flesh.

Oh my, this was a lot . . .

But I needed more.

"I'm going to taste you everywhere, Noel. Are you agreeable to having my mouth exploring every inch of your body?"

I groaned in anticipation of how amazing his mouth on me would feel. "Very agreeable. You can start now."

He pulled back enough to bless me with a smile that promised satisfaction, and then he carried me to my bed. His mouth and my mouth were at war again until my body sank into the mattress.

There was a frantic rush to get our clothes off, then Kanton dropped to his knees at the foot of my bed and buried his face between my legs.

"Fuck. I knew it. Perfect." The greedy swipes of his tongue and the vibration of his voice against my sex was a brilliant combination. His expression was dangerous when he lifted his eyes to watch as he slid a finger inside me. "So glad you're agreeable to what I'm about to do to you."

Definitely not more than me.

I gasped when his tongue moved down my slit. A moan escaped my trembling lips, and my pussy pulsed and tightened. The rush was already taking over, building from deep within, threatening to erupt.

Magical.

My breathing was disrupted, and I couldn't think clearly, but I also didn't want to. Delusion was great as long as it felt this amazing. All I wanted at the moment was to reach the finish line because the reward would be a sweet and sinful victory.

I was close. So close. And then I was there . . .

"Oh . . ."

While his fingers thrusted smoothly in and out of me, with his tongue and lips working my clit, my orgasm jolted through me. The added vibration of his voice thrumming against my heated, slick skin had me pulsing and shuddering blissfully while Kanton continued pushing my limits. Every skillful stroke of his fingers and tongue coaxed my body into a weightless, satiated state, one I was thoroughly enjoying.

But he didn't stop.

I felt his body move up to mine, warm lips latched on to my very sensitive nipples, one at a time, sucking hard while he continued thrusting his fingers at a steady pace between my legs. The buildup began again, and before I knew it, my pussy was pulsing and clenching with need. I groaned and exhaled a long, drawn out breath seconds before his mouth connected with mine. While I struggled through a second orgasm that felt ten times more powerful than the first, his tongue connected with mine, coaxing me through the release.

"Still agreeable?"

I choked on a laugh as my brain slowly began to process again. "Are you *really* asking me that?"

"I am. I aim to please."

"You pleased. Very much. I'd like for you to keep pleasing."

"Good to know, but we might have a slight issue."

I frowned, and he closed his eyes briefly as if it pained him to say the word. "Condoms."

"Nightstand, and before you start assuming, I have them as a precaution, not a purpose."

"At this point, I don't care. I was debating how good my pullout game would be, but I wasn't sure you'd agree to that as an option."

"Um, definitely not. Now, can you get the condoms so that we can move this along?"

He chuckled, leaving me to get to my nightstand, and I instantly missed the weight and warmth of his body. I also enjoyed the visuals of him and his very nice package while he covered himself in the most painfully slow manner.

Or maybe I was being impatient.

By the time he dipped his shoulders under my thighs and slowly pressed into me, I knew I was done for. About halfway in, he thrusted his hips forward until he was completely seated. Another orgasm was already pulsing and growing with each purposeful thrust.

How?

Kanton groaned, moving out slowly, but his thrust landed hard when he pressed forward again. It was slow and a torturous ache, leaving me feeling painfully full . . .

Of him.

With each plunge, he angled himself perfectly, guiding my climax, pulling it from somewhere deep within until I felt it crawling to the surface. I had never in my life come so many times, so fast, but I wasn't complaining.

"Again. Oh. My. Fuck," fumbled from my mouth.

Kanton groaned in satisfaction. My pussy began to shudder, throbbing and clenching him until I no longer had control. I shattered again as ecstasy swept through me with long, hard pulses. I was lost in an overload of pleasure while Kanton continued pressing into me with hard, controlled thrusts until I felt his last one. He wasn't far behind me, finishing with a deep, throaty growl and then the weight of him pressing into me so that my thighs spread wide and angled back toward my stomach.

My muscles ached. Our bodies were slick and warm, and I sighed from a satiated feeling that was settling into every inch of my body. After a few minutes of heavy breathing, Kanton's mouth grazed the curve of my neck, and I would swear to feeling the curve of his lips against my skin just before he murmured, "You might have convinced me that Christmas isn't so bad after all."

Kanton.

THE FOLLOWING DAY, I woke with the feel of Noel's limbs tangled with mine. The memories of us last night had my dick so hard again I could barely stand it, but I needed to think and not get sucked back into this beautiful woman's allure.

I carefully eased away, escaping the confinement of her sheets, and quickly collected my clothes from last night. Once I left the room, I slowly closed the door and headed straight for the bathroom. The only shower was in Noel's room, so I slipped back into my clothes, washed my face, and brushed my teeth before returning to the living room.

It was just after seven in the morning, which meant I had silence and time to think. Think about the way Noel's mouth felt on mine, the way her soft hands brushed over my skin, the way her delicate fingers firmly wrapped about my dick just before her tongue glided across it.

The dream had nothing on the real thing. Not a damn thing. Damn!

I needed to clear my head, so I settled onto the sofa with my laptop, determined to do a little research, but this time, Brighton wasn't my focus. I knew everything there was to know about the guy: his business preferences, his spending habits, and his determination to keep control of his family legacy.

The guy was basically in a last-ditch effort to keep this family's hard work under control and managed by someone who shared their blood. If he failed to turn a considerable profit by the end of the first quarter, then the board, a conglomerate of six men who held shares in his company, would take over. Individually, they didn't have enough to make any real difference, but if they stood together against Brighton, he would have no choice but to step down.

But Brighton and his family legacy would have to wait. Right now, I needed to call in a few favors to see if I could help Noel with her failing business. Although there wasn't anyone threatening to step in and take over, she personally would lose everything if she didn't secure the clients to support her financially.

The look in her eyes when she explained the issue was enough to have me ready to strong-arm a few people into some solid, lucrative contracts. I had access to a few very prestigious companies that could use her services. The problem was, I had no idea if she was even good at her job . . . nor did I care. I had to help. I was going to help because there was something about Noel's smile that ignited a fierce motivation for me to ensure it was always there.

After a few hours of scouring my client manifest, primarily people who would be open to paying me a favor, I came up with a few who were finalizing growth and expansion plans. Companies like Centric Property Management, which was building condominiums in multiple states, and Griffin LLC, which owned construction companies with multimillion-dollar projects to build properties in Georgia, Florida, and the Carolinas. They had design teams in place, but I might be able to convince them to work with Noel to handle the virtual staging for their properties. Nowadays, visuals were the key to selling. If you could give each buyer a customized experience to allow them to visualize themselves in the properties, it would be much easier to get their money.

Once I decided, I called the one person who could pull it all together for me.

"It's very early, Kanton. What happened to 'enjoy your Christmas holiday'?"

I smiled at Shelby's groggy voice and clipped tone, but I knew her well enough to be assured that she wasn't annoyed by my early-morning call but more amused that I reached out, which meant that I needed something. I promised I wouldn't. Shelby liked being right.

"You're usually up with the sun, and considering that you sound like you're still in bed, I'd say you *are* enjoying your time off."

"I've been up for about an hour, but because of too much spiked eggnog, I can't guarantee that my brain is functioning properly."

"Spiked eggnog?" I questioned with a smirk. "You're more of the cognac kind of girl."

"I am, but Gordon's sister is not."

"His sister? I thought this was a romantic getaway. What did I miss?"

"I told you he's going to propose. His parents and sister arrived last night. They're spending Christmas here with us."

"He proposed?"

"Not yet, but he's going to." She perked up, and I shook my head.

"Well, I won't hold you, and I pray that things go as planned."

"Trust me, they will." She sounded so sure I decided not to argue.

"I need a favor . . ."

"You ready to evict your housemate? I already had Howard look into things, and you'd be totally justified to have her removed—"

"I'm not kicking Noel out of her apartment."

"Technically, it's your apartment until 11:00 a.m. on December 27th. According to Howard, the rental agreement is legal and binding. You can call the cops to have her removed . . ."

Howard, my lawyer?

Shelby wouldn't be Shelby if she didn't already have him on standby with this situation.

"Shelby, focus. That's not why I'm calling."

"Then why are you calling?"

"I would like for you to set up a meeting with Calvin Davis and Marshall Clayton. Preferably sooner rather than later."

"Why? What's wrong?"

"Nothing's wrong. I'm doing a favor for a friend."

"*Her?*"

"Yes, *her*. She owns a virtual interior design company, and I'd like to ask if they would be willing to take her on."

"Kanton . . ."

"What?"

"Are you *serious* right now?"

"Very, is there a problem?"

"Hell yeah, there's a problem. She's there. You didn't make her leave, so I can only assume what you two have been up to, but I'm guessing it has something to do with your newly found interest in helping this woman by pawning her off on your clients—"

I cringed at the thought. "I'm *not* pawning her off on them. I'm only suggesting she might be a good option—"

"Is she any good?"

Shit. I had no clue.

So I lied.

"Yes."

"And I assume she has references . . ."

Noel said she had a few clients, just not enough, so surely, they'd be willing to offer a reference.

"Of course."

"What's her website? Let me take a look—"

Shit.

"You don't need to do that; just set up the meetings, Shelby," I mumbled, not wanting to dive into my motivation behind this. I was more driven by my feelings for Noel than what I knew to be her ability to do the job. I was indeed pawning her off on clients. Clients who trusted me to make proper decisions for their businesses. After all, I was the person who managed their finances and pulled them out of the red so that they were now thriving. Wasting money on a company such as Noel's that couldn't deliver went against everything I drilled into them. But I didn't know that she wouldn't deliver.

"Kanton, what you do in her personal life is none of my business, so if you're stepping out of your norm to enjoy a little holiday nookie, I applaud you. It might do you some good to break the mold and explore something or someone new. But when the decisions you make in your personal life affect your professional affairs, it's my job to step in. Your clients are what keep your name in high standing. Asking them to take on this woman just because she is gifted at making you come is not a thoughtful decision. Let me be the impartial voice to ensure you're not making a mistake with this. What's her company information?"

As much as I hated to admit it, Shelby was right, so I rattled off what she asked for. I was being irrational. I hadn't taken the time to check. I believed in Noel, which meant I trusted her word.

"Design Dreams."

I heard rustling in the background and then the cadence of Shelby's nails pecking away at a keyboard. I listened, silently waiting.

"This is awful. You can't be serious right now."

My brows pinched, and I immediately opened my laptop.

"Her site is a mess. It's cluttered, the fonts are terrible, too much color, overloaded with pictures, and to be honest, I have no damn clue what the hell this woman does. It looks like a Pinterest page on steroids."

Shit.

As her page came into view, I cringed. Shelby was right. The page was awful. Very artsy and very colorful, much like Noel. It screamed of her personality, which had me smiling, but it was disastrous for branding a business.

But . . .

"Look at her designs, and they're good, Shelby. Really fucking good." I moved through images of three living rooms: modern, a farmhouse, and one which was a blend of both. There were also visuals of what looked like a study and two bedrooms.

"They're good . . ."

"Better than good."

Shelby sighed in annoyance. "I agree, but you and I both know that if any real prospective clients look at her site, they'll laugh at you, thinking you've lost your mind. As good as these designs are, she's not good with business, or at least not with presenting her business. This site is a disaster. I can't single out how to contact her if I wanted to hire the woman."

I glanced through the landing page and agreed, nodding with a painful realization. In the bottom corner was a list of hyperlinks, one of which said, "Contact Me."

"She's a creative. Maybe the business side needs a little work, but we can help with that."

"Just so we're clear on your plans, you're offering to take her on as a client?"

"No, I'm helping as a friend. She can't afford me, and I would never take her money."

Shelby was quiet. Too damn quiet, which meant she was moving through the only possible scenario that made sense. She knew me better than anyone. This wasn't my thing. I'd toss it to one of my team, but I would never have gotten personally invested in taking on a business like Noel's.

"A *friend*?" she eventually spoke.

"Yes."

"Okay, then. Give me a few days. I'll see how I can make her more presentable before I set up the meetings."

"Thank you."

"Don't thank me just yet. I'm not sure I can do much with this."

I nodded stiffly. "You love a good challenge. I have faith you'll make this work, one way or another."

"If this is your way of testing me to ensure I'm still on my shit, I assure you, I am. This wasn't necessary."

I chuckled. "I don't need to test you, Shelby. I hired you because I know what your abilities are."

"Even I have my limits. Give me a few days, but it's Christmas, so I'll do what I can. This may have to wait until the first of the year."

I understood but hoped for the best.

"Got it."

After I ended the call, I stared blankly at the newly decorated living room. Not only had I been bullied into decorating a tree, but I had also provided the manual labor that hung garlands and twinkly lights across the back of the bar that lined the kitchen and around the fireplace mantle.

With the sun beaming through the floor-to-ceiling windows, it didn't give the same magical feel as last night, but it presented an aura that screamed *"Happy, cheerful Christmas."*

Magical?

I grunted at the thought. When had I ever considered anything about Christmas to be magical?

Since you experienced her . . .

My head swung slowly toward the back of the apartment where Noel was sleeping, and my dick swelled with the need to want to climb back in bed to join her. But not to sleep. To settle between her legs and thoroughly enjoy every inch of her body the way I had last night, but before I could fall too deeply into the memory of that visual, I had a new one.

Noel came down the short hallway from her bedroom, stopping at the perimeter of the living room, wearing black spandex shorts, an oversized cream T-shirt that had a big red circle dead center, which, I realized, was supposed to be Rudolph's nose based on the antler ears that topped her head sitting just before the messy chaos of hair that she twisted into a bun.

This woman was so damn perfect in all her quirky weirdness that I couldn't help the smile that eased onto my face just before I greeted her.

"Rough night?"

Her smooth brown skin hid the blush of red that I was positive crawled up her neck and crept onto her cheeks, but it wasn't like Noel to not have a witty comeback.

"Very. I shared my bed with a snorer and barely got any rest until he snuck out of my bed this morning."

I chuckled as she dipped into the kitchen and began removing things. Curiosity got the best of me, or maybe it was the void I felt from missing those pretty brown eyes and a sea of smooth, rich skin. It also could have been the way her perky breasts pushed against the fabric of her tee or the way her soft hips stretched out the spandex shorts, but either way, I was off the sofa and entering the kitchen to see what Noel was up to.

I noticed a glass bowl on the counter next to a carton of eggs, a loaf of bread, and a milk carton.

"French toast?" I questioned when she turned to me and offered a smile and a soft nod.

"Dinner last night and breakfast this morning. I'm starting to think you're setting me up."

She turned away from me to open a cabinet where she retrieved a measuring glass and a large mixing spoon from a nearby drawer.

"Setting you up how?"

"They say you shouldn't feed strays, or they'll never leave."

Noel laughed, rolling her eyes before turning toward the sink to wash her hands. When she dried them on a hand towel she tossed on the counter, she pointed at me with one of the eggs she lifted. "You're

not a stray. You're my houseguest until the 27th, and I'd be willing
to bet it would take more than a few meals to keep you here."

I crossed the kitchen, stepping behind Noel, boxing her in as
I placed my hands on the counter and lowered my face to the side
of hers. I felt a shiver travel through her body when I kissed her
temple. "I elevated from Scrooge to houseguest?"

"You did decorate a tree last night."

I kissed a trail down her neck, leaning my body into hers. "I
did, didn't I?"

"You did." Her breathing was labored, and my dick twitched
as it swelled against her.

"And you thanked me very nicely for my services, if I recall."

"I did, didn't I?"

"You did." I smiled, planting a kiss on the back of her neck.
"The hospitality is great, but the host is even better." I pulled back.
"Do you need me to keep you company while you cook?"

"Uhhh." She stumbled over the word, shaking off the flush
she felt from my having been so close. "No, not really."

"Great. I'm going to jump into the shower and change then."

"That's good because we have a busy day ahead of us."

I turned back toward the kitchen to find Noel cracking an egg
on the edge of a glass bowl. The thought of her in my kitchen or her
cooking for me daily was not a visual I would turn my nose up at.

"We had a busy day yesterday."

"And I promised you a true Christmas experience you can't
get from one day. Now, go . . ." She flicked her wrist, shooing me
away and where I would typically argue about the idea of being
fully submerged in all things Christmas . . . I was actually looking
forward to whatever Noel had planned for me.

Noel.

THE MORNING WAS perfect. Kanton and I had breakfast. Then we cleaned the kitchen together. We worked like a well-oiled machine, moving together as if this were our regular daily routine. And I liked it. A little too much.

"This feels very elementary school arts and crafts-ish. I can't believe you're making me do this."

I grinned at Kanton's long, nimble fingers as he kneaded the salt dough we mixed to create our handcrafted ornaments.

"Is that your fancy way of calling this activity 'childish'?"

He grimaced and cut his eyes toward me, lifting the mound of dough which his long fingers formed into the perfect consistency for making ornaments. "If I say yes, are you going to pout?"

"Pretty much, so keep your negative thoughts to yourself." I reached for the cookie sheet layered with parchment paper and placed it on the counter next to the floury mess we created. Kanton watched me roll the dough flat enough to move to the next step.

"Pick."

"Pick what?"

"The shapes you want. We have to use the cookie cutters to shape them. Once we're done, I'll bake them, and after they've cooled, we can paint and decorate." I beamed, and he groaned, reaching for the tree, but I popped his hand.

"That's mine."

He arched a brow, turning toward me. "You're forcing me to do arts and crafts, but you won't allow me first pick at what shape I want?"

"Nope."

He chuckled and reached for the star, shifting his eyes toward me. "May I?"

"You may."

We filled the cookie sheet with several trees, stars, snowmen, and Santa heads, which I carefully placed into the oven and set the timer. After cleaning up, we settled onto the sofa for our next activity.

I sat on one end of the sofa, my back against the arm and legs crossed at the ankles, while Kanton sat on the opposite end.

"What's next on the torture list?" he asked smugly, bringing a grin to my face.

"Two Truths and a Lie, Holiday Edition."

"I have no idea what that is, but it doesn't sound like anything I'm going to enjoy."

I narrowed my eyes. "You don't know what Two Truths and a Lie is?"

"Don't have a damn clue.

"You're kidding, right?"

"Nope."

"It's an icebreaker. Sort of a get-to-know-you kind of thing. We played all the time in college, but if the person got the answer wrong, then shots were involved." I smiled widely.

"Shots might make this more interesting. Should I get the bourbon I bought the other day?" He flashed me a smile as his eyes raked down my body, and I rolled my eyes.

"Well, too bad, and no. We're doing the sober edition. I need you functional so that you can decorate your ornaments when they're done . . ."

"Or hear me out . . . A few shots might make me less subjective and much more creative." The sexy grin he delivered had my stomach taking flight, but I stuck to my guns.

"No shots, and I'll go first."

He groaned, but I ignored his displeasure. "As a kid, I refused to sleep on Christmas Eve because I wanted to see Santa but never made it past midnight. I couldn't open my presents until we did family breakfast and photos, and my parents had to hide my presents at the neighbor's house because I would always search for them and ruin the surprise."

"I'm assuming I'm supposed to pick the truths and the lie."

I nodded, and he frowned slightly while processing what I said. Then, he gave his answer. "Considering what I already know about you, I'm going to say the lie is that you refused to go to bed on Christmas Eve but not because you wanted to see Santa. You wanted to complain about his process. I imagine you in snowflake-covered pajamas, with a list of tips on how old Saint Nick could make Christmas ten times better."

I belted out a laugh seconds before lifting a throw pillow, which I launched at his head. Kanton was stealthy enough to dodge my attack, and his smile expanded.

"I'm guessing I was right."

"You absolutely were not. The lie was that my parents had to hide my gifts with the neighbors because I would go looking for them."

"You didn't?"

"No, I didn't."

"Hard to believe."

"Not really. I love surprises. That's part of the magic. Ripping open presents on Christmas morning to see if Santa delivered all the goodies on your list."

"And did he?"

I beamed. "Almost every single time. I realized as I got older that my parents cheated by making copies of my letters to Santa to ensure I got what I wanted, but who can be mad about that? What about you?"

"I never wrote letters to Santa and never got what I wanted for Christmas."

"What? Why not?" My face crumpled.

"I told you, Christmas with my family was more of a production. The details are always well thought out and planned. It was never about me or getting what I wanted or being surprised Christmas morning. It was about capturing the perfect moment on camera or in a photo. A six-year-old writing a letter to Santa didn't make the list."

"And you didn't get presents?"

"I did. Very nice, expensive gifts that fit the narrative of my family's wealth. When I was ten, I donated my entire *Christmas* to needy families. When I was six, I was gifted a foundation for wayward families in my name. And when I was eight, I received a scholarship fund for a student of excellence also in my name, all of which looked amazing and prestigious, and I still write a check for it to ensure the tradition holds, but those gifts were about others and never for me. I'm grateful to give to needy families, but my family was wealthy. Ensuring I had a new bike, a basketball, or a Nerf gun wouldn't have put a dent in their finances. I was a kid. I didn't understand why I couldn't have one thing for myself."

"No toys for Christmas, ever?"

"No."

"That's . . . *sad* . . ."

"Yeah, it is."

"It sounds like you didn't have much of a childhood."

"It wasn't terrible. My parents loved me. I had everything I needed, more than most could ever imagine, but my family functioned like a company."

"It all makes sense now."

He frowned. "What makes sense?"

"Why you're so . . . *you*."

The guy was all business, no fun, very disciplined, and very much controlled.

"You make it sound like I'm a tragedy or dysfunctional, and I assure you, I'm not."

I smiled slowly. "No, not at all, but you are a little too structured. Being here is good for you . . ."

And me.

Really good for me.

"You think so?"

"Yes, even if you suck at holiday games, decorating, Christmas crafts, and spreading holiday cheer." I smiled smugly.

Something in his eyes shifted, and then one of my ankles was dragged forward seconds before Kanton was planked over me, his lower half pressing in between my legs. His arms caged me in, and my, oh my, was I loving how this felt.

"I'm terrible at games, but I can think of a few things that I'm really good at."

"Oh yeah? And what's that?"

"This . . ."

His head dipped low, and he moved down my body, tugging at my shorts, which I lifted to help him remove. When my legs ended up draped over his shoulders and his face buried between my thighs, I silently thanked the universe for small favors.

Because he hadn't lied. With each swipe of his tongue, I agreed. He was really, really, *really* good at this.

"Are you going to tell me where we're going?"

"Nope. It's a surprise."

"I don't like surprises," Kanton muttered as he opened the rear door of the car that was waiting for us once we exited the lobby of my building. "And why aren't we driving?"

"You promised not to complain . . ." I reminded him of our conversation earlier that afternoon, telling him we had plans for the evening. He promised not to complain as long as it didn't involve any glitter, paint, or ribbons.

"I'm not complaining. I'm just asking questions." He settled in next to me, exchanged greetings with the driver, and then yanked me into his side since I had elected to sit on my side of the vehicle. Considering we had been laid up together most of the day, I thought he might want his space. I thought wrong.

"We're not driving because there will be alcohol where we're going, so just in case either of us wants to indulge, then there won't be any issues with us getting home safely."

"Are we going to a club? I don't do clubs." He frowned, and I offered a smile.

"No, we're not, and why don't you do clubs?"

"Because clubs are pointless unless you're looking to get drunk or laid."

"You don't like getting drunk?"

"No, do you?" He arched a brow, and I shrugged.

"I have at times, but mostly not by choice. Sometimes, the drinks just keep flowing, and well, shit happens."

"Nothing is appealing about being so intoxicated you can't think straight, you feel physically sick, and/or pass out with no memory of what happened before that."

"I agree, but it's also nice to throw caution to the wind and just go with the flow."

Kanton leaned into me, and the warmth of his mouth against my neck created a chain reaction. A shiver trailed down my spine, my muscles locked and then released, while my pussy pulsed when he spoke. "You a little tipsy might not be such a bad thing. I actually like the idea of your willingness to go with the flow."

"That's not a problem I have. More your thing than mine. You could stand to loosen up a bit and allow some fun to slip past that hard exterior of yours."

"I would prefer being hard in your interior to loosen *you* up."

A flood of fire shot through my veins, and a wave of sensitivity settled into my body with memories of what his being hard and loosening me up felt like.

"Can we stay focused, please?"

"I am. The topic was getting drunk and getting laid. Speaking of which, why didn't you ask me if I like to get laid?"

"Because I already know the answer to that one." I turned my face to him, and he smirked before kissing me.

"Indeed you do. Finally, something we share in common."

Was he keeping score? Trying to find things about us that made sense, and if so, why? I refused to let my mind wonder about things that didn't matter. This was temporary. *He* was temporary. We were just living in the moment . . . a moment that would end after Christmas, and as much as I knew that the end was undoubtedly coming, I still found myself wishing for more.

After a half-hour drive to a quiet, little neighborhood in West Atlanta, we pulled up to a one-level ranch house I had been to more times than I could count. Kanton glanced at the house and then back at me with a skeptical look.

"Who lives here?"

"Friends."

"Friends?" He frowned a little more, and I reached across him to yank the handle to the door.

"Yes, friends. No complaining, remember?" He eased out of the vehicle and accepted the bag I brought with holiday treats and a bottle of wine from my stash. He then helped me out of the car after I thanked the driver.

We walked to the house, with Kanton guiding me with a hand at my lower back while he carefully avoided slick spots from the light snowfall that morning. It was about all we would see this year. As soon as we reached the door, and it swung up, granting a visual of a round face, bright eyes, and smile as beautiful as her spirit, I felt at ease.

"You made it, and you brought your guest."

"I did. I hope that's okay."

"Absolutely. I always cook too much anyway. An old habit I can't break from when Carlie was home. Come in, please."

Once we were inside and relieved of our coats, which were tossed on the rack near the door, we moved through our introduction. "Kanton, this is Cleo, Lewis's wife. Cleo, this is Kanton. He's staying with me for the week."

Kanton's eyes darted to me, and a playful smile creased his lips before he greeted Cleo. I was sure the smile was because of the "staying with me" part.

"Nice to meet you." He extended a hand that she swatted away and hugged him.

"Oh, you're nice and firm, and you smell good. Now I see why this one didn't toss you out on your ass."

"Cleo . . ."

The low rumble of Lewis's voice had all of us turning in his direction. He was standing at the head of the hallway wearing jeans and a sweater—a huge contrast from his typical uniform.

"What? You're the one who said she didn't kick him out because he was good-looking. I'm only agreeing."

I cringed at the two of them discussing my reasoning for allowing Kanton to spend the week with me, which had me blurting out, "I let him stay because he threatened to sue me. You know how anal and demanding corporate types can be."

Kanton chuckled but didn't debate my lie. Instead, he approached Lewis and extended a hand. "Well, either way, I'm here. Thank you for the invite."

"I didn't invite you. I invited Noel." He shook Kanton's hand, grinning as his eyes shot past him. "Thank Noel for the good food you'll enjoy this evening."

"Noel's been blessing me with many things since I've been here. She's been such a gracious host."

When Kanton's eyes found mine, I blushed at the look he gave. It was a thank-you for not just tonight but other things as well.

"I bet she has, as cute as you are," Cleo mumbled lowly, but I was sure Kanton heard her even if Lewis hadn't. "Follow me. I have something I want you to try."

Cleo offered up a teasing smile as she followed the same path that her husband had taken. I was about to follow when Kanton stepped into my path.

"Is that why you agreed to let me stay? Because I'm cute and firm and smell good?"

My eyes flashed wide, and he inched closer when I hissed my answer. "Absolutely not. You threatened to sue me, or have you forgotten? And I needed the money. Me agreeing to our deal has nothing to do with how good you look, feel, or smell."

Kanton's hands landed quickly at my hips, and my pelvis was yanked forward until I collided with him and his . . .

"You sure about that? These are your friends, right?"

My brows furrowed. "Yes, why?"

"Friends tend to know you best, and Cleo and Lewis both seemed confident that you have a thing for me. I have it on good authority that you have an affinity for my mouth, my tongue, and my . . ."

He rocked his hips forward, and my body felt weak with the reminder of that last thing.

"You're awfully sure of yourself." I smirked and tried to pull away, but he dug his fingers in deeper.

"Are you?"

"Sure of myself?"

He leaned closer so that our lips were a breath apart. Mine twitched with the need for a connection to his until they tilted at the corners seconds before he made clear, "No, sure of *me*." And then he walked away, and I stood hating how right he was.

Kanton.

"THIS IS REALLY good."

"I assumed it was, considering that's your third one." Cleo pointed to the glass mug I protectively cradled after I finished off what remained of my eggnog. She had miscounted. This was my fourth, not third, but I wouldn't fess up because, after all, who was counting?

"She gets me every year with this stuff. You would think after thirty-eight years, I'd know better than to travel down that rabbit hole, but this is hard to resist." Lewis lifted his own mug after taking down another healthy swallow of his wife's special brew.

"I've been trying to convince her to hand over the recipe, but she refuses." Noel cut her eyes at Cleo, who smiled proudly.

"This is a special brew. I can't just hand it over lightly. Isn't that right, babe?" Her eyes shifted to her husband, who nodded with a twinkling in his eyes. These two were the real deal.

"Sure is. She got me sloshed on this stuff the first year we dated. Had a ring on her finger by Valentine's Day, and we married by spring."

"Because of eggnog?" Noel's brows pinched as her eyes bounced between the two.

"Because of what happens *after* the eggnog," Lewis said, winking at his wife.

"Huh . . . *oh* . . ." Noel muttered and then cut her eyes at me.

"Speaking of, are you single, dear?" Cleo's eyes landed on me, and I nodded.

"I am."

"Good to know. Our girl here has been single for long enough. Maybe I should send some home with you tonight."

"That would be a hard pass." Noel's spine straightened, and her eyes narrowed on Cleo. Lewis chuckled, and Noel added, "And I haven't been single for *that* long. You make it sound like I'm a spinster or something."

"You're making yourself sound like a spinster using that word," Cleo teased before she continued. "And although it hasn't been too long since you rid yourself of that last disaster, you might as well have considered yourself single while you were together. He was never around much. Certainly couldn't bother himself enough to sit down at our table and share a meal with us." Cleo didn't sound happy about his lack of attendance at their home.

"He—"

"*Worked* a lot. Yeah, I know, but people find time for what's important to them. Don't you agree, Kanton?"

This felt dangerously close to treading in territory where I had no business venturing. "Most of the time, yes. Sometimes, work can't be avoided."

Lewis chimed in. "You're a lot like him, you know."

I frowned, and he added. "Her ex. All business and no fun. The career-driven type with more focus on their money than—"

"They're *not* the same." Noel defended me, causing something primal to swell in my chest, but the conversation about her ex sidetracked me. She mentioned being single. Neither of us had gone into depth about our situations.

There seemed to be a story based on the tension brewing in Noel, which screamed for me to leave it alone. She was uncomfortable, which made me angry. My first thought was that he had done her wrong, and the idea of anyone hurting Noel made me want to hurt them.

"No, not the same because he's here. Evan would never have come." Lewis smiled softly at Noel and then turned to me. "You smoke cigars?"

"Never turn down a good blend. You offering?"

"I am. I've got some from Flavor that I've been dying to try. Cleo makes me smoke outside, so I hope you can handle the cold."

"I think I'll survive."

"Let's go then."

Noel offered to help Cleo clean up while Lewis and I headed out back. We both bypassed coats, so I was grateful when we ended up on a glass-enclosed porch. It was still nippy, but we weren't out in direct air. Lewis collected his humidor and single-blade cutter.

"Are things going well with you two?"

Just jump right in. I had a feeling this was why I received the invite.

"They are, but I wouldn't exactly call us a 'you two.'"

"Hmmm." He nodded with his back to me as he clipped the ends of two cigars and passed me one. He blazed the end of his and then handed over a lighter for me to do the same. We stood staring out into the darkness of his backyard, which was littered with colorful lights. It was similar to the front yard, although there weren't any reindeer back here.

It was gaudy and overkill, but somehow, it felt more welcoming than the professionally installed decorations my mother paid thousands for each year.

Lewis and Cleo were the real deal. They were not just happily married but also in love. I could feel it radiating from them, from their home. Nothing like my parents. They loved each other and possibly had been in love at some point, but the older I got, the more I realized they were more or less a business rather than a marriage.

"You have a lot of lights."

Lewis scoffed as if irritated, but his tone was the same as when he responded. "Too many damn lights, but Cleo loves them, so I drag them out every year and let her boss me around telling me where they go, even though we've been doing this dance for over twenty years the same way, in this same house. We did it for another fifteen in the one before this one."

I grinned. "Sounds exhausting."

"It is, but I love every minute of it. What about your family? I'm sure they have their own traditions. You said you were here for work. They're not missing you?"

"My mother is, but mostly because I've disrupted her visually perfect Christmas."

"Huh? One of those types. I bet being here with Noel is a bit of culture shock then if you're used to visually perfect and not the real thing." He glanced at me with a smile tugging at his lips before he puffed on the cigar dangling in his fingers. I did the same and nodded as I enjoyed the smoking flavor and then exhaled.

"It's been an experience. She's very Christmassy." I turned to him. "Speaking of, you could have warned me about the tree."

"I did," he asserted. "You didn't listen, and she *is* very Christmassy. She's also thoughtful and very selfless. It's why she and her ex didn't make it."

When I glanced his way, his eyes were on me. "You didn't like him very much, did you?"

"Didn't really dislike him as much as I disliked the idea of him with our Noel. Not a good fit."

"Why not?"

"Polar opposites. She's more of a free spirit. Kind, smiles a lot, wants everyone around her smiling too. She'll find a way to make it happen if they're not. He was a guy in a suit with a busy schedule and no time to make her smile."

Interesting.

"But they were together."

"They were together for a little over a year, but that's how women are. They bind themselves to men who will never make them happy. It's like they love to torture themselves, making all the wrong decisions, and then punishing us good guys for showing them the life and happiness they deserve." Lewis grunted and added, "When I met Cleo, she was dating a musician. He was artsy, played the sax, and had all the women chasing after him . . . even my Cleo . . . until I showed her what a real man was. Had to drag her kicking and screaming at first because she refused to believe that I was the man she'd fall hopelessly in love with, but you see how that turned out." He smiled, and I chuckled.

"I do."

"I said the two of you were a lot alike. You and her ex, but I meant in appearance. I think you're a much better fit than he ever was."

"Oh, we're not—"

"Not saying the two of you are into anything, only that you could be a better fit. He liked the idea of Noel. She's hard to resist. She's like an explosion of energy that you find yourself drawn to but don't know why. You just know that you've gotta be around her. With Cleo and me, she fills the void of our daughter Carlie. She got some fancy job and moved to London. We only see her a couple of times a year, so it's nice having someone like Noel to look after."

"Then I'm glad you all have each other."

He nodded but kept going.

"And with her ex, he never gave her what she needed. Didn't support her the way he should have. You know she wanted to start her business a long time ago, but he discouraged her?"

I knew men like that. They wanted their women to look the part and be available to be at their beck and call . . . basically, bodies to show off, fuck, and feed them. The type of woman my mother wanted me to marry, the type of man she assumed I was. She couldn't be more wrong.

"He didn't want her to be successful?"

"More like he didn't want to support her dreams. That would be one more thing: he had to make up excuses for not being present. He made her choose him over her career, and she did for a while, but she realized he was an ass and she should make herself a priority since that was obviously what he was doing."

The more Lewis talked, the more I wanted to meet this guy. Or rather, wanted his face to meet my fists.

"He didn't deserve Noel. Never made her a priority. He'd send her expensive gifts but wasn't ever around. He had the means, so the gifts meant nothing to him. I'd deliver them to her, see the smile that never reached her eyes, and want to punch him in the face. She'd rather have his time than his money, but guys like Evan don't really understand that. Got to the point where she finally had enough. They had some big argument that ended things. He left and never looked back. Can't say I was upset about it. She could do better."

"She should have better so she can be happy."

"I want her to be happy." He stared at me in an unwavering manner. "You keep that in mind while you're enjoying your time here. We clear on that, Kanton?"

And there it was. The threat to do right by Noel . . . or deal with Lewis.

"Very."

He gripped my shoulder, and we finished our cigars in silence, although my thoughts were very loud. Noel had brought me to meet her extended family.

She was inviting me deeper into her world, and I wasn't sure what to do with that. This was one week of my life, and then I had to return to everything I knew. No matter how good this felt, how good she felt, it couldn't be much more than this . . . right?

"Tonight was fun," Noel said quietly as she clutched the massive glass mason jar that Cleo sent home with us. I had a container of her famous sugar cookies tucked under my arm while I keyed the code to enter her apartment.

"It was. Thank you for inviting me."

We stepped into the apartment, and I reached for the mason jar. Noel shed her coat, and I walked into the kitchen and placed the cookies on the counter and eggnog in the refrigerator.

"Thank you for going. I think Cleo felt bad for me. She knows I'm usually home for Christmas, and she wanted me to have some semblance of being with family." She turned to me after hanging her coat on the rack near the door and then reached for mine. "And I think she wanted to see you."

"Me?"

"Yep. The text she sent me earlier said, 'Got a home-cooked meal and some eggnog waiting if you're interested. And you can bring a friend if you want.'"

"Not subtle at all."

"Nope, but Cleo's just like that. They're good people and adorably cute."

"They are, and they're very protective of you."

She turned around with an apologetic expression. "Oh God, what did he say to you out there?"

"Nothing you need to be worried about. Just that you're a very special person, and I agreed. I also ensured he knew he didn't have to worry about me mistreating you. I'd be on my best behavior while here, and then I'll be out of your hair so that you can get back to your life."

"Oh . . ." Something passed in her eyes but didn't linger long enough for me to catch what it was because she quietly rattled off, "Well, it's late. I think I will turn in for the night, get some rest, and you should too."

"This seems way too easy. No Christmas movies or baking ornaments planned for the evening?" I arched a brow.

She slowly shook her head. "No. You get the night off. I've been consuming your time and pushing you into Christmas overload. You get a hall pass for the night, and besides, I need to check in with my parents and Simone to assure them I haven't fallen into a severe depression behind missing them. I'm sure you also have work to do since I've been monopolizing most of your time. We've got the Brightons' Christmas party tomorrow."

"Right, we do."

"Okay, then, I'll see you in the morning." She hesitated, and so did I. Something was off. I couldn't tell what. Maybe she realized that things with us were a bit too much. Maybe Cleo had warned her against the idea of more with me because I was too much like her ex.

Her ex.

Fuck, I hated the guy, and I didn't even know him.

"Good night, Kanton."

"Good night, Noel."

She was gone, and then I heard the soft click of her door. A reminder that she was shutting me out. I stood in the same spot, staring down the hall, watching the same path she took. Something in me felt unbalanced. That something was the presence of Noel, but who was I to force the issue? A few days. That's all this was, and with that, I headed to the living room and flopped on the sofa, folding my arms and tucking them behind my head as I closed my eyes. Only I couldn't settle my mind, so I was up again,

untangling lights for the tree and mantle. The mindless work kept
me occupied until exhaustion settled in enough for me to sleep.

When I got comfortable on the sofa again, I thought about
Lewis's story of how he decorated every year for his wife. I could
only wonder what that would be like if I did the same for mine.
But Noel wasn't my wife or even my anything, so with a huff of
annoyance, I closed my eyes and allowed myself to drift.

I woke up the following day to the sound of low-hissed profanity,
which had me smiling as I peeled my eyes open, slowly turning
my head to find a very nice visual of an ass that I had become
intimately acquainted with over the past few days. Although
covered in tight jeans instead of my preferred spandex, tiny silk
shorts, or my all-time favorite . . . nothing at all.

"Shit, shit, shit."

As soon as she lifted the keys, which was why I woke to such
a tempting visual, I cleared my throat, and she quickly straightened
her posture and spun on her heels, turning to face me.

"Well, good morning, and I have to say, as beautiful as you
are in this very moment, I was rather enjoying the view I just had."

She frowned at me and rolled her eyes. "Sorry to disappoint,
but I have somewhere to be. You'll have to find something else to
entertain you."

"Not possible," I murmured, throwing my legs over the side of
the sofa and rolling my neck a few times to work out the stiffness.
"You heading out?"

"Yes, I need to get a dress for tonight."

"You don't have something you can wear?"

She was only going to Brighton's party as a favor to me, so the
idea of her having to purchase a dress didn't sit right.

She quickly shook her head. "No, it's semiformal, and I've seen pictures. They really go all out, and nothing I have will work."

"I find it hard to believe you don't own a cocktail dress with embossed snowmen for such an occasion."

"Cute, and I said, semiformal."

"I would believe that to be semiformal and acceptable for the Queen of Christmas."

She rolled her shoulders back and lifted her chin. "For me, it would, but it's not my party, so I think it's best if I complied with their dress code."

"Do you mind if I tag along? I probably need to grab something also."

Her face crumpled. And I wasn't sure what that was about.

"You don't have a suit? You were planning a meeting with Brighton."

"I do, but it's gray and plain as shit. You said formal, right?"

"Well, yes, but—"

I stood and cut her off. "Give me fifteen minutes to shower and throw something on."

"Kanton, you really don't have to—"

"If you're complying with the dress code, then, as your guest, I should too. Fifteen minutes."

She groaned and stomped into the living room, plopping down on the sofa I had just vacated. I grabbed a pair of jeans, a thermal shirt, and the rest of what I needed and hurried to the bathroom, praying she didn't change her mind and leave me.

For whatever reason, whatever had been bothering Noel last night was still bothering her today, but I'd deal with that later. At the moment, I needed to shower and dress in record time so that I didn't get left behind.

Noel.

Me: Would it be rude if I left him?
Simone: Yes, why would you? What happened? Did he do something?

*B**ESIDES THE FACT** that last night he made clear that he was only here for a week of fun, and then he was going back to his life . . . Nope, nothing happened at all.*

Me: No, but I don't want to go shopping with him. You know my situation. I was going to grab something inexpensive, prayerfully on sale, and then maybe even return it. I can't do that with him there.
Simone: Why the hell not?

Because I'm in between blessings, and he's rich, and it will only further convince him that we don't fit. Not that it matters. He already knows we don't.

Me: Because it will be weird shopping with a stranger.
Simone: Shopping with a stranger or shopping with a wealthy stranger?

I chewed my lip, hating how easily she could read me.
Me: Both.

Those three dots danced. Stopped. Danced again. Stopped once more, and then the message came through.

Simone: If he can't love you for you and all your bargain-dress-buying-glory, then fuck him, Noel. And I don't mean the way you've been doing all week. I mean Queen Bey style: middle-finger-up, boy-bye kinda fuck you. Rich people who are rudely rich aren't real people. They're assholes, and I hope that's not who he is, but if that is, in fact, the truth, then again, fuck him.

I smiled widely, proud of how much she truly loved me and would tear down a total stranger just to make sure I was okay.

Me: I love you for loving me, and you're right. Fuck him if he can't love me in all my bargain-dress-buying-glory. Gotta go. I'll send pictures.
Simone: You better, and I love you more. Slay, bitch, slay.
Me: I will!

Ten minutes later, rounding out our fifteen to twenty-five, Kanton came hurrying out of the bathroom, leaving a trail of citrus and bergamot lingering in the air as he passed me, dumping his things on top of his suitcase and then putting on his shoes. How could I dislike someone as sexy as this man? He made it really hard.

Hard.

Stop it.

"Ready?" He glanced at me on his way to the door, where he grabbed the fleece scarf I had forced him to wear when we went tree shopping. My heart melted at the sight because I knew he did that for me. It matched my bright green skully because the two came as a set.

"You're wearing that?"

"You're wearing that." He pointed to my hat. "And I thought that tacky Christmas attire was a requirement for holiday shopping."

"Tree shopping and it's not tacky. It's nostalgic." When I lifted my chin, he ignored my defiant rebuttal and nodded.

"Since I'm forcing my way to tag along, I figured I might as well keep my guide happy."

"You're a very smart man, Mr. Joseph."

"I've been told a time or two."

Kanton drove us to Shops at Buckhead using my navigation system since he insisted on driving. I was grateful because traffic was terrible, overloaded with what I could only assume was last-minute shoppers and possibly travelers driving through the city en route to their families.

The thought made me sad with the reminder that I couldn't be with mine, and although I'd talked to Mom and Dad several times, it just wasn't the same. The good thing was my week hadn't been so terrible thanks to the very attractive man whipping my car through traffic like he lived here. He drove with skill and very confidently as if daring anyone to get in our way. I was grateful they didn't because I wasn't sure how that would end.

We parked and walked inside the crowded mall, dodging bodies. At some point, Kanton and I ended up hand in hand, shoulder to shoulder. It was easier to stay together until we reached our location.

The directory.

I aimed to send him on his merry little way while I went on mine.

"You can search there and see what stores you want to try. We can meet back up in about an hour, OK? Is that enough time?"

He arched a brow and stepped closer. "Or we could go together. It might help to know what you're wearing so I can decide what to get."

No, not happening.

"We don't have to match."

"I disagree. You're my date, and I'm yours." His smile was sexy, and, oh, so hard to resist, but still . . .

"It's not exactly a *real* date. More like you're my plus-one. Matching is not required."

"Again, I disagree. Where to first?"

"Kanton . . ." I huffed.

"Noel . . ." he returned with an adamant challenge.

"Fine. Neiman's."

"Perfect. I'm sure I can find something there."

"Of course you can," I murmured, feeling annoyed.

We were moving again, and after a long pause of silence, Kanton stepped in front of me, causing my body to slam right into his chest. His hands on my arms righted me so that I didn't fall, but the frown on his face matched mine.

"Did I do something wrong?"

"No, why?"

"Because you've been a little distant, maybe even annoyed, since we got home last night, and based on how you've been acting today, it seems like you'd rather be anywhere *but* near me. If I said or did something—"

"You haven't," I huffed and relaxed some. It wasn't his fault that I was stressed about spending money I didn't have. Nor was it his fault I wanted one night to dress up and feel pretty, standing next to a man who I was falling for and who would be gone soon . . . leaving me with yet another disappointment. "I just . . . This has been a lot, but none of this is your fault."

"This as in *us*?"

"Yes, but spending time with you hasn't been a bad thing. This is just me being me . . . well, never mind. It's not a big deal."

He frowned harder, searching my face. "You sure?"

"I'm sure." I forced a smile and slipped my hand into his. "Let's go find something for tonight."

As soon as we entered the store, I browsed dresses with the ability to check the prices because Kanton accepted a call and stepped away for privacy, but that didn't mean he wasn't keeping tabs on my whereabouts.

When I moved too far, he moved with me, keeping a respectful distance and ensuring he was within reach. For what, I didn't know, but based on the way he followed my every move with those intense eyes, I could pretty much guess. He liked looking at me just as much as I enjoyed looking at him, and that, within itself, was an issue.

When I made my third trip to the dressing room with several new dresses, I was convinced that I couldn't find the right one. At least, not one that wouldn't consume the entire free balance I had on Emmie.

Nothing worked for a plethora of reasons. Too short, too long, too tight, too full, exposed too much cleavage, didn't show enough. Nothing worked. Not one of the dresses I tried screamed, "This is the one!"

This time, when I came marching out of the dressing room, feeling defeated, I was startled at the low rasp and deep brown eyes that were waiting.

"Still no luck?"

"No. I give up."

He smirked, turned away from me, and when he was back in view, he held up a dress. "May I offer a suggestion?"

Kanton lowered his eyes to the dress. It was absolutely perfect. Beautiful, so perfect . . . and so expensive . . .

I didn't have to see the price tag to know I couldn't afford it. I hated how much I really wanted to try it on but wouldn't because I'd be heartbroken when it fit as perfectly as I knew it would . . . so I picked a fight.

"I'm sorry if my economical selections don't suit your taste, but unfortunately, that's all I can afford right now. I'll pick one of these."

"You think I picked this dress because of how much it cost?"

The look on his face crushed me. Kanton was offended. And he should have been. Not once had he thrown his money or status in my face, and here I was doing it for him. But I was already invested, so I stood my ground, crossing my arms over my chest, cradling the armful of dresses I tried on against my body.

"Didn't you?"

I wasn't backing down, but neither was he. Offended or not, he stood his ground as well. "No, I didn't. I saw the saleswoman passing by with this dress. Another customer had it on hold and called to release it after finding another they liked better. She was about to return it to the sales floor, but I asked if I could see it. The minute I got a better look, I knew it would be perfect. And not because of the price. Because of the pattern, layers, and unique details. It's also incredibly sexy, and I could literally visualize how amazing you're going to look with it on. I picked this dress because it fit *you*, Noel. Not because it fits some nonexistent budget that you're assuming I like to adhere to while shopping. I honestly don't have a damn clue how much the dress cost."

Again, I felt like shit . . . but I stood my ground. "A lot. I can tell, and I can't afford to pay whatever it costs. Not right now."

"I wouldn't expect you to pay for it. I'll buy the dress."

"No."

Kanton's expression shifted again, and I could sense he was doing his best to keep his cool, but when he inched closer, instead of arguing or saying fuck it, his hands moved lower, taking possession of the dresses I was holding. He held out the one he selected until I accepted it, and then he relaxed his expression.

"I'm *not* your ex. I don't need to buy expensive things to make up for not seeing you how you deserve to be seen. I don't give a damn what you wear tonight. You can wear one of those ugly-ass sweaters or those adorably sexy satin pajama sets if that's what you prefer. I would still stand proudly beside you, Noel. You like this dress. I can see it in your eyes, so try it on, and if you still love it, then allow me the *privilege* of buying it for you."

"Okay."

How could I say no after that very compelling argument?

"Okay?" He was surprised by my one-word response.

"Yes, I said okay. I'll try the dress on. If it fits, and that's a big *if*, I'll let you buy it for me."

"It will fit."

"You don't know that."

"I do. I might have asked the saleswoman to gauge your size for me, and she assured me that that dress would be a perfect fit."

I smiled, rolling my eyes. "Of course you did."

I tried on the dress, which was a perfect fit, as promised. And as he promised, I loved it, and so did Kanton based on how his eyes devoured me. I asked him to take a few pictures, and he insisted on taking them on his phone and sending them to me. I had a suspicion that was so he had his own to keep. He purchased the dress, and then we headed to the men's section. And while he browsed, I sent the pictures to Simone so she wouldn't murder me.

After the first picture was delivered, I received an immediate response.

Simone: You better do that shit, bestie.
Me: You like?
Simone: Bitch, I love. Looks expensive, though.
Me: It is. He paid for it, and no, he's not rude rich.

Simone: Then fuck him again and again and again . . . the right way. In the dress, because he deserves it.
Me: I'm already in over my head.
Simone: Then it's too late to worry about it. Get the dick, friend.

That was followed by a string of very inappropriate emojis, which made me lock my phone and search for Kanton. When I located him and approached where he was standing, I instantly regretted it.

"Noel, hi." I was greeted by Kenya, one of Neiman's personal shoppers, who I had, on occasion, used to help me shop, but not for myself. Her eyes bounced between me and Kanton, and as soon as recognition set in, she smiled bigger.

"Oh, wow, this is Evan, isn't it? We finally meet after all this time of helping Noel pick the perfect gifts, more helping than selecting, so don't worry." She paused to wink at Kanton. "I was beginning to believe you didn't exist."

"Sorry to disappoint, but you're still not meeting Evan."

Her eyes bounced between us again, and she frowned apologetically. "Oh, I'm sorry. I assumed—"

"It's fine. He and I aren't together anymore. This is Kanton. A friend."

"Friend, right. Again, sorry," she said to me and then turned to him. "Give me just a minute to check on that suit for you. Black on black, right? Will you need it altered?"

"Yes, all black, and if you have those measurements, then I won't need alterations."

"Perfect. Be right back."

"Evan, the ex?" he said as soon as she was gone.

"Yes, Evan, the ex," I repeated.

"You must have shopped here a lot if she remembers you and who you were shopping for."

"Let's just say enough. He had specific tastes. It was easier to stick to what I knew he liked."

"I see."

"But you knew that already, didn't you?" I peeked at him as he fingered through a display of ties.

"What makes you say that?"

"The 'I'm not like your ex who needs to buy you expensive things' comment. I'm guessing Lewis told you about him?"

"Briefly, but not much, though. Mostly that you two didn't fit."

I smirked, nodding. "They didn't like each other."

"I imagine not. Lewis and Cleo seem very protective of you."

"They are."

"What happened between you two, if you don't mind me asking?" He turned to face me, and I wanted to say I did mind, but what did it matter? He wasn't asking for a reference of what not to do. More to fill in the blanks of what Lewis left out.

"He traveled a lot for work. He's a corporate attorney with clients all over the country. I decided that being in a relationship was no fun if I was always alone. He didn't put up much of a fight, so we ended things. I'm sure you can understand that. The 'not having time' part because you're busy."

"Sounds like that was best for *him*, not—"

"You're in luck. I have the measurements you need. Would you like to try it on?"

"No, but I do need a shirt."

"Black?" He glanced at me when she asked, as if he was requesting my approval. I nodded, and his eyes shifted back to her.

"Yes, and that will be all."

"Okay, perfect." She left with his suit and added a shirt, and shortly after, we were on our way.

As we left Neiman's, Kanton walked incredibly close, carrying the garment bags holding my dress and his suit. I was beginning to appreciate what his closeness felt like, and that made me inch away with each step we took.

"How about we grab some lunch before heading home?" he suggested, and I scrunched my nose, peeking up at him when that word he had been using so freely found its way through his lips again.

"Home for you is New York."

"It is, but for now, *your apartment* is your home for me."

I huffed a sigh and gently shook my head.

"So, lunch?"

"Sure, but I'm treating. It's the least I can do." My eyes lowered to the garment bags draped over his arm, and his steps paused as we entered the lower level of the Food Pavilion just outside of California Pizza Kitchen.

"This isn't a competition, Noel. I'm not keeping score, and neither should you."

"I'm not—"

I didn't care about his money. I cared about how people with his type of money made me feel because I didn't have it. I also realized that was *my* issue, not *his*. Evan treated me like an accessory. Similar to the expensive cars he drove. Some days, he chose to show me attention, and I'd get to make a few rounds; others, he elected to have a driver because he couldn't be bothered by the hassle.

I wasn't on his level, so he didn't have to respect me. In his eyes, I should be happy that he considered me worth what little time and attention he offered. It took me a while to figure that out, but I did.

It also took time not to feel the sting from how little he respected me. Being around Kanton was a reminder of sorts, no matter how different he and Evan were. Evan started off great, and then one day, he wasn't.

"You are. Let it go. Pick your poison. I can eat just about anything." The way his eyes traveled down my body temporarily derailed my thoughts, and a flush of warmth traveled through me.

We settled on pizza since we were right there, waiting outside the opening to be seated, and we ended up in a booth near the back. We ordered, and I decided to stop overthinking and just enjoy the moment, but curiosity got the best of me when I decided to do a little digging of my own.

"You know all about my ex, but I don't know anything about yours."

"Do you want to?" Kanton grinned at me, and I shrugged nonchalantly.

"I wouldn't say I *want* to, but it seems appropriate since you know about mine."

His smile expanded. "You really like keeping score, don't you?"

"Maybe."

He chuckled and leaned back, resting one arm on the table, the other in his lap. The position opened his body more, and my eyes traveled from his face down to his chest until I caught myself, and they snapped back up.

"What would you like to know?"

"What did you do to run her off?" I flashed a cocky grin.

"What makes you think she didn't run me off?"

"It's possible, but my money is on you being the problem."

He laughed lightly and drummed his fingers on the table. "You'd be wrong. Neither of us were necessarily the problem. We just didn't fit and never should have been together in the first place."

"That means she wasn't Mommy-Résumé-Approved?"

He belted out a laugh. "Most definitely not. Jordan is an influencer, for lack of a better word. My mother would hate that about her. Our issue, however, is I'm more structured, whereas she loathes the idea of schedules and responsibility. It never would have worked."

"Didn't you know that when you met her?"

Evan knew who I was. I never pretended to be someone I wasn't. Yet, he *pretended* to want me until he decided he and I didn't fit. Even though I was the one who ended things, he would have.

"In some ways, yes, but there's always the 'opposite attract' theory. I enjoyed it for what it was . . ."

"She was a temporary fix for the days when you wanted to explore a less-structured lifestyle."

He frowned at me, staring intently for a long moment. "No. I never play with anyone's emotions, Noel. That's not who I am. She wasn't some toy or distraction. We both tried something new, enjoyed the relationship while we were in it, but we realized that we were two very different people. Our long-term goals didn't align, which posed a problem when considering anything real."

"Oh . . ."

His eyes never left my face when he asked, "Is that how *he* made you feel?"

"What? No . . ." I squared my shoulders. "And this isn't about me. I was asking about you."

"You were." He nodded, lifting his drink.

"Maybe we should keep things neutral. No more relationship talk. Agreed?"

His eyes narrowed slightly, but a smile was there. "Agreed."

I switched the subject. "What's the big plan to convince Brighton that you're his guy?"

"No big plan. The goal is to tell him why I'm the best."

I frowned slightly. "That's a terrible idea."

"Why?"

"You weren't even on the list to begin with, which means he doesn't care about all the reasons you're the best. I'm sure he knows what he needs and presumably hand selected the firm he wanted to use. If you want to close the deal, you'll have to do better than rattling off facts about you and your company."

"Yeah?"

"Definitely."

His eyes flicked with amusement. "Then what do you suggest I do?"

"I don't know, just, you know . . . Do what you do. You can be pretty charming when you want to. *Charm* him."

Kanton smiled arrogantly, and I realized my slip when the corners of his mouth tilted higher. "You think I'm charming?"

"Annoyingly so, yes."

He chuckled and lifted his beer again. "I won't disagree, but charming Brighton might not be as easy as charming someone like you."

"Why not?"

His eyes dragged down my body again. "Let's just say there's not a chance in hell that he will pique my interest enough for me to invest fully . . . the way that you have."

My cheeks heated, and I rolled my eyes, knowing what he hinted. "Well, either way, you'd better try because your plan sucks, and I doubt that listing facts will be enough."

"Noted." He grinned. "I'll think of something. Can't have you disappointed in me now, can I?"

"Nope. That would be a travesty."

Kanton chuckled again, and we left the topic there, which was good for both of us if we would survive the rest of his time here.

Kanton.

GORGEOUS.

Elegant.

Stunning.

Beautiful.

So fucking perfect.

That was the bottom line. The moment Noel stepped into the living room wearing the gown I purchased for her, something primal in me took over. This woman was gorgeous. Her wild curls were no longer, and, instead, her hair was straight, twisted, and pinned at the nape of her neck, with a few loose tendrils floating around her face.

Light makeup layered her skin, but naturally so. The only reason I knew for certain was because of the hints of gold around her eyes, the way her lashes lengthened, and the bronze color that coated her lips.

Those damn lips.

Fuck me.

No, fuck her. I wanted to fuck her right here in the living room while she was in that dress.

"Well . . ." Noel smiled and slowly twirled, offering me a full view of every inch of her. My dick was the first to react, and when the rest of me caught up, I moved closer. Brushing a finger down her cheek over the curve of her jaw, I said, "You're trying to sabotage my efforts to win over Brighton."

She frowned slightly, those bronze-painted lips pushing into a subtle pout. "Why would you say that?"

I leaned close, inhaling deeply the light scent of brown sugar and vanilla, speaking as my mouth grazed her ear. "With you in this dress, there's very little chance he'll give me his full attention tonight."

"Then I'll change because his full attention is the only reason we're going tonight." Her voice was teasing, and while I pulled back, granting a full view of her beautiful face, those lips were in a soft smile.

"Not happening; now, let's go."

I rolled my shoulders back and walked to the kitchen counter where the candles and case of cigars that we purchased for Brighton and his wife were sitting. I lifted them both, and we were on our way.

We took the elevator to the penthouse floor and walked out to the end of the hall, where two black double doors awaited us. A doorman greeted us and opened the doors. I waited while Noel entered first.

The space was elegant and reminded me of my mother. She would have approved. Hints of red and green dominated the silver and gold theme. There were beautifully carved ice sculptures of snowflakes positioned throughout the space, and holiday music was performed by a seven-person live orchestra. Horns and keyboards created a soft background noise that was not too overbearing but just enough to set the tone for the evening.

"Noel, you came." A woman came into view, wearing a silver gown that hugged her body and brushed the floor. With her golden brown skin and soft eyes, she was just as elegant as the decorations. I was sure that had been the intention. My mother was the queen of graceful subtlety.

"Kristian. Hi. Thank you so much for inviting me."

"We invite you every year, Noel. This is the first time you accepted, and although I understand why, I'm grateful you're here."

"Me too. I hate I couldn't get home to be with my family, but this is so perfect. It feels like Christmas magic in here. You did an amazing job."

"My *team* did an amazing job. I'll be sure to pass that along, but for now, I thank you for the compliment on their behalf." She winked and then turned to Kanton. "And who do we have here?"

"This is Kanton Joseph. He's—"

I didn't know if she would announce my company or fumble over why I was here, but either way, I needed to ensure she didn't put my intentions out there, so I balanced the gifts on one arm and extended my free hand to her.

"A good friend of Noel's. I hope you don't mind me tagging along as her plus-one."

Kristian's eyes bounced between us as she accepted my hand and then focused on me. "No, not at all. You two are adding to the ambiance." She grinned smugly.

"Thank you. And those are for you." I motioned to the candles and cigars. "You and your husband."

"Handsome and bearing gifts. I like him, Noel."

"With me crashing the party, I thought it was best not to show up empty-handed."

"Hmm, smart man, and it seems you've done your research. These are our favorites."

I glanced at Noel. "I had a little help in that department."

"It appears you did, but regardless, I appreciate the effort. I would be grateful if you don't mind placing those over there. Grab a drink and enjoy the evening. I'm going to continue doing my rounds. It was nice to meet you, Kanton, and Noel, I'm pleased you could join us this year."

"Thanks, me too," Noel said from beside me.

After placing the candles on the small credenzas, I snagged two glasses of champagne from the silver tray of one of the servers walking around.

"I wasn't going to introduce you as my boyfriend. You didn't have to cut me off." Noel grinned behind her glass.

"I wouldn't have minded if you had. What I didn't want was for you to spill about my company or why I was here."

"Then it's a good thing you did interrupt. I surely would have done that."

"I want the conversation with Brighton to be organic and not forced. No one likes to feel like they're being worked over."

"Charmed," she added.

"No matter how you phrase it, I don't think it will work in my favor if I immediately force my hand."

She nodded, smiling up at me, which had my eyes narrowing. "What?"

"You do have a plan."

"More like a strategy, but for now, I *plan* to enjoy this beautiful space with a beautiful woman." I paused and extended my elbow out to Noel. "Shall we?"

She shifted the glass from one hand to the other and placed her empty hand on my forearm.

"Let's go shake up some shit."

I laughed, peering down at her. "Shake up some shit?"

"Seemed wildly inappropriate to say, so, of course, it felt right."

"Of course."

We spent the next hour talking to guests. There were about fifty or so people in attendance, most of whom I learned were employees of the Brightons, a handful of friends, and some relatives. I purposely avoided any conversation with Brighton and, instead, enjoyed the evening with Noel at my side.

She was amazing, so full of life as she chatted with guests, asking questions, giving compliments, and handing over Christmas puns that kept smiles on everyone's faces. She was a natural, and once again, I noticed that everyone was naturally drawn to her.

As was I.

By her third glass of champagne, she had a lazy smile on her face, lowered eyes, and clung to me for support. She wasn't drunk, just a little buzzed, but I enjoyed the way she kept contact with me, leaning into my side, holding onto my arms, or when I stood behind her, slightly to the right or left, she leaned back into my chest, fitting perfectly with my frame.

We fit.

That was the one thought that remained in rotation throughout the evening. However, no matter how much I enjoyed my time with Noel, I kept an eye on Brighton. I watched who he spoke with, how he seemed relaxed, and when he stood quietly off to the side with employees wearing a tight expression. I had to make my move at some point, but this was no longer just about me.

I wanted Noel to enjoy her evening. I wasn't sure why I cared so much that she did, but it mattered. She understood why we were here. This had been her idea, but knowing didn't mean I couldn't kill two birds with one stone. Close the deal with Brighton and allow Noel a perfect evening.

"Hey, aren't you going to talk to him?" She frowned lazily as her eyes darted over to Brighton and then up to me.

"I am, but it's not just about him."

"Actually, it is. It's why we're here."

"Part of the reason; the other is—"

My phone vibrated, and after I took it out of my pocket, I held up a finger. "It's Shelby. I need to get this."

She nodded and stepped away as I answered. "Hey?"

"How's it going,"

"It's Christmas Eve. Aren't you supposed to be getting engaged?"

"Already done. Now, how's it going?"

"Shit, congratulations. He really did it, huh?"

"Didn't I tell you he would? I'm a bit like your mother regarding planning, which you know because you pay me well. Now, answer the question."

All business.

"Things here are going well. We're at the party, the setup is nice, Noel's having a great time—"

"Please don't take this wrong, but her enjoyment is not my concern. I want to know about Brighton. You talk to him yet?"

"No, I haven't. I didn't want to walk right in with 'Hi, I'm Kanton Joseph with Global. I'm crashing your party to convince you to choose my firm to help your company stop hemorrhaging money. I can guarantee you'll turn a profit by the end of the first quarter. I also know if you don't, you'll lose control of your company—'"

"Can you do that?"

I frowned at the soft but assertive feminine voice that came from beside me instead of through my phone.

Kristian Brighton.

"Shelby, I have to go."

"Wait, no. First, let me tell you what I think you need to—"

I ended the call and turned to Kristian, lifting a brow. She stepped closer, hand on her hip in the most dominant yet elegant way. "I don't pride myself on intruding in personal conversations, but that one was about two people I'm partial to. Noel and my husband. If you intend to use either one of them—"

"It's not," I asserted.

"Good. If it were, I'd throw your ass up out of here. Now, back to my question . . . can you?"

"I assume you mean, can I help your husband turn a profit by the end of the first quarter?"

"You would be correct."

"I can."

"How?"

"You have a lot of bad debt and pointless spending. You also need to bring in new clients, which won't happen if you don't appeal to those willing to splurge on your services."

"And you have a solution?"

"I do."

She paused, thinking about what I said, and then gave me her answer. "It's Christmas Eve, and we're here amongst family and friends to celebrate as such. I put a lot of time and effort into ensuring tonight is perfect. There will be no business discussed this evening."

Fuck.

"But I've been watching you all evening like you've been watching my husband." She smiled smugly. "Most of my husband's business partners are suits in his boardroom. I, on the other hand, hold much more power than they do because I wear nothing in his bedroom." She winked, and I smirked.

Understood.

"Are you offering to help me sway his decision to choose my firm?"

"I'm offering you access to him, just not tonight. If he's impressed, I will do the rest to persuade him to take you on. I trust his judgment, and he trusts mine, but please understand that the only reason why I'm agreeing to help is because, like I said, I've been watching you. You seem genuine in the way you've handled Noel."

"I'm not using her to get to your husband. Me being here was her idea."

She grinned. "I'm sure it was. She's a sweetheart. Very selfless but also very biased about the men she allows to get close to her. I think maybe this time, she's made a good choice, huh?"

The statement was both a question and a warning.

I simply nodded to agree.

"Great, then go, enjoy your evening, and you'll hear from my husband soon."

I opened my mouth to object, but she cut me off. "I'm giving you my word. You can count on that."

I had to take what I could get. "Thank you."

"Now go, and remember, no business talk tonight. Enjoy yourself."

My hands were tied. I understood the dynamics of a marriage such as the one Brighton and his wife shared. It mirrored that of my own parents. My mother could persuade my father to do whatever she wanted. They tolerated each other most days. Brighton, however, seemed to love his wife.

That much I'd learned from my research about them. They were the real deal, so having her on my side was necessary. I could prove my worth if she got me in the room with him. Then she would seal the deal for me if he wasn't wholly convinced. For now, I would do as she demanded and enjoy my evening.

My eyes moved to find Noel. I smiled brightly while she chatted away with a woman wearing a bright red dress. The two contrasted greatly. Both were elegant and beautiful, but Noel was still Noel. A little less polished based on the way she laughed too loudly, slapped her hand over her stomach, and snatched hors d'oeuvres from servers as they passed by. The woman in the red dress sipped her champagne in an elegant, poised fashion, stood with perfect posture, and smiled softly as if she were posing for a magazine shoot.

It was a complete contrast, but I preferred my awkward, wild child over her practiced perfection.

My . . .

Noel wasn't *mine* . . .

But she could be . . .

I shook the thought and approached, moving behind Noel, who tilted her head back into my chest and smiled up at me.

"Hey, you."

"Hey," I returned her greeting and then turned to the woman she had been talking to.

"You mind if I steal her away for a moment?"

"Not at all," she offered, focusing on Noel. "It was such a pleasure meeting you."

"Same, and try the chowder puffs. They're to die for."

"I will."

After she was gone, Noel turned again to me but remained close. "How did it go with her over there?"

Kristian Brighton.

"Good."

"When are you meeting with him."

"Not sure, but Kristian gave me her word it would happen."

"Not tonight?" She frowned a bit.

"No, not tonight."

"I can talk to—"

"Noel, it's fine. She gave me her word. Now, I think you owe me a dance."

"I never promised you a dance." She lifted her eyes to me, placing her hands on my chest. Mine lowered to her waist and moved a little farther down, brushing over her hips.

"You in this dress was a promise of the two of us being close. The minute you put it on, you guaranteed me whatever I want with you tonight."

Her breath hitched, and a smile eased onto her face. "I guess that means we dance."

For now.

I guided her to the small area designated as a dance floor, separated by four concrete pillars that held ice sculptures of snowflakes. They were illuminated with lights on the base, which made them sparkle like diamonds.

Hanging from the insanely high ceilings were matching crystal icicles and snowflakes, making the small area appear as a winter wonderland. Perfect for dancing with the Queen of Christmas.

I held Noel close and pressed her into my body with my hands at the small of her back. She placed her hands on my chest, and I lowered my forehead to hers, trying to decide how on earth I was going to walk out of that apartment when my time was up and pretend like everything about me hadn't changed.

Noel.

TONIGHT HAD BEEN perfect.

Better than perfect, but words failed me. Mostly because I was tipsy from champagne and emotionally lifted from the overpowering allure of the man who closed us into my apartment after we left the Brightons' Christmas Eve party. It was just after eleven, and the night couldn't have been more . . .

Perfect.

Mom and Dad had called to make sure I hadn't drowned my sorrows in eggnog, and after a short chat and a few I love yous, they were convinced I was okay. They were also thrilled that I had chosen to go to a party instead of sulking at home alone.

Simone texted to check in. She would have called also, but she knew my plans to attend the Brightons' party and wanted pictures to ensure I was having fun. I assured her I was and would give her details later.

Now, we were back home . . .

Home.

It was strange how we both felt so comfortable with that word on our tongues regarding my apartment. This was my home, but not his, although it surely felt like it. He'd hung the lights, helped me decorate the tree, and spent hours on the sofa with me, watching terribly cheesy Christmas movies at my insistence.

His scent lingered in the air, and his presence was overwhelmingly throughout every inch of my place. Our coexistence made me smile, but at the same time, my chest ached, realizing it was all ending very soon.

He was leaving, and there wasn't a damn thing I could do about it. Kanton had a life and a business in New York. Mine was here. While he was thriving and surging forward, I was at a standstill of chaos.

The last thing I needed was to be falling for a man who I couldn't have. Not because I didn't deserve him. I did, but primarily because of timing. It wasn't the right time for either of us. The most I could do was enjoy the last of what I had left with him for what it was.

I watched as Kanton worked his way out of his jacket and draped it neatly over the back of a chair. He approached me slowly, stopping about an inch away. "So . . ."

"So . . ?" I repeated, smiling up at him.

"What's the plan?"

"Plan?" I frowned a bit.

"You promised me the perfect Christmas experience, and up to now, you've delivered. Tonight, however, is the most important evening with all of this, so you have to have plans for us. Otherwise, I'm going to be sorely disappointed."

"You hate my plans."

Strong hands were on me, pulling me close.

"I might have been opposed initially, but I hate to admit that I like the idea of Christmas with you. I'm still, however, on the fence, so you have the rest of the night and tomorrow to convince me."

"What makes you think I care enough to go the extra mile?" I arched a brow, and he smiled arrogantly.

"Just a feeling."

My smile was slow and easy. "Okay, I care, but today was kind of busy, and I didn't have time to make any plans. But if you give me a minute, I'm sure I can come up with something. We could write a letter to Santa. I'm sure that would be amusing to watch, or we could bake cookies, or—"

His mouth landed hard on mine, cutting off my final words. "Or we could do this—"

He slid his tongue into my mouth with an urgent, greedy exploration. The hints of bourbon and champagne ignited the buzz I was already feeling. I returned the kiss, leaning into him, eager for more and annoyed when he separated to say, "Or we could wing it."

My heart raced faster.

"Winging it sounds good."

I smiled against his mouth while he kissed me again. This time, his hand moved up my back, tugging at my zipper, which he lowered. I yanked at his shirt, freeing it from his pants, and moved my hands beneath it, enjoying the warmth and hard planes of his abs . . . and then lower. When my fingers brushed over his belt buckle and gave a little tug, his jaw set, and his eyes lowered.

And so did mine. He had been very gracious. It only made sense that I was too.

"Noel . . ." It was a low growl that I took as a warning. One I planned to ignore.

"Hmmm?"

"What are you doing?" He sucked in a sharp breath when my fingers eased beneath the waistband of his briefs.

"I'm pretty sure you know *exactly* what I'm doing, and if you don't, give me a second, and I'll show you."

"Oh fuck . . ."

I wrapped my lips around his head and sucked him in nice and slow. My hand moved up to the base, applying a generous amount of pressure. I was grateful for the heels I was wearing. They served as a perfect tool for balance, meaning I could concentrate on the task at hand.

The groan above my head indicated that I was doing a decent job, but I didn't want to be "decent." I wanted to blow his mind. Bringing Kanton the same pleasure he blessed me with sparked something in me. I sucked harder, using my tongue, gripping firmly to the base, peering up at him to gauge his reaction. Kanton growled his approval, and those heavy lids lowered in appreciation.

His hand moved to my chin, fingers fanned out over my cheeks, applying enough pressure to guide my motions, and I grinned around him, feeling accomplished.

"Fuck . . ." he hissed, and then I was yanked from beneath him, lifted out of my dress which pooled around my ankles, then lifted around his waist. I hadn't realized we were moving until my ass chilled from the cool surface of the kitchen counter seconds before my thighs were spread wide, and Kanton thrusted into me hard and fast.

I groaned in satisfaction, and he continued landing deep with hard, punishing thrusts until we fell in sync. He bit down on my lip and then kissed me, murmuring between my lips, "My first Noel. So fucking gorgeous."

"Your *only* Noel." I kissed him back, narrowing my eyes when he smiled arrogantly at my demand.

"I won't object to that."

Maybe it was the evening, the sex, or just the perfection of the moment, but I wanted to be his *only* Noel. I didn't have long to process the thought because Kanton began rocking into me harder, with long, deep thrusts that had my body spasming. I felt warm all over and satisfyingly full as the pressure built to an unbearable degree.

"I'm . . . oh shit . . ."

He yanked my hips forward, and I panicked, feeling unsteady, no longer having the counter beneath me, but my palms landed flat on the sleek surface, gripping the edge for stability.

We came at the same time, and Kanton's hands slid beneath me, tugging me into him. My body settled into a haze of satisfaction as endorphins flooded my system. Once again, we were moving, but this time to my bedroom.

Two more earth-shattering orgasms followed, and then I drifted to sleep, with the weight and warmth of his body, feeling completely and utterly satiated with the delicious ache that lingered from the way he thoroughly handled my body.

Merry fucking Christmas.

The next morning, I was up early, tossing covers back, making Kanton growl and yank them back over our bodies. I repeated the act, and he peeled one eye open, peering at me. "Where are you going?"

"Not me, *we*. It's Christmas. We have to shower and get dressed." I was giddy because . . . well, it was Christmas.

"Or we could lie back down, get up later, shower, and then lie back down again." He smiled, tugging me back toward him with his eyes closed, but I forced a halt to the motion by placing my hands flat on his chest so that I remained upright. Bad idea because the feel of him under my palms and fingertips had me ready to explore, only further south.

"Nope, my day, my rules," I asserted, climbing over him, grateful that he allowed me to escape. That didn't stop him from growling his disapproval as he flopped over, burying his face in the pillow.

"Kanton . . ." I whined, and he growled again.

"I'm coming. Five minutes, but since you're forcing me out of bed at this ungodly hour, I get to fuck you in the shower before you torture me with whatever Christmas plans you have."

My body pulsed with the threat that actually wasn't a threat. "Okay, fine, but you'd better hurry because if I'm done in there before you join me, you miss out."

That got him moving, and before the water temperature was fully adjusted to the right level, he joined me. We brushed our teeth with our naked bodies flush against each other, and his very hard dick between us while we stood in front of the sink. Then we showered together, with me orgasming twice with my legs wrapped around his waist while my back was pressed against the tiled wall. We dressed in pajamas I managed to sneak and order online.

I had asked Lewis to keep them downstairs where resident packages were held, and he had them brought up to my apartment while Kanton and I were at the party last night, along with the presents I had for him.

"I knew this was going to be very painful," he mumbled, entering the living room wearing clothes that matched mine. Black pants with tiny reindeer and a bright red T-shirt that said, "*Dear Santa, I regret nothing.*"

"You don't like them?"

"On you, yes; on me, not so much."

"Well, humor me."

I grabbed my phone, pulling up the camera app. I snapped several pictures of him scowling, but he smiled when I leaned next to him, sliding under his arm and extending mine to capture selfies. I barely caught the shot before he was pushing his face into the curve of my neck, kissing me there and then on my temple, but he faced the camera again for the last picture, pressing his face close to mine.

"Now for presents."

"Presents?"

Kanton's face crumpled, and I grabbed his hand, pulling him with me as he mumbled, "I didn't know we were doing presents."

"*We're* not. *I* am. This is *me* providing *you* with the perfect Christmas, remember?"

"But it won't be perfect if I can't give you a present as well."

We stopped in front of the sofa. "I don't need presents, but if it makes you feel any better, you gave me a present last night. Plenty, actually, if I count how many times I enjoyed your . . ." My eyes lowered to his *present*. "Now, sit."

After gently shoving Kanton's chest and encouraging him to sit, I left and moved to the tree, gathering wrapped gifts. I knew Cleo had to have handled this task since they were neatly wrapped. Lewis had defied me when I made him promise only to store them. He took everything home and allowed his wife to wrap them. But I wasn't complaining. Wrapped gifts would make the moment much more satisfying.

I set them next to Kanton on the sofa, and he frowned at me while I lifted my phone again, bringing up the camera app. Only I planned on capturing both video and stills.

"Stop growling and open them."

He frowned again and then hesitantly lifted the first one. I held up the camera to capture his reaction while Kanton slowly ripped into the paper. His eyes lowered to the bright blue and orange cardboard casing that held his first gift. Then he lifted his eyes to me. His brow lifted at the same time the corners of his mouth slanted. My stomach clenched with memories of where that mouth had been last night.

"You bought me a Nerf gun?"

"I did. Keep going," I beamed, capturing the picture of his amused face as he moved to the next one and began ripping into the paper—a box of Nerf bullets.

Next was Hot Wheels.

"I'm sensing a theme here."

"Good. Keep going."

When he got to the last one, he smiled bigger than I'd ever seen before. He was genuinely happy, which had me imagining the same face but only years younger, opening gifts on Christmas morning. According to Kanton, he never had that experience, which made me angry with his parents. *Parents* I didn't know but wasn't fond of because they cheated their son.

"This is . . ." He shook his head and lowered his eyes to the collection of toys. "Thank you."

"You like them?"

"I do, but more than anything, I love that you cared enough to try to give me something I've never had."

"Oh, speaking of, I have two more things for you." I jumped up and moved the tree, grabbing the basketball tucked in the corner and a small box I had wrapped myself and handed over to Kanton.

He smiled at the basketball, setting it aside. "I think I know what this one is."

"Basketball. I saved it for last because I figured you'd guess."

He grinned and lifted the lid of the last box. His eyes shot up to mine, narrowing as they held me in place. After a long pause, they moved slowly back down to the ornament I snuck and made for him.

A square shaped and painted like a present with Kanton's First Real Christmas. I hesitated when making it, not wanting to overstep. No matter how complicated things were with his family, they were still his family, and this wasn't his first Christmas. The longer he sat quietly staring at the ornament, the more nervous I became, and that had me rambling.

"I know it's not your first, but in a way, it kind of is because it is a first and—"

I was yanked with no finesse and landed awkwardly on his lap, but before I could complain, he kissed me hard, passionately, and with so much of himself that all I could do was submit. When he pulled back, he pressed his forehead to mine.

"It *is* my first real Christmas. And it's also my first Christmas with *you*. It's appropriate. Thank you."

"You're welcome." This time, I kissed him, but then those feelings surfaced again. His first and last Christmas with me. I needed distance because this was too much. I eased off his lap just in time because my mother was calling.

"It's my mom. I have to take this, and when I'm done, I'm making you a Christmas breakfast."

"Please promise me it doesn't involve elves or Santa."

"No can do, sir." I swiped to answer and ducked off. "Hey, Mom . . ."

I welcomed the distraction because this was starting to feel like too much.

"Merry Christmas, honey."

"Merry Christmas. Where's Dad?"

"In the kitchen burning pancakes. You know he likes to make breakfast to give me a break . . ."

He did but ended up making more work. Mom had to salvage what he didn't destroy and then clean behind him, but she loved every minute of it.

"He's sweet for that. Stop acting like you don't look forward to it."

"Charred pancakes, lumpy grits, and crunchy eggs. Sure, I look forward to it, and let's not forget that he uses *every* pot, pan, bowl, and utensil we own to get it done."

I grinned at the amusement in her voice hidden behind the sass. "You love it, and you know it."

"I do. The mess, not so much, but that he loves me enough to try—that part, I won't complain about."

"Because you shouldn't. He does truly love you. And I love you. I hate I can't be there to help clean up his mess this year."

"I know. Me too. I thought things would work out for you to make it. I held on to hope, but . . ."

"I know, me too."

"I hate this so much that things were ruined."

Initially, it was, but now . . .

My eyes darted toward the living room. I was leaning against the linen closet in the hallway. I inhaled a deep breath and released it slowly.

"It hasn't been terrible."

"You're alone."

I wasn't. But I wouldn't tell her that.

"I haven't been alone. I had dinner with Lewis and Cleo and then the party last night. It's not like being home with you guys, but it made the time more bearable."

He made it perfect.

"That's good, Noel."

"But next year, I'll be there."

"Maybe with someone?"

I should have expected that.

"Maybe, but honestly, with everything I have on my plate right now, I don't have time for anything else in my life. Especially not a relationship. At least, not until I get a handle on things. There's already so much I'm struggling to get a handle on."

"I thought things were good?"

"They are, but working for someone and running your own business takes much more time, hard work, and discipline. That means a huge investment of not just my money but of me. Once I find my footing with this, I can consider bringing someone home for Christmas."

"There will always be an excuse, Noel. You can't put your life on pause waiting for the perfect time."

"I know, Mom. That's not what I'm doing. I just need a year or two to find my footing with the company. Then I'll focus on my personal life. I promise. A relationship doesn't make sense right now."

"I'm holding you to your promise. Would you like to speak to your dad?"

"No, not right now. I don't want to disrupt his focus on those crunchy eggs . . ."

She groaned, and I added, "Tell him I love him and Merry Christmas. I'll call you guys later."

"Okay, honey. I love you."

"I love you too."

I ended the call and glanced down the hall, smiling at the thought of bringing Kanton home to meet my parents. They'd love him. But then I quickly pushed the idea to the back of my mind because, well, yeah, that wasn't happening.

Kanton.

"**• • • RUNNING YOUR OWN** *business takes a lot of hard work and discipline. That means a huge investment of not just my money but my time as well.*"

"*I just need a year or two to find my footing with the company. Then I'll focus on my personal life. I promise. A relationship doesn't make sense right now.*"

The goal was to put a smile on Noel's face, but I demolished the one on mine. She had promised to deliver the perfect Christmas experience, and she had . . . until I stood in the kitchen with my laptop with the intent of showing her the website Shelby emailed me a few minutes after Noel took the call from her mother.

It was only a mockup because my guy was off until the first of the year, but he did spend a few hours pulling photos and information from her site and social media, which were linked to her site, and dropping them in to make it feel more natural.

I would bet that his last-minute scramble cost me a pretty penny, but that was money well spent. I didn't mind at all. I didn't mind anything when it came to Noel. Not her quirkiness or her quick-witted assumptions of spending my money to put a smile on her face, or mine, like that dress did last night.

But overhearing Noel talking to her mother further proved that I was overstepping. No matter how great my time with her had been, it was time to head home. She wasn't looking for anything and, instead, invested in her business. A business that I was now helping her navigate.

Although she didn't know that.

I considered how busy she would be if my contacts agreed to offer her contracts and how busy I would be accepting the deal from Brighton. I was optimistic about both, and adding in that she lived in Atlanta and I called New York my home, that sealed our fate.

This wasn't possible. I didn't want a long-distance relationship with anyone, and I was sure she would want one with me. Her life was hers. Her friends, her chosen family, Lewis and his wife.

Asking her to give that up was absurd. The idea of me moving here wasn't fathomable either. My company was based in New York, and yes, I could work remotely, but I worked just as hard as my team, and being present was important.

No, the idea of us wasn't possible, and I refused to present it only for Noel to choose me or try to make it work and then realize that she'd chosen wrong. I refused to put that on her shoulders, which only meant one thing: Today was all we had left. Tomorrow, I would leave, and Noel would return to her life. I would begrudgingly get back to mine.

I buried any thoughts of considering something with Noel and plastered on a smile, determined to enjoy what little time I had left with her just in time to see her heading toward me.

"Sorry about that. I had to convince my mom that I was enjoying my Christmas."

"Don't apologize, but I have to ask, are you?" I swiped my fingers over the trackpad of my laptop to clear the visual of Noel's mock website and placed the device on the counter.

"Enjoying my Christmas?" She beamed. "Hell yeah, I am! Seeing a grown-ass man all but crying over toys was a highlight I will never forget."

A bark of laughter shook my shoulders as I turned to the sink to wash my hands, lifting a hand towel to dry them when I faced

Noel again. "I'm pretty sure you're exaggerating. There were no tears involved."

"I have the video. Would you like to watch?"

"No, I'll pass. Since I dropped the ball on your present, I was thinking I could do something nice for you. Maybe cook you breakfast or something?"

A weird look passed behind her eyes, and I almost retracted the offer, but she swallowed thickly and narrowed her eyes on me.

"I thought I nailed the Christmas thing."

"You did."

"Then why are you offering up food promising a return on my investment?"

I threw my head back and laughed again. "You're terrible for that."

"I'm not. You can't cook. You're the one who told me you couldn't."

"I did, and I can't, but I can read recipes, and what can be so hard about holiday pancakes with green eggs and ham?"

"First of all, that's Dr. Seuss, and pancakes are a lot more complicated than you think."

"Shouldn't be. Some flour, food coloring, a couple of cups of oil . . ."

"What! No! *Cups* of oil do not belong in holiday pancakes." She looked mortified, and I chuckled, kissing her cheek.

"I'm kidding. I've got this. Go . . ."

I bumped her hip with mine, but before she could get too far, I hooked an arm around her waist and pulled Noel into me, leveling my mouth over hers. "Thanks again for my presents. They were perfect."

So are you.

I kissed her once. She blinked up at me and smiled before I let her go. "I'm glad that you loved them."

I did. A little too much, but mostly, the person who made it happen is what stole my heart.

"Now go."

I pulled up a search field and typed holiday pancakes. I found one that didn't take much and seemed simple enough before I started searching for the needed ingredients.

"Hey, do you have food coloring?"

"Uhh, you don't have to do that. Just regular pancakes will be fine."

"It's Christmas, Noel. You're not a 'regular pancake' kind of girl. Do you have it or not?"

"Pantry, top shelf, in the corner. Please don't overdo it. I'm not interested in cleaning up red goo from the stove and floors."

I grinned after locating the food coloring. "I'll do my best to keep it in the bowl and microwave."

"*Microwave?!*" she screeched.

"I'm kidding; relax."

"I can't. You're making me worry."

"Well, don't. Trust me. I've got this covered. I run a multimillion-dollar business. I can make Santa cakes."

She peeked around the wall that separated the kitchen and living room. "Santa cakes?"

"Yes, now go."

I turned my back and began measuring the flour. But I felt her watching me. Sure enough, when I glanced over my shoulder, I found her grinning, phone in hand, recording me.

"You *really* want me distracted while I'm measuring things?"

"Oh God, no. Okay, I'm done."

Our day together was a combination of food, good conversation, plenty of flirtatious teasing, but, more importantly, good vibes. We stayed in all day, and I was content with the day just being about the two of us.

Even now, as we were cozy on her sofa, this was the best end to a wonderful day. Although she was at one end of the couch with her knees drawn into her chest while my frame was slouched, one foot on the floor, the other extended in her direction, I felt her presence. That presence had me angry that this was all we could be.

"What time is your flight in the morning?" Noel was staring at the tree. She had been doing that a lot this evening. Her eyes were everywhere but on me. I sensed her walls coming up, and as much as I wanted to tear them back down, I decided it was best for both of us to let things be what they were.

"Eight, which means I should be leaving here by five."

"You should probably get some rest then." Her eyes flickered over to mine. A stoic expression settled onto her face.

"I should."

The silence lingered a bit longer before she smiled softly. "It's going to be weird with you not being around."

"Will you feel weird or relieved?" I teased, and her smile expanded.

"Maybe a little of both, but at least you can get back to your life, and I can get back to mine."

"Sounds like you're leaning more on the relief side of things. Have I been *that* much of an inconvenience?"

Her brows pinched, and she softly shook her head. "No."

I chuckled, brushing a hand over my head. "You're lying."

"I am not . . ."

I narrowed my eyes, and her smile expanded. "Okay, maybe a little. It was hell getting that food coloring off the counters. But honestly, the week wasn't unbearable. You weren't any more of an inconvenience than I must have been to you. I'm willing to bet when you booked my place, you hadn't in your wildest dreams planned on spending the week with the most stubborn Christmas enthusiast known to man."

"No, I did, but you weren't all that bad."

This time, it was her brow lifting in challenge, which had me shrugging. "What person who loathes Christmas doesn't mind being forced to overindulge in holiday romance movies, forced to wear Christmas attire while shopping for a tree that they were threatened to decorate while listening to the very off-key rendition of every holiday song ever written?"

She threw her head back and laughed, extending her leg, which allowed a foot to shove playfully against my thigh. I reached to grab that same foot, but she was quick enough to pull it back before I had possession.

"I'm only admitting to a few of those things."

"What aren't you claiming?"

"Threatening you to decorate the tree and singing off-key. My voice is lovely."

"If you favor the sound of a cat being tortured."

"You're mean." She pouted, and I lifted with the intent of inching closer. I wanted to kiss that pouty mouth, amongst other things, but the universe intervened, and my phone vibrated with a call.

My eyes shot over to the trunk where it was resting, and I internally groaned when I realized it was Shelby. I had every intention of ignoring the call. I was seconds away from doing so, but Noel swung her knees to the side and dropped her feet on the floor.

"You should get that." Her brows pinched like she was struggling with something.

"It can wait."

"It's late, and I need to call my parents before they're off to bed. You also have a very early flight, so it's best if you get some rest."

The call ended, but it started back seconds later, which had me lifting the device and growling out a command.

"Shelby, hang on a second."

"You'll likely be asleep when I leave."

"You know the code. Make sure you lock me in." She smiled, and I nodded. "You have all your things?" She turned her head to the corner where my luggage was sitting: all but the duffle by the sofa. I had already showered, so all that was left was to clean up in the morning, which I could do in the half bath, change my clothes, and then shove them in my duffle. There was no reason for me to bother her in the morning. She knew this as well.

"I do."

"Great." She inched closer to me, hugging my waist, which prompted my arm to lift around her waist. "Thanks for not calling the cops."

"I would have never done that."

"You sure because you seemed pretty adamant about forcing your hand?"

"I needed to stay. You didn't want me to. I had to use what I had."

"Right, frivolous threats. Either way, this was fun. Having you here. My Christmas wasn't so terrible after all."

"Mine either." Our eyes locked, and she kissed my cheek after a minute, but I turned, allowing my lips to graze hers. It was quick because she pulled away, and I let her.

"Good night, Kanton. Safe travels."

"Good night, Noel."

I stood in place and watched her walk away. I didn't move an inch until I heard the soft click of her door separating us. It wasn't until then that I lifted my phone to address Shelby.

"What's up?"

"Sounds like I was interrupting."

You were.

"No, my flight is early. Just saying good night."

"You sure that's all it was?"

I reeled in my annoyance. "Yes, Shelby. That's all it was. Did you need something?"

"Brighton reached out. He's on the books for Jan 2. I guess things went well."

I glanced toward the tree after I settled back onto the sofa. "On the books?"

"Yes, he's flying in for a meeting on the second. I assumed you set that up."

"No, I didn't, but I know who did."

"Care to share?"

"Not now. We'll discuss it when I return, but he asked for an in-house meeting?"

"He did, and he called personally."

"How did he get you?"

"Your business line was transferred to my work cell since you left."

"You're supposed to be on vacation."

"I am, and apparently, so are you, but the point is, he's going to sit down with us, and it pretty much sounded like his mind was made up about becoming our client. What did you say to him?"

"Nothing."

"Nothing? You *had* to say something, Kanton. He said he talked everything over with his business partner and—"

"I didn't say anything to him, but I did talk briefly with his wife at the Christmas party Noel invited me to. She forbade me from discussing business last night, and if I kept my promise, she would guarantee me a meeting with her husband."

"You finessed his wife?"

"I was honest with her after she overheard me talking to you."

"I knew that pretty face of yours would become a valuable business tool for you. Good job, boss."

"I've learned from the best. Use what you have, which is the motto you live by."

"I would be offended, but I can't be because that is the motto I live by. If I can seal a deal by smiling pretty, then so be it."

"Which makes you a dangerous woman. Brains and beauty."

"You should keep that in mind and keep me on your team."

"I hadn't planned on letting you go, Shelby."

"I know, but just in case you've considered doing so, I'm laying the groundwork. Your car is scheduled and will be outside the building by 5:00 a.m. sharp. Safe travels and I'll see you in a few days."

"Safe travels to you as well, Shelby, and Merry Christmas."

"That it has been," she sang with a little too much amusement before the call ended.

After a few moments of staring at the spot where Noel had been, the need to be near her crawled beneath my skin, but my rational brain took over, and I decided to leave things as they were.

It was the best thing for both of us, so I stretched out, closed my eyes, and decided to get a few hours of sleep. It was time to return to my life, which didn't include a spirited woman who somehow managed to change everything about me.

Noel.

TWO WEEKS LATER.

"**A**RE YOU READY to order?" I kept my eyes on my phone, swiping mindlessly through emails, when I heard Simone's voice.

The Coleman Group was supposed to let me know their decision by the first of the year. It was the second week of January, and I still hadn't heard anything. Part of me was hopeful that no news was good news, but deep down in my core, I was well aware that they had elected not to bring me on as their interior designer. I really needed that job.

"I already ordered. Endless mimosas," I murmured, and in my peripheral, I saw the menu Simone was holding lower to the table.

"Food, Noel. You can't just drink mimosas."

I grinned but kept my eyes on hers. "Can't I, though?"

"You can, but it's not smart, considering you're a lightweight. Now, pick something, or I'll order for you. I can't treat you to brunch if you don't eat."

"Chicken and waffles." I briefly lifted my eyes to hers, wrapped my hand around the base of my champagne flute, and took two uncouth, hefty gulps of my mimosa.

"Thank you."

A few minutes later, she was flagging over our server and rattling off our order, my chicken and waffles, and her caprese salad with added grilled chicken. I wasn't sure how the conversation went because an email caught my attention, or rather, the subject line.

Updated Website For Review.

196

I assumed it was spam because I hadn't made any updates to my website, and the company that sent the email wasn't one I was familiar with. It wasn't anything these days for companies to use creative marketing, such as sending an email that says, "Your order is ready to ship," and then for you to click the email thinking you had been hacked only to find a prompt and a link saying, "You're a few clicks away from finding a prospective product."

A sales tactic that often worked. I'd fallen victim a few times, getting the same email from a few of my favorite companies where I hadn't shopped in a while, and ended up placing an order after their fake order email.

But this wasn't that. The more I read, the more my face and body grew tense.

Greetings, Ms. Anderson.

I apologize for the delay, but considering the rush order, the site took a little longer than planned. Please take a look, and if you have any questions, let me know.

The links attached will take you to the visual of what your new site will look like. I've offered several versions of the template for you to choose from. Once you have selected, please forward the information I've requested below so that I can transfer it to your domain. The graphic team was able to pull most of what was needed from your original site. Please verify the information is up to date and valid. If you need any changes, please email them to me as soon as possible, as I'm sure you're eager to launch your new site.

The design package Mr. Joseph purchased on your behalf is a complete design with three years of maintenance. Any changes, updates, and certifications are included. Please allow forty-eight hours for all changes or additions that you request. You can contact me personally, as I have been assigned to service your account.

Sincerely,
Spencer Lowery

Kanton.

"What the fuck," I mumbled, and Simone leaned in to see what I was looking at.

"What's wrong?"

I ignored her and clicked the first link. My eyes narrowed on the clean, organized layout with all my information, photos from previous work, and mockups.

"How?"

"How what, Noel? What's wrong?"

"This . . ." I shoved the phone at her, and she took it from my hands, slowly scrolling, tapping, and moving her finger across my screen.

"This shit is the bomb, Noel. When did you get a new site?"

"I didn't."

"What?" She looked at me in confusion.

"I didn't do that . . ." I pointed to my phone, and she frowned.

"But all your stuff is on here. Shit. Did someone hack you?"

"There would have to be something worth hacking for that to happen, so no." I shook my head. "Well, maybe, but I wasn't hacked in a bad way."

"Girl, what the hell?" She frowned harder.

"Kanton."

She tilted her head to the side, peering at me. She and I had discussed my time with him. Well, not everything because she didn't get a play-by-play of that fantastic sex, but she, in fact, knew it was amazing. To her dismay, she also knew that I missed Kanton and was struggling not to pick up the phone and call, but reaching out would be crazy, right? He left. He didn't offer any inclination that he wanted to be in touch.

"He made you a new website?"

"No, but he paid someone else to. And it comes with three layouts to choose from and a three-year site management budget based on what the email said. I have my own personal web tech who has been assigned to me."

She lifted her eyes and grinned. "The sex was good for both of you then."

I rolled my eyes and snatched my phone. "This isn't about sex. He offered to help with my business before *sex* happened."

"Mmhmm, but do you know how much web design and site management cost? A lot."

"He's rich. He can afford this, and he probably enlisted somebody he already has on his payroll, so doing this was just another layer of business for the guy."

"Stop it."

"Stop what?"

She narrowed her eyes, communicating what she meant.

Stop downplaying this man's efforts to justify my fear of wanting something with him.

"The site is bomb."

"*My* site was bomb." She nodded, sipping her mimosas but not responding. "You didn't like my site?"

"I loved your site. It was very colorful and creative, which is basically very you, but . . ."

"But what?"

"It wasn't as professional as it could have been."

"What the hell, Simone? You're just *now* telling me that?"

"I kind of already told you, but you didn't hear me."

"You did *not*."

"I did. When you asked what I thought, I said it's creative."

"That's good. I'm a creative."

"Creative *is* good, but when it comes to business, you need that . . ." She pointed to my phone. "It's still very you and creative but organized, clean, and professional."

"Again, why didn't you tell me?"

She shrugged. "Because it was just after you had that argument with Evan where he told you designing was a hobby unworthy of a business venture. You were so determined to prove him wrong. I didn't want to hurt your feelings, and you loved the site so much."

"You're a shitty friend." I narrowed my eyes as the lie left my mouth. She wasn't a shitty friend. My feelings were hurt.

"I'm a good, supportive friend, and it wasn't terrible, just a little chaotic. But problem solved. Kanton fixed it for you. You should fly to New York to personally thank him with your lady parts."

I burst out laughing. "My *lady parts*? Who the fuck says that other than a gynecologist."

"Me, when I'm trying to be proper in public."

"Please don't ever say that again."

"Fine, so are you going?"

"I most certainly am not."

"Why? The dick was good, the man is fine, he obviously is interested in your career goals. Based on that and—"

"And he was just doing me a favor. He made a promise, and he's keeping it. This . . ." I held up the phone. ". . . does not mean anything other than he's a man of his word."

"Can we talk some real shit for a minute?"

I knew it was coming.

She allowed me two weeks of hardcore denial.

"Yep . . ." I said nonchalantly, lifting my mimosa. I needed it for what was coming.

"You really like this guy, Noel. Why aren't you doing anything about it?"

"Because there's nothing to be done. The week was fun, and then it ended. He left."

"And you let him."

I snorted, rolling my eyes. "I didn't *let* him do anything. He's a grown man."

"He was feeling you, and you were feeling him. Did you even consider the prospect of something more?"

"No, but neither did he."

"Men are stupid. How many times do we have to acknowledge something that will never change? You watch enough of those dumbass movies to know the happy ending only happens when someone forces them to see what they know but refuse to acknowledge."

"True, but that's in a fictional world. My life is *very* real."

"Okay, so then, let's acknowledge another realism. Kanton is not Evan."

I frowned hard, narrowing my eyes her way. "He's nothing like that asshole. It's disrespectful for you even to put them in the same sentence. Evan never cared about me. He liked the idea of this quirky, weird woman who he could dress up and show off. The woman who he could brag about to his friends, telling them how he made *me* better, like I was some fucking charity project and not already the most amazing woman he would ever have the pleasure of meeting. He made me what he wanted me to be—a clone of all the women he was fucking behind my back. But the thing is, I would never be them—an ego stroker and submissive. His fragile ego couldn't handle my refusal to look pretty and shut up, so he got bored and found other women to occupy his time. He was too much of a coward to admit that we didn't work. He never knew or saw me because he didn't want to. Kanton and Evan are *not* the same."

When I finished my rant, she sat quietly, smiling in victory, and I realized she set me up. Sure, thinking that Evan and Kanton were somewhat similar was a red flag. I didn't want to be another "project" for a man who had his life together, only for him to get bored, and I would be left feeling inadequate again. I knew I wasn't. I knew my worth, but holding firm with what I knew was sometimes hard when others kept knocking me down.

"I don't want to travel down that road again," I said quietly.

"You're not. You just gave me all the reasons why this time could be different—*will* be different. He has money, sure, and he has his life together, but he sees you, Noel. Not once did he try to change you into something you're not. Hell, if anything, you tried to change *him*."

"Showing someone that Christmas is the most glorious holiday of all is *not* changing someone. It's a duty on my part and theirs."

She rolled her eyes. "It's you being you, and he allowed you the space to do so, and based on what you told me, he loved every minute of it *and* you. Isn't that proof enough that you should at least consider something more?"

Yes.

But . . .

"I need to focus on my business. I can't fail. Distractions are the last thing I need."

"A distraction that understands how important your business is might not be such a terrible thing."

"It's just a website," I argued, running out of valid points.

"He made you pancakes."

Oooh, she's playing dirty.

"He's not my father."

"God, I hope not. That would be . . . eeeh, but *he* is a version of the man that loves your mother. Tell me you haven't considered the obvious. He made you pancakes, Noel."

"He made me pancakes." I closed my eyes and released a sigh. "He also hasn't called or texted or—"

"He made you a website. Other than Christmas, that's pretty much your only other love language."

"It's not."

She narrowed her eyes, and I rolled mine. "Okay, it is, but that's not the point."

"That is *very much* the point. He's trying to get your attention. At the very least, you should reach out to say thank you. Did you ever consider that maybe he's second-guessing too? It's not like *you* called or texted."

"I don't have a reason to."

"Well, now, you do, but if I were you, I would take this a step further. You could get a round-trip flight to New York pretty cheap or possibly even free. I have miles."

"And why would I use your miles? I could simply send an email in return to say thank you."

"You could, but you won't. Sending a simple email is not who you are. You're a 'grand gesture' kinda girl. The 'catch a flight and show up unannounced to say thank you for my website. Now, let me thank you with my lady parts' kinda girl."

I shot her a stern look, and she grinned. "Did you *really* want me to say pussy out here while in the presence of all these lovely people?"

"You just did."

"Oh well, you get my point." She lifted her phone. "Now, am I finding you a flight or not? You know, ever since I've known you, you've been dying to live out one of those movies."

I have.

"Okay, fine. Find me a flight but with an open ticket just in case I get there, and we called this all wrong."

I really wanted us to be correct and that the site was his way of asking for my attention, but . . .

"I forgot how little you travel. Open-ended tickets no longer exist. That was a '70s to '80s thing when there weren't a gazillion people traveling. But I can book a business class for you. The dates are much more flexible, and some airlines don't charge a fee for changing the dates if you book for business and not personal."

"Problem solved then," I muttered, knowing there was no way out of this.

I can't believe I'm actually doing this.

"*And* when this works, just remember there's a rule about you naming your firstborn after me."

"That is *definitely* not a rule."

She lifted one shoulder into a shrug while tapping away on her phone. "Well, it is now."

Simone came through with the plane ticket, and since she is the most amazing best friend ever, after brunch, we got mani and pedis before she drove me back to my building to pack. I would have to do something really nice for her when I could afford it.

My flight was at 1:45 the following day. I showered and polished my body, grooming enough to make myself feel presentable, tossed a couple of things in a carry-on, and then settled onto my sofa with a glass of wine. My tree was still up, far beyond its expiration date. The needles were falling off daily, but I couldn't bring myself to get rid of it. Doing so felt like bringing closure to the time I spent with Kanton. So, yeah, maybe I was an optimist and sad at the same time.

I quickly pulled up my photo gallery and began swiping through the photos I hadn't been able to bring myself to look at since he left. It felt like torture revisiting something I couldn't have, but tonight was different. Who knows, I might have new photos to add to the collection by tomorrow.

The smile that crashed my face while viewing the video of Kanton hanging lights along the mantle because I was unreasonably lusting over the way his sweats hung low on his waist, not to mention the way his shirt stretched and flexed with every movement he made . . . So, yeah, I captured the moment. A moment the universe didn't want me to enjoy. Or maybe it was a warning that this was a horrible idea. My phone rang, and I was so annoyed that I didn't think twice about answering the call and growling into the phone.

"What?"

"Well, hello to you too, Noel. I see much hasn't changed."

I rolled my eyes at Evan's sarcastic tone. To think that voice used to bring a smile to my face . . . Now, it had two reactions: either rage or a strong desire to vomit.

"Why are you calling me?"

"You have something I need."

Not possible.

"I'm pretty sure you dialed the wrong number. Delete me and try again." I was about to hang up, but his following sentence halted me.

"My golf clubs are there. My very *expensive* clubs, and I need them."

"They're not. You took everything that belonged to you."

"Not the clubs, remember? I tried to get them several times, and you were conveniently unavailable."

Shit.

He was right.

They were here, and the reason they were here was because I didn't want to see him. So, each time he reached out, I made an excuse about being unavailable. The guy was rich. He could buy a new set. I should have sold them.

"Right. I can leave them with—"

"Are you insane? You will *not*. They're worth a lot of money. That's a Bentley Graphite set with cart bag. I've promised them for an auction. They're rare, and I don't trust minimum-wage security guards handling my property."

Wow!

"Lewis wouldn't steal from you or anyone else."

"I'm not saying he would, but he might mishandle or lose them—a risk I won't take. I'm sure you have no intention of seeing me any more than I have of you, so we can make this as painless as possible. I'll be in town in a few days. I can swing by and get them. In and out. You don't have to talk to me."

"Sorry, but I'm heading out of town."

"I need those clubs, Noel."

"I'm sure you do. You've made a promise to someone, and we both know you would like to show off."

"Is that necessary?"

Very.

"I won't be here, but I will tell Lewis to expect you. He can bring you up and get the clubs for you."

"Just give me the code. I'm sure it's changed by now. I can get them myself."

"No. I don't want you in my place."

"You're being childish."

"And you're being an ass. I'll let Lewis know to expect you. It's that or nothing."

"Fine."

He hung up, and I rolled my eyes. For a split second, I thought about Kanton. Evan was a different person when we met. Charming, funny, attentive . . . and then things changed. Everything I did annoyed him. My thoughts were childish. My dreams were dumb, and he tended to spend more time traveling for business than with me. He had even refused to meet my family—a clear sign that he had no intention of being a real part of my life.

But Kanton wasn't Evan. I felt that in my soul, so I pushed the thoughts to the back of my mind and finished my wine. I was catching a flight to New York, and that was that. If I were lucky, I would be taking flight with some much-needed orgasms not long after I landed.

"How was your flight?"

"Good. It pays to have friends who are willing to share their miles. They bumped me up to first class too."

"Oh wow, that never happens to me. I'm a little jealous."

"Good, as you should be. You're the reason I'm here. I could have called or sent a text. I'm in a filthy city with pushy people about to surprise a man who very well may not want to see me."

"He wants to see you too. You two are just too chicken shit to be honest about what you want, so you're welcome."

I grinned as I navigated out of the airport toward Rideshare. Thank goodness I didn't check a bag. That whole scene was very chaotic and very scary. The way people were shoving each other and their luggage around to get to their bags or to get to where they were going gave me anxiety.

"What's the plan? You going to his office or his house?"

"Not sure. Maybe I should just call him. I'm here now . . ."

"No, absolutely not. The element of surprise always wins. If you call, you'll give yourself time to back out if he says even one thing that makes you second-guess being there."

She knew me, and she was right.

"Office then. Besides, I don't have his home address. The one used for the Shared Space booking was his office."

"That won't work. Now that I think about it, if you go to the office, he'll have the opportunity to put you in a hotel while you're there. If you show up at his house, he'll have to let you stay."

I paused my steps. "Wait. So you're anticipating that he won't *want* me to stay? What happened to you fully supporting this trip?"

"I do fully support the trip. I'm the one who gave a gentle push to get you there, but again, men are stupid, and you're not me. I would demand what I want. You'll dance around it."

"More like hard shove—not gentle push. You really have no faith in me. I'm here, aren't I?"

"You are . . ." Her tone elevated. "And I'm so proud of you for going after what you want. First Design Dreams, and now, Mr. Fuck Me. *Me* being *you*."

My smile expanded as I peered across the surrounding area, locating the Rideshare station. "I love you. You're the best friend anyone could ever have, so thank you for this. I have to go. I need to schedule my ride and mentally wrap my head around what I'm doing."

"You should have already done that."

"Schedule my ride?"

"That too. You're in New York, Noel, but also wrapping your mind around getting your man. You better not back out."

"I won't. I can't. I'm here, and you'll never let me live this down if I do back out."

"Good. At least you know. Text me after your first round of orgasms and tell me everything. I mean it. Love you."

She ended the call while I shook my head, happy and horrified that she was my best friend. While standing at the Rideshare station, I scrolled through my phone and found the listing for Kanton on my Shared Space app. After locating the phone number listed, I stared at the digits for what felt like forever until someone bumped into me, almost launching my phone from my hand.

He didn't bother to say a word. Not even a simple look of sympathy. Instead, he glared at me like *I* was the one who had plowed into *him* when, clearly, I was standing still, and he had been moving. Carelessly. I tugged my carry-on closer to my side and made the call. After several rings, through which I held my breath, someone answered.

"Thank you for calling Global. How may I direct your call?"

"Uh, I'm trying to reach Kanton Joseph."

"Hold, please."

After a short pause, she was back.

"Mr. Joseph is in a meeting. I'll transfer you to his office. Have a good day."

I opened my mouth to speak but wasn't given the chance. The phone rang again, and another voice was flowing, but not his—a female.

"Kanton Joseph's office."

"Hi, I'm . . . uhh. My name is Noel Anderson."

"Yes, and?"

I frowned at her tone. It wasn't rude, but not exactly friendly. "I'm a friend of Kanton's, and I'm visiting—"

"*Here*, in New York?"

Strange. Her voice did a thing.

"Yes, I wanted to surprise him. I was thinking about stopping by the office to see him . . ."

"He's in a meeting."

"Oh, well then—"

"*But* he shouldn't be long. However, he'll be leaving immediately after. It might be best to surprise him if you met Kanton at his apartment instead of here at the office."

Shit.

"At his apartment?"

"Yes, you have that address, don't you?"

"No, I don't. We haven't seen each other in some time and . . ."

"Are you sure you're friends and not some crazy ex from his past trying to seek revenge for crushing your heart years ago?"

She sounded amused, like she was possibly making a joke, but I couldn't be a hundred percent sure.

"No, not a crazy ex. Just friends, that's all. Maybe I should just come there to meet him instead. If he knows I'm coming, I'm sure he would wait."

Or run.

"I had to ask. Do you have something to write with?"

"What?"

"I'll give you his address so you can surprise him at his apartment. I'm sure he'd much rather you meet him there."

"Oh, sure. Hang on. Let me put you on speaker. I can type it into my phone."

She rattled off the address, and I typed it in notes, immediately removing the phone from speaker afterward.

"Got it. Thank you. How long do you think he'll be?"

"It's four now. He should be there no later than six."

"Six?"

"Yes, six. There's a quaint little café in his building. Why don't you grab a bite to eat until then? That is, if you want to surprise him."

More like an ambush.

"Okay, thank you."

"When you're ready to head up to his place, go straight back to the elevators on the left. You'll have to key in a code to get to the twenty-first floor. Use 1943."

"Got it. Thanks again."

"You're very welcome, Noel, and welcome to New York."

She ended the call, and I frowned a bit. That was too easy.

Maybe she's setting me up.

Or maybe I'm just looking for an excuse to sabotage this.

Clearing my thoughts, I keyed in the address she gave me to schedule my ride, and a few minutes later, they were pulling up.

Here goes nothing.

By 6:00, my nerves were all over the place. I sat in the café enjoying a turkey and Swiss while working on a few new designs for my site. But I kept looking up the entire time, expecting to see Kanton walk into the building.

I didn't have a vantage point of the entrance from the café, but that didn't stop my eyes from wandering each time I noticed a body in my peripheral. Whoever the woman was that answered his line had mentioned he'd be there no later than six, so I decided to stop stalling and do what I came here to do.

Get the guy!

Hopefully, the guy wanted to be *got*.

Stop it, Noel.

I cleaned my table, packed up my laptop, which I shoved into my travel tote, and dumped my trash on the way out. After navigating to the elevator and following the instructions I had been given, I stepped inside and keyed the code that would provide me with access to the twenty-first floor.

As each number illuminated, making it painfully clear that I was getting closer, my stomach knotted and tensed. My nerves were frayed, but deep down inside, a bubble of excitement blossomed. Once I stepped off the elevator, my eyes scanned the first door I could find, giving me directions for where I needed to go.

21-A.

Inhaling deeply, I knocked and waited. My anxiety kicked in, but I plastered on a smile that dropped immediately when a woman and not Kanton greeted me. A woman wearing a skimpy dress, her feet bare while she held a glass of wine in one hand and a lacy piece of lingerie in the other. She lifted a brow, taking me in, but smiled smugly the minute the question flew out of my mouth.

"Who are you?"

"Jordan. Who are you?"

Jordan. His ex.

Or maybe he lied, and she's not his ex. Now with her here, dressed like that, sipping wine, looking very comfortable in his apartment . . .

Of course, he lied, but still . . .

"Is Kanton here?"

"No, but I'm guessing he should be any minute."

"How did you get inside his apartment?" I frowned at her again, taking in her appearance. She was here, comfortable, drinking wine, and holding lingerie she was likely about to wear for him.

"With my key, and you didn't answer my question. Who are you?"

My spine straightened, and I closed my eyes briefly, getting a grip. This was *precisely* why I didn't want to come here.

"No one. Sorry to bother you."

I turned to leave, but her voice followed. "You're not bothering me. If you want to come in and wait—"

"No, thanks," I muttered. This was my fault—not his. He didn't ask me to come. I shouldn't have, and now, I was taking my ass back home where I belonged and forgetting about Kanton Joseph.

Or at least I'm going to attempt to.

While in the back of my scheduled ride, I pulled up outgoing flights to Atlanta. There was one leaving in an hour. If I was lucky, I could be on it. If not, I would have to stay the night and catch the first flight out in the morning. Spending another minute in this city wasn't an option, so I sent up a prayer that I could be on that flight and leave behind this city and the man who brought me here.

Kanton.

EARLIER THAT DAY . . .

SHELBY WALKED INTO my office and placed a stack of papers on my desk, then settled onto the armchair that sat a few feet away from my desk and crossed one leg over the other, staring at me.

"What's this?"

"Another one of your not-so-indiscreet love letters."

I looked at her, and she pointed. "The contract from Brighton. Read it."

"Did you add the provisions I asked for?"

"Yes."

"Did he agree?"

"Of course, he did. You saved the man millions in one week. He will do whatever you ask to ensure you pad his bottom line."

This was true. With a few clicks of a mouse, I showed Brighton how to dump several business expenses that cost him more than he had realized.

Some things were easily overlooked, and by the end of the month, he would be singing my praises once my firm had done a deep dive to finalize ways to increase business and lower expenses. A huge part of growing business was rebranding, and Noel would help.

I hoped.

"One year and complete control to rebrand not only his stateside locations but also the international ones."

"It's what you asked for."

"And the hundred grand," I clarified.

"Payable as soon as she signs the contract."

Noel needed the money. Offering a hundred grand up front of the 250 grand she would make for the year would hopefully sweeten the deal and force her to overlook the fact that I personally handed over what would likely be her biggest contract ever. She was proud, and if I learned anything about the woman, she wouldn't appreciate feeling like she was getting a handout.

This wasn't a handout. I had seen her work. She was competent. Shelby agreed, which eased my mind a bit that I was thinking with the proper head. Both heads missed Noel something terrible, but I didn't want her feeling obligated to see me because I presented the option, and she was too kind to turn it down.

This was simply a gentle nudge to, at the very least, have a conversation. Even if it was Noel yelling at me about meddling in her business. Which reminded me . . .

"Any word from Spencer yet?"

"Nope. He sent the email midmorning yesterday. She hasn't responded."

"You checked . . ."

"Today, yes. A few minutes before I came in here to bring you that. I had a feeling the topic would come up."

My eyes narrowed on her, and she smiled smugly. "I'm good at my job, Kanton, but you know this."

I do.

"What I'm confused about is why you won't just pick up the phone and call her instead of manipulating things with her life."

"I'm not manip—"

"You are. You had her website redone."

"Only so that she was more presentable, and that was *your* idea."

"My idea after *you* insisted on adding Design Dreams as an à la carte selection to your service for *your* clients. *Clients* that trust you. I refuse to allow Rainbow Brite the ability to damage your brand

and have them questioning your reliability. Presentation is everything, and you have a reputation. A *flawless* reputation, I might add."

I leaned back in my seat, massaging my chin. My fingers mindlessly stroked over my beard, reminding me of Noel, and then my dick began to play as well, lengthening in my briefs with the memory of her naked body on my chest while her fingers mirrored the same motion of massaging my beard.

"She's a good person who has had some tough breaks. Why is it an issue for me to help?"

"To help is one thing, but a quarter-million-dollar job?" Shelby arched a brow, and I shrugged.

"You negotiated the terms. I only requested she receive an advance on the salary. Standard practice when accepting such a huge undertaking."

"You also knew I would broker the best deal possible, and the standard is 30 percent. You demanded 40."

"Is she qualified?" I challenged.

"No." I narrowed my eyes, and Shelby clarified. "Talent-wise, from what I've seen, I believe she can do the job, but you and I both know she's never handled a job this large. If she were someone who was not privileged enough to speak from personal experience about the joys of receiving orgasms from you, would you be so open to demanding that type of payout? Her résumé does not support the demand."

"Brighton doesn't know that."

"But you do, and so do I."

"He agreed."

"Because he trusts you. What happens if Noel doesn't deliver?"

"She will."

"But it's possible she won't."

"Anything's possible, Shelby. Brighton could suffer a heart attack while fucking his wife and never know if Noel delivers or not."

"Let's not kill the guy. . ."

"I wanted you to get my point."

"You wanted me to fuck off and leave this alone. I won't. Not until I say what I have to say."

I gave her my full attention. Not that I had a choice. Shelby was ruthless that way. It was why I paid her so much. She would likely be heading one of our branches one day when I saw fit to open a new one, but I also wasn't interested in accepting anyone in her place, so I wasn't rushing the idea. She was me in female form. Damn good at her job, and she knew it.

"I've never seen this version of you before."

"You disapprove? I thought you were all for me finding the love of my life and delivering on the kids thing." I smirked, and she returned one.

"I am, but that's not what you're doing. If that were the case, you would pick up the phone, call the woman, and invite her to the city for a weekend. Instead, you're adding her account to the company technology expense and securing quarter-million-dollar contracts for a woman who's never cleared more than ten thousand on any project she's managed."

"I'm not seeing your point."

"What's the deal, Kanton?"

"There is no deal."

"Did you proposition her, and she turned you down?"

"Proposition her?" I laughed at the thought.

"You had sex, clearly, and I'm not mad because, apparently, sis has a platinum pussy, but obviously, you want more, and she doesn't."

"You think I'm trying to buy her with a website and a job offer?"

"No, because that's not your standard mode of operation, but you are clearly trying to get her attention."

"I'm helping a friend."

It was a lie. Shelby saw straight through it, but what I wouldn't admit was that I wanted Noel to choose me. I had already chosen her. I didn't want to place the possibility of us on the table for her to consider out of obligation.

I wanted Noel to think about me and come willingly to the conclusion that she and I were a perfect fit. Her career was important. That much I understood, and I would never want Noel to choose one or the other, but in a way, she had.

I just need a year or two to find my footing with the company. Then I'll focus on my personal life.

I didn't have a year or two. Or rather, I did, but I refused to wait that long. I wanted Noel in my life now. The past two weeks without her had been very mundane. I was still trying to figure out how one week with her had shifted my entire outlook on life.

I was tired of pretending she hadn't, so it was time to do something about it. What's the point of being rich with accessibility if I didn't do rich-people shit? That was why I was working so hard to cancel any argument Noel could use as an excuse for why a relationship with me would not work.

The year contract and advance from Brighton solved the issue she had with building her career. Once her name was attached to the rebranding of his companies, her opportunities would be endless. With a thriving career, she could focus on other things.

Me.

Noel wanted more. I saw it in her eyes, I felt it in her touch, I sensed it in the way she didn't want me to leave the night before my flight. She had been placed in the position to choose before, and she lost in the end because of a man who didn't deserve or value her. I didn't want Noel to feel a sense of déjà vu. This was how I needed to handle the situation.

"You're 'friends' now?"

"Yes."

"You're full of shit. Just call her and get it over with. You're a very calculated man. You live your life by planning, following those plans, and executing with precision."

"Planning and executing with precision has made me wealthy and successful."

"With business—but the same might not be the case regarding relationships. It might actually backfire."

"Says the woman who planned her own engagement."

Her eyes lowered to the ring on her finger, and she smiled. "Gordon lives by the same rules you do. The same rules I understand, so that works in our world. Do you really believe the same will work for her? She's not like us."

Like always, Shelby had very valid points.

Regardless, I released a sigh and remained steady with my feelings on the matter.

"I know what I'm doing."

She stood from the sofa. "I hope you do because, if not, this will end badly."

Which I had already considered.

"Ten minutes until we meet with Johnson."

I nodded and rolled my neck, feeling the tension building in it and my back. Since returning from Atlanta, I'd been hoping that getting home and sleeping in my bed again would help, but it hadn't. As comfy as Noel's sofa was for sitting, it wasn't the best option for sleeping.

"I'll be there," I murmured.

Shelby paused at my office door. "Physically, sure, but I need your head in the game, Kanton. This is an important meeting. Once you're done with Johnson, you can head home."

"Are we confused again about who works for whom?"

She flashed me a pointed smile. "Although the lines often get blurred, absolutely not. You're the boss. I'm in your employ." She winked. "I'm only telling you because Kiara will be at your place by seven." *My chiropractor.* "You should have already seen her, but you're stubborn. I'm starting to think you're personally suffering through this as a reminder of *her.*"

She didn't wait for a response because she didn't have to. The truth was painfully obvious. I missed Noel and held onto whatever I could that connected me to her. Even this pulsing pain in my neck and back.

PRESENT TIME . . .

Traffic was a bitch right now. I was grateful that I elected to have a driver today, or the tension in my neck and back would have been a lot worse from the frustration of navigating through the overly crowded New York streets. By the time we reached my building, I was also grateful for Shelby ignoring my persistence about not seeing Kiara. Once she had me realigned, I planned on taking a hot shower, cracking open a few beers, and figuring out what the hell I was doing with my life.

The short answer was avoiding the obvious. I wanted Noel. I wanted her in my life, and I wanted her to welcome me into hers. The way I was currently handling things would no longer suffice, which meant I had to make some tough decisions, one of which was how to fix this problem because my mind was made up. Noel was mine. The rest would be decided once I convinced her of such.

"Evening, sir." I nodded at Gerald and immediately thought of Lewis. I chuckled lightly at how different my world was from Noel's. I was familiar with the rotation of people who worked here at my building, but we weren't friends. I didn't gift them personal things for Christmas, nor did I know the intimate details of their lives as Noel did of those she encountered daily.

That was a *Noel* thing. A layer of who she was. She cared about people. It wasn't that I didn't. I simply allowed myself to be so absorbed in my own life, which often couldn't be avoided, that I rarely crossed boundaries with others.

However, Noel didn't just cross boundaries; she demolished them. The thought made me smile as I stopped at my door and removed the keys from my pocket to enter. Only before I did, a frown marred my face at the sound of music playing behind the door.

What the fuck?

The minute I stepped inside, I realized why.

Jordan.

When the door slammed with my annoyance for her being here a week late and unannounced, she peeked her head from my bedroom. "Oh, hey. You're home."

I ignored the pleasantries and barked out a question. "What are you doing here?"

"I told you I was coming back to get my things."

"You did, and you were supposed to have done that last week."

"I know, I know. I'm sorry. Plans changed, but I'm here now, and I'll be packed and out by tomorrow. You don't mind if I stay tonight, right?"

She peeked over her shoulder, but my eyes were moving around the explosion of her things that cluttered my bedroom. There were several large suitcases and two trunks, all expensive and very much Jordan's signature style.

"You don't mind, right?" she repeated because I had yet to respond.

"No. The sooner you're done, the sooner you can be out of here, but pick a guest room. You're not sleeping in here. That's a bad idea." I knew she was coming at some point, and I wasn't really upset, but Jordan being here disrupted my thoughts about what I would do about Noel. I might not have been as courteous as I usually would have been.

"It could be a good idea. One last hurrah, you know?"

She lifted a glass from the dresser, swirling the ruby-red liquid, and then turned to lean against the dresser. Sex with Jordan was one of our good points, but the offer no longer enticed me. I simply wanted her out.

"I'll pass."

"You're in a mood."

"You're a week late, your things are everywhere, and you're drinking my wine."

"It's my favorite."

"It's *my* favorite, which you became partial to. I stock it for me, not because you like it, Jordan."

She grinned and shrugged. "True, but this . . ." She tipped the glass in my direction. ". . . is not what that mood is all about. Did she call you because I swear I didn't say anything inappropriate? I even offered to let her come in and wait."

"What are you talking about?"

"The woman who showed up here."

"Kiara?" I mumbled, still confused about what the hell she was talking about. I glanced at my watch. It was a quarter to seven. Kiara was punctual but rarely ever early, and Jordan knew Kiara so that she wouldn't have described her as "*the woman.*"

"No, not her." She smiled wider. "Now it makes sense. She was surprising *you*, and I surprised *her*."

"*Her* who, Jordan? Did she give you a name?" Not that it mattered. I wasn't expecting anyone.

"No, but I can describe her. My height, natural hair, my complexion, and she had amazing skin. She was cute, but not *me*. Not really your type."

I shot her an amused look. "*You're* not my type."

Her lips tilted up before the glass was hiding the expression. "I used to be."

In both of our delusional minds.

"What else? That's not much to go on."

"Nothing else. She was cute. Had a kinda sweet and innocent vibe, even though I could tell she wanted to claw my eyes out when I answered the door. She had a suitcase with her . . ."

My mind jolted.

There's no way!

The woman she was describing could have easily been Noel, but . . .

"How long ago was she here?"

"Twenty, maybe thirty minutes. You just missed her."

"Fuck."

I snatched my phone from my pocket and dialed her number. It went straight to voicemail, so I tried again. Three more times, back-to-back, and the same result. She was either ignoring my calls, or her phone was on "do not disturb."

Because she was on a plane.

But not that fast, so she was definitely hitting ignore or blocking me.

"Damn it."

I hurried to the living room and lifted the cordless linked to my landline. I pulled up her number in my cell and dialed. It rang twice, and then she answered, thank God.

"Noel . . ."

She didn't speak. Not one word, but she was there. I felt it.

"Noel, you're in New York—"

"Don't worry. Not for long. I'm leaving. I shouldn't have come. It was a stupid idea to come in the first place. No hard feelings, but please don't call me again. This time, the asshole didn't change, and the girl didn't get the guy."

Just before she ended the call, I heard "Welcome to LaGuardia" in the background.

She's at the airport.

She's leaving.

"Fuck," I mumbled again, making another call, but this time to Shelby.

"I need you to book me a flight to Atlanta. The first thing out that you can book me on."

I stepped back into my room to find Jordan sorting through her things as if she wasn't the reason behind my current problem. I couldn't deal with her right now, so I bypassed her and headed to the closet.

"Although I'm glad you're finally coming to your senses about Noel, you don't need a flight to Atlanta. She's here in New York and should have been at your place by now," Shelby said.

I froze, reaching for my duffle. "How do you know she's here?"

"Because she called the office while you were meeting with Johnson. She wanted to surprise you, or at least, I assumed she did because she pretended you were 'old friends.' But when she offered her name, I knew exactly who she was. I gave her your address so that she could surprise you at home. It's why I told you to leave after the meeting."

"You said it was because of Kiara."

"Originally, it was. I already had Kiara booked, but after Noel called, I wanted to ensure you didn't miss her. Consider it the universe aligning."

"Damn it."

"What?"

"The universe didn't get the memo about aligning. She's on her way back to Atlanta. I need a flight."

"What do you mean on her way back to Atlanta?"

"When Noel arrived, I wasn't here. Jordan was. I called from my cell, and she ignored me. I called from the apartment because she wouldn't recognize the number and got lucky. She answered but didn't give me a chance to explain. She's back at the airport. I heard the announcement about LaGuardia in the background before she hung up on me."

"Then you missed her. I'm looking now. There's a flight at 7:45, which she's probably on."

"When's the next one?"

"9:45—"

"Book it. I'm packing now. That gives me plenty of time to get there."

"That's 9:45 in the *morning*, Kanton. There are no more fights this evening."

"How is that even possible? There are at least fifty flights a day to Atlanta."

"Normally, but they've had weather issues, so they've limited flights."

"What about private?"

"I can try, but that might not work either. If one's at a nearby airport, I can try to charter it for you, but it will cost. Also, if they're limiting commercial, that likely applies to private."

"I don't give a damn about the cost. Just try. I'm packing now. Call me back as soon as you have an answer."

"Will do, but you know this is *your* fault, right?"

"I had no idea Jordan was going to be here."

"That's not what I mean. You should have called long before now. When a woman makes a grand gesture like this, and it ends badly, they typically don't forgive easily . . . or at all."

This time, the asshole didn't change, and the girl didn't get the guy.
Noel and those damn movies!

"I haven't done anything wrong. I'm not with Jordan. She shouldn't even fucking be here."

"Nope, she shouldn't, but that's a conversation for another day."

"Can you save the lecture and find me a way to Atlanta?"

"Sure thing, boss." Her tone was light and laced with amusement. She was enjoying this far too much, but she was right about one thing. It wasn't going to be easy to sway Noel on the truth. The lie she walked in on was far more convincing. Either way, I was going to Atlanta to plead my case, but first, I needed to deal with my current problem.

I left my closet and tossed my duffle on the bed, gaining Jordan's attention.

"Didn't take you long to move on." She didn't sound upset, but I hadn't expected her to be. We split amicably.

My eyes found hers, which danced with curiosity, so I nipped that immediately. "Not your concern. I need you to finish this up and be out of here by tomorrow, and this time, for good. No more excuses. No more pop-ups."

"That was the plan."

"Good, and leave the key with the concierge."

She smiled, slowly lifting her wineglass. I felt her watching me as I moved around my room, yanking things from my dresser and tossing them on the bed. When I was tired of her eyes following my movements, I turned to face her.

"What?"

"She's important." The look I gave said, "Leave it alone," but Jordan smiled wider. "I'm not upset."

"If you were, you wouldn't have the right to be. We're not together, and you've also moved on."

With multiple people—another issue that got in the way of us working. Jordan wanted the freedom to explore various partners. I did not.

"No, we're not, and I have, but you're wrong. I *do* have the right to be upset. This person you are now is someone you never offered me the opportunity to get to know. You're catching a flight to chase a woman. When we ended things, it was like ending a business endeavor. Very polite and to the point."

She was right. Yet another reason why I knew that I had to make this right with Noel. Ending things with her would be loud and messy, and we hadn't even begun anything that needed to end.

But if that day came, I'd argue why her not being in my life was not something I could accept, and I would be happy to do so. The thought of doing the same to keep Jordan never even crossed my mind. I was more relieved than anything.

"We both understood that you and I would have never been more than what it was."

"We did, but it still stings a bit. Every girl likes to believe they're the one, or at least, have the potential to be."

My eyes lifted to hers, and she smiled. "I'm happy for you, Kanton."

"Are you?"

"I am. I hope this works, and if you would like me to clear things up with her, I'd be happy to help out."

"Absolutely not. You've done enough."

"Maybe I have, but unintentionally. I didn't know who she was, and I didn't purposely try to sabotage things with her."

I believed her.

And that was the end of things. Jordan went back to sipping her wine, and I packed my things, praying that Shelby could find me a flight before morning. And if she didn't, I wouldn't be getting any sleep until I was on my way to fix this.

Noel.

I THINK THE UNIVERSE felt sorry for me. All the stars aligned, and I was able to secure a seat on the last flight back to Atlanta. Thanks to weather concerns, I was on the last flight out. They didn't upgrade me to first class, but that didn't matter much. Not even premium snacks, a complimentary pillow, and a blanket could satiate the ache pooling around my bruised heart.

No matter how often I told myself things with Kanton and I wouldn't work because of all the obstacles between us, I secretly hoped they would. Seeing his ex at his place was clearly all the proof I needed to convince myself that he and I weren't supposed to happen. Even if they weren't together, she was there. I wasn't. How could I trust that he wouldn't continue to see her in my absence if I did give him a chance?

I didn't want half of a man. I had that with Evan, and frankly, it sucked. I wanted a man who would offer himself to me wholly and completely because that was what I would give. Having a man committed to me and only me was what I deserved. That man wasn't Kanton, no matter how much I wished it were.

I was exhausted and drained when I sluggishly entered my building, dragging my rolling carry-on behind me. Atlanta got snow instead of sleet, but nowhere near what was expected, so the flights were slowly coming back up, but the chaos at the airport and in the city had already begun. Not even Lewis's smile helped to turn my mood around.

"Hey, you. That was a quick trip."

I nodded. "It was."

"Everything okay?"

Nope.

Not even close.

He knew I was going to New York. I hadn't told him why, but I was sure he assumed because he also knew that was where Kanton lived.

"Not really, but it will be." I smiled softly, and Lewis moved closer, granting me a hug. I allowed myself the comfort that wouldn't cure my broken heart, but it would make it ache a little less. When I pulled away, he peered at me with guarded eyes.

"Want to talk about it? If not with me, then maybe Cleo? She's always available for you."

"No, I'll be okay once I take a hot shower and get some rest. It's been a long day. It's also late . . ."

"She's up. It's not a bother if you want to give her a call. You know she won't rest until I'm home."

I wanted what they had. It was sweet and imperfect, but it was everything I could imagine. Much like my parents, Lewis and Cleo were goals.

"I know, but I promise I'm fine. Just tired."

He narrowed his stare at me. "You sure that's all it is?"

There was a silent question.

Did he hurt you?

And yes, *he* did, but unintentionally. But truthfully, it was my fault for expecting more than I should have.

"I'm sure."

Lewis nodded, but I could tell he wasn't satisfied with my answer. He wanted to hurt the person who hurt me.

Kanton.

But Kanton didn't deserve Lewis's fury. "I'm going to head up. You have a good night, and hug Cleo for me."

"Will do. You should come to dinner soon. I'm sure she'd love to see you."

"Give me a date, and I'll be there."

Again, he nodded, and I headed toward the elevators, feeling physically and emotionally drained. When I was showered and in my pajamas, I crawled into my bed, burrowing myself beneath the bedding. After flicking on my TV, I almost chucked the remote at the screen when I realized I was still on the Holiday Movie Channel and up next for my viewing pleasure, *Big City Holiday Surprise.*

Great!

I certainly got a surprise in the big city, but it wasn't one fit for a holiday movie or pleasant. No matter how terrible my life felt at this moment, and it truly felt like a bottomless pit of never-ending unhappiness, I still snuggled deeper into my pillow. Then I tugged my comforter tight under my chin to watch the movie.

Even if I didn't get the guy, maybe this woman would. What was I thinking? Of course, she would, because this was a movie and fictional people got their happily ever after. It was only in the real world where the girl didn't get the guy . . . where I didn't get the guy.

Okay, Noel, get yourself together. One night of sulking is all you're allowed.

Kanton's not meant to be your guy, but you do have a guy. He's out there somewhere, just waiting for the perfect meet cute so you can fall hopelessly in love and relish in your happily ever after.

I had to believe this to be true. What else was a hopeless romantic supposed to do?

"Stop watching these stupid movies; that is what you can do," I mumbled, and then I pressed the power button to shut off my TV.

I wasn't in the right mindset to watch anything at all, especially not this. It would be best if I just called it a night. I would work on pulling my life together tomorrow. Now that I didn't have Kanton occupying space in my head and heart, and no viable work opportunities, I needed to get my shit together so that I wasn't in a different type of Christmas movie . . .

Homeless for the Holidays.

I must have been more exhausted than I imagined because I wasn't up until just after ten the following day and only then because I heard my front door slam, which had me jumping up in bed in a panic until I heard a familiar voice.

"I can't believe you didn't call me . . ."

I closed my eyes at the sound of Simone outside my bedroom door just before she pushed it open.

"Call you for what?" I mumbled as I climbed out of bed and headed to the bathroom to hide. Only I wasn't granted the opportunity to escape without scrutiny. The minute I sighed in release, emptying my bladder, she appeared in the doorway, glaring at me.

"Uh, excuse me. Privacy, please?" I narrowed my eyes, and she rolled hers.

"You don't get privacy. I'm angry with you."

Well, join the club. I'm angry with you for making me embarrass myself.

"I'm sure you are, but can you be angry with me out there and let me finish in here."

"Fine . . ."

She turned to leave, and I finished using the bathroom, flushed, washed my hands, and then proceeded to wash my face and brush my teeth after staring in the mirror at my ruffled appearance. I looked a hot mess—hair all over the place, puffy eyes from lack of restful sleep, and pure disappointment.

I suppose I took too long because she appeared in the doorway again with a frown set in place. "Why didn't you call me?"

"Because I needed to process everything, and I wasn't ready for you to tell me all the reasons why I should have handled things differently. I went to sleep instead."

"I meant, why didn't you call before you left New York? But you just answered that question. What happened?"

I shoved my toothbrush back into my mouth and continued cleaning my teeth. Simone's impatience grew with every second that passed. I finished up with mouthwash before I turned to face her again, asking a question instead of answering hers. "How did you even know I was home?"

"I booked the flight. All I had to do was check. When you didn't answer my text or calls, I searched the booking this morning and found your flight home. *Last night.* You should have called."

"I probably should have, but I knew what you would say . . ."

"Noel, I'm your best friend. If you need me, I'm there. Always, and regardless of what you think, I choose you over everything, so I wouldn't have argued if you had a valid reason for leaving."

My shoulders deflated. "I know. You're the best friend I could ever ask for. I need to be a better friend to *you*. You're always here, making things work in my life, and I'm—"

"The same. Who let me live with them for almost six months when I broke up with Davis, packed my things, and moved back home without a job or plan?"

"Me."

"And who created my résumé as I applied for jobs and kept me from drowning in my own sadness because Davis was a dick who totally broke my heart? Not to mention doing all this while covering all the expenses around here because I didn't have a dime to my name?"

I grinned. "Me."

"And who—"

"Okay, okay. I get it. I'm not a shitty friend."

"Do you? Because it feels like you're keeping score."

I cringed, and she tilted her head to the side in question, so I explained. "You sound like Kanton. He kept telling me that I was obsessed with keeping score when it comes to doing nice things."

"Well, he's right. You are, and I wish you wouldn't be. That's not what friendship is about. We don't keep score. We do what's necessary for the people we love. You love me, and I love you, so we step up. There's no running total on either side."

"I know, but it feels like you've been the one holding me together lately—"

"I have, and I don't mind. Again, I love you and know you would do the same. You *have* done the same. Can we get past that and talk about the *real* issue here? What happened with Kanton?"

I sighed and flopped on the foot of my bed. "He's still with his ex, but based on what I know now, she was probably never his ex to begin with."

"He told you that?"

"No, she did."

"*She* did?"

"Well, not in so many words, but her actions absolutely said she was with him. She was at his apartment."

"And what did he say?"

"He wasn't there. She used the key that he gave her to get in. When she answered the door, she told me he would be home soon, and I could wait if I wanted."

"Why the hell didn't you? He owes you an explanation."

"Does he?" I turned to her, and she opened her mouth to argue her point but then hesitated. We were both well aware that he didn't. I was the one who blindly hopped on a plane and showed up at his apartment unannounced. "Right, so you see my point. I left."

"But how do you know she wasn't just there for—"

"A friendly, platonic visit? Stopping by to catch up, say hello?"

I'd slept with Kanton. Experienced him while he was here. Any woman who truly knew him wouldn't let go so quickly. No, it wasn't a "stopping by to offer a friendly hello."

"It happens, Noel."

"She was wearing a skimpy dress. She was also barefoot, drinking wine and holding lacy lingerie that she would wear to greet him at the door when he got home. I'm sure I interrupted her selection process. It wasn't just an 'I'm dropping by to catch up' thing. It was more like 'I'm dropping by so you can drop your dick in me' thing."

Simone nodded and removed her phone from her pocket. She didn't say anything. She kept swiping the device and then tapping the screen before calmly stating, "They have a flight at three today."

"Are you confused? Did you hear *any* of what I just said? There's no way in hell I'm going back to New York. I'm done with this *and* him. It's time to move on."

"Oh, we're not going to see *him*. We're going to see *her*, and by 'see her,' I mean see her face getting acquainted with our fists."

I laughed hard. "No, we are not. She's not the problem . . ."

"She *is* the problem, Noel."

"She's not. The problem is that no matter how much fun we had or how perfect it seemed like we would be together, the stars just didn't align. He's not my person, and I'm not his. I'm okay with accepting that we're not meant to be."

"You're not just fine."

No, I'm not.

"I am, or rather, I *will* be. I need you to let me be whatever I am right now, and I can't if you keep pushing me toward something that didn't work."

Her face softened. "I want you to be happy."

"I know, and when it's right, I will be happy."

Hopefully.

"Okay, then, I'll let it go."

"Thank you."

"I brought gifts," she said, perking up.

"Please tell me you did not."

"I did, but it's not what you think. I have cinnamon rolls, extra cream cheese icing, and Jeni's Skillet Cinnamon Roll Ice Cream."

My stomach sang its approval.

"That's a breakup care package, and this isn't a breakup."

"All things considered, I decided this qualified. Now, let's go. I also have tequila."

I stood after she did, heading to my bedroom door. "Tequila?"

She shrugged, glancing at me over her shoulder. "I wasn't sure how bad it would be, but considering you were only in New York for a few hours, I thought things might be tequila kind of bad."

They were, but I refuse to drown my sorrows in tequila.

"*You're too good to me*," I sang, hugging her around the waist, halting her steps in the middle of the hallway.

She clasped her hands over where mine rested at her stomach. "I am, but only because you've shown me what being a good friend looks like. Now, let's go overindulge, and then we're dismantling that tree. It's two weeks overdue."

It was. She wanted to take it down on New Year's Eve when we stayed in, drinking champagne and dancing around my apartment in a lazy, inebriated bliss, but I refused.

"I'm going to need the tequila for that," I mumbled, and she smiled, lifting the bottle after we reached the kitchen.

"Then it's a good thing I got the *big* bottle."

I groaned, rolling my eyes at the thought of the two of us taking down a Christmas tree drunk off our asses. Not a pretty picture, but the tequila would surely help me survive the process.

Cheers to moving on with life.

Kanton.

I HADN'T SLEPT SINCE I woke at seven the previous morning. My body was screaming at me to find a comfortable place to crash and burn. I thought maybe I would get some rest on the plane.

Didn't happen.

My mind was all over the place with how I would handle things with Noel. I refused to grant her the option of not hearing me out. I refused to allow her to accept that she and I weren't meant to be. We were, and I was here offering a grand gesture to make sure she understood just how serious I was about proving my point.

I laughed to myself as I exited the car that brought me to her building. She loved those damn movies, and now we were right in the middle of a perfect plot for one. Guy fumbles girl and leaves without telling her how he really feels. Girl lets him go without doing the same. Girl flies to his city to make it right, and instead of finding him, finds a woman he would no sooner spend his future with than a stranger on the street, but she storms off, destroyed by a misunderstanding. All the elements were there.

Unexpected attraction. Passionate connection. Third act breakup over a misunderstanding, and then the happily ever after where love wins.

Love.

Did I love Noel?

Yes, I did. It was fast and unexpected and not easy, but I loved her.

It was possible she didn't feel the same, but deep down inside, I thought she did. What I did know was that she was mine, and I was hers. Here I was, walking into her building, only to be hit with another gut punch with what I heard when I stepped inside the lobby.

"I'm well aware that she was supposed to be out of town. I talked to Noel. She's expecting me."

Lewis's back was to me, so he hadn't noticed I entered the lobby nor noticed when I bypassed him and the guy he was talking to. I almost considered tossing this guy the hell out of the lobby, but instead, I focused on my reason for being here. If she was expecting him, I needed to get to her first so that there wasn't another barrier between us, forcing Noel to second-guess.

I quickly made it to the elevator, but it took too long to arrive, and whoever the hell this guy was, he managed to get on with me. I discreetly checked him out, and when I realized who he was, I wasn't sure he would walk off the elevator. Expensive clothes and shoes, a hundred-thousand-dollar watch. Pretentious and entitled demeanor. He was annoyed, which meant that any interaction he had with Noel wouldn't sit well with me.

I laughed to myself, shaking my head. How ironic. She showed up at my place to find my ex, and now, I was here at her place, on the elevator with hers. Only I refused to give a damn about this guy. He wouldn't get anywhere near Noel. But still, a part of me needed to know why he was here and if she was, indeed, expecting him.

We got off the elevator on the same floor, en route to the same apartment, but he hadn't cared enough to acknowledge me beyond a quick glance in the car when he first stepped on. I was seeing everything Noel and those closest to her told me about this dick, up close and personal. Seeing him made maintaining restraint, instead of knocking him on his ass and kicking him back into the elevator, a daunting task.

While he approached Noel's door, I hung back, remaining slightly out of view at the corner, waiting. I heard the beep from him entering the wrong code, and my fists clenched. Was *he* expecting access? *Had* she granted him that? He did tell Lewis Noel was expecting him.

For what exactly?

After a few failed attempts, he knocked more aggressively than necessary, and as soon as I heard the door open, he wasted no time proving how much of a dick he truly was.

"I guess you did change the code. I'm glad to see you're capable of successfully completing something. I was beginning to wonder if that were even possible."

"As if you know what I'm capable of," she shot back.

"It doesn't matter. Are you going to pretend to have manners and invite me in or not?"

"No, but you already knew that, didn't you? If I recall, you know everything except how to treat me."

"Why are you being so childish? I see not much has changed."

The muscles in my chest had tensed with the possibility that she wanted this jerk here loosened, but the tension in my arms and back coiled tightly, needing either to destroy or maim. I would deal with that in a minute, but for now . . .

"A lot has changed. Starting with you watching how the fuck you talk to her unless you want to deal with me not giving a damn how I handle you. I'm not much for talking to dumb fucks like you."

"Kanton . . ."

Her eyes shot past the ex and landed on me. He spun on his heels, turning to see who had been so bold as to speak to him in that manner, and the glare in his eyes expressed just how much he *didn't* appreciate my words *or* my presence.

"Who the hell are you?"

"Not *you*, which means I have the right to be here, but more importantly, a problem you don't want. Is there something I can help you with?"

"Oh, this is interesting." Another woman stepped up next to Noel, smiling smugly as her eyes moved between Evan and me.

She didn't hold my attention long, however, because the dumbass thought it would be the right thing to do to further express how little Noel meant to him in the most disrespectful way possible.

"You can't help me with a damn thing, but I can help you. Don't waste your time. She's not worth the effort you'll have to invest, but if this is just you slumming it and having a little fun, then, by all means, enjoy. That's about the only bonus to being with her. She's a great fu—"

Before he could finish the sentence, I finished him. My fist hit his face, and he spun and hit the wall, landing so awkwardly that he stumbled to the floor.

"Well, damn. That was impressive," the woman who was standing next to Noel said calmly, like I hadn't just punched a guy. My eyes moved from her to Noel, who was staring at me with a scowl in place. I couldn't tell if she was angry about me hitting the guy or just angry.

"You son of a bitch—" Evan growled, holding his face while scrambling to get off the floor, but he also backpedaled to be sure he wasn't near me when he managed to get to his feet.

"I told you I wasn't a problem you wanted. You didn't listen. Now, again, is there something *I* can help you with? If not, you might want to leave *now*. You being here is not smart."

"I'm not going anywhere until I get what I came here for." He turned to Noel. "Give me my gotdamn clubs."

"Sure thing. If it gets you away from me, I'll be glad to . . ."

I wanted to knock him on his ass again, but the idea of Noel moving when he said move had me following behind her. As soon as I found her in the hallway opening a closet I never paid much attention to, I grabbed her wrist.

"What clubs? What's he talking about?"

The heat from her eyes seared me, but I stood my ground.

"None of your business, and what are *you* doing here?"

"You didn't let him explain. Obviously, he's here to explain and to punch your ex for being a dick," the woman who was with Noel said in an amused tone.

"Simone . . ." was what she received in return.

"What? You're the one who told me you didn't let him explain. He's here, giving Evan exactly what he deserves only a few hours after you left New York. My final assessment: Kanton is here to get his girl. And I approve."

"He could have called," Noel sneered and then delivered me a death stare like she was considering punching me the way that I punched Evan. I would have laughed because it was all quite amusing, but instead, I offered . . .

"I tried to call. You either blocked me or kept hitting ignore every time I called."

"Problem solved. He called. Now, he's here. If you'll excuse me, I'm going to give Evan his clubs and then head out." Her eyes swept me from head to toe, lingering in certain areas as she did a full assessment and then added, "Now, it all makes sense."

She smirked, moving past me to drag the clubs out of the closet. I reached for them, but she slapped my hand. "Nope. I got this. I can handle Evan. You two have some things to work out. I'll take care of these, and then I'm leaving. You . . ." She narrowed her eyes on Noel. "Listen to whatever he has to say." She turned in my direction. "And you better have something really good to say which will fix this."

She dragged the golf bag behind her, bypassing me but stopping at the counter to lift a bottle of tequila. "And I'm taking this. As sexy as he is, he should be enough of a high. Call me tomorrow, Noel. And it was nice to meet you, Kanton. We'll do dinner when you two come up for air."

I chuckled, watching her leave. I liked Simone. She and Noel made sense as friends. Speaking of her friend . . .

She glared at me a few feet away until something crashed, followed by Simone sticking her head in the door for the last time. "Clubs delivered on the *floor*. You kids behave now, or don't . . ."

And then she was gone. I almost asked her to stay. I wasn't sure if I was ready to go to war with Noel alone, but I was here and not leaving like she had.

"You flew to see me and then left . . ." I stared at her, and she didn't waste time getting to the point.

"You have a girlfriend. Who was at your apartment. Why would I stay?"

"I don't have a girlfriend, but I'm here working on that."

She narrowed her eyes more.

"Jordan was at your apartment. She used the key that *you* gave her, and answered the door wearing little to nothing, drinking wine. Didn't look like much of an ex to me. At least not what I consider an ex."

I stood grinning at her, and that only pissed her off more, which had her growling, "What?"

"How do you watch all those unrealistic movies, which all have the same storyline and plot, and not see what's happening here?"

Her eyes narrowed more, and I moved closer, stating one word: "Misunderstanding."

"Possibly, but it still proves that this won't work. You're there, and I'm here. None of this makes sense."

"Because you don't want it to. I'm *not* with Jordan. Right before my trip here, she got a job and had to fly to the UK at the last minute. She was supposed to be out of my apartment before I got home, but she called and asked if she could have more time while I was here. I agreed. What you saw was Jordan at my place packing up her things so that she could ship them to the UK, where she will be living for the next six weeks."

"And where will she be living *after* those six weeks end?"

"I don't know, and I don't care. Not my problem. She *is* my ex, Noel."

"What else do you have?"

"Huh?"

I moved closer, and thankfully, she didn't move back, but I didn't touch her no matter how badly I wanted to. I wanted to do more than just touch her, but I had to be patient. "You know why I'm here."

"Do I?" She lifted her chin, and I smirked.

"You do, but for argument's sake, I'll tell you so we don't have any more misunderstandings. The past two weeks have taught me something very important."

"Which is?"

"My life doesn't work without you in it, and I'm willing to bet you would say the same if I asked and you answered honestly."

"You're awfully confident."

"I always am when my gut tells me something is a sure thing, and that's what it's been telling me about you, about *us*, Noel."

"You left . . ." she said quietly, like it pained her to get the words out.

I did, and that was a huge mistake.

"You let me . . ."

"Why wouldn't I?"

I inched closer. Damn, I wanted to touch her so badly, but I also needed us to get this figured out, and sex would only temporarily distract Noel from doubting.

"Because you didn't want me to go, that is why, but I did, and so here we are."

"Now what?"

"Now, you give me your top three reasons why I shouldn't stay, and if I can't find a solution that eases your concerns, I'll leave."

"Only three? I have way more than that."

I nodded. "I'm sure you do, but I'm only taking the top three."

Her brows pinched, and she chewed the corner of her lip before doing what I asked. I didn't expect she wouldn't. "I live in Atlanta, and you live in New York, which I've only visited once, and I don't like the place very much. It's crowded, the people are pushy, self-absorbed, and no one smiles."

I smirked. The no smiling thing likely ranked higher on her list of cons than the fact that the city was too crowded. Noel was a people person.

"I can't force anyone to smile, but I can promise you that not all of New York is overcrowded. My apartment is actually very spacious."

She glared at me, and I chuckled, knowing where her thoughts went. I wouldn't make the mistake of getting stuck on the Jordan thing. She was about as relevant as Noel's ex, who, at the moment, was likely trying to figure out who I was so that he could sue me. I doubted anyone here would help him figure that out.

"As spacious as your apartment might be, you're proving my point. You live *there*. Your life is there, mine is here . . ."

"I like it here."

"Kanton . . ." She frowned.

"Until we find a resolution to the location problem, we travel. We can both work remotely."

"And what if we can't solve the problem? I would never expect you to leave New York."

"And I would never expect you to leave Atlanta . . ."

She opened her mouth to finish the argument, but I cut her off. "But being with you is important to me. You don't have to expect or assume, Noel. I'll be wherever you are if you're willing to give this a real chance."

"You have an entire company there." She was breaking down, and I kept pushing.

"When I have to travel . . ."

Her face tensed. She was thinking about the asshole I just punched, so I asserted with confidence. "*When* I have to travel, you can travel with me. If you can't, I'll make you come enough times before I go to ensure you don't miss me too much, and then I'll call, text, and FaceTime to make sure you know that I'll be coming back to you because *you* are all that I want, Noel. I want *you*." I closed what little space was left between us. "*You* want *me*. There's no reason why we can't have each other."

"I can't afford to travel, and don't you dare say you'll pay for it." She was trying her best not to give in to this. I refused to let her succeed.

I gripped her hips, pulling Noel into me. "I will pay for whatever I need to because I can, but I told you I would help with your business, and I have."

"You built me a website. That only helps so much."

So damn stubborn. She was going to go down fighting.

"And Brighton agreed to bring you on for his rebranding. It's a $250,000 contract. One hundred grand up front. You can afford to travel to me and with me as well as wherever else you want to go, as long as I'm involved."

I would never allow her to pay, but she could if she needed to feel satisfied. I'd let her have it for now.

She rolled her eyes, most likely at the "as long as I'm involved" part, before she asked, "Brighton is giving me a contract because you asked him to?"

Yes, basically, but . . .

"He's giving you the contract because he's seen your work. Yes, he trusts me, but I didn't ask him for this as a favor. Shelby sent him your designs, and he made the decision himself. If you want verification, you can ask whenever you want. Well, almost whenever. Not tonight. I have plans for you tonight." I smirked and felt her body shiver against mine. "I know you wouldn't want a handout. You would want to earn this, and you have."

"Not all of it."

"Noel . . ."

She stared at me and slowly smiled. "That's a lot of money and a really big job."

"You can't handle it? If I recall, you handle really big things very well. With expert skill." I pulled her harder against me, but she didn't allow the closeness to distract her.

"I can do the job."

"Then you don't want it?"

"I do . . ."

"Then it's a done deal. All you have to do is sign the contract when he sends it over. Now, what's your last thing?"

I lowered my face into the curve of her neck, kissing and teasing her skin with my lips and tongue. She smelled so damn good. I missed her smell and the way she felt.

"Huh?"

"I asked you to give me three reasons. You only gave me two. Location and your job."

"Oh . . . I don't have a third."

"Too bad because I have an argument for the third."

"How can you have an argument when you don't know what I was going to say?"

I pulled away, using one hand to grip the back of her neck. "I didn't have to know *what* you were going to say. My argument would be the same regardless."

"Okay, so let me hear it."

"It's more of a 'let you feel it' type of argument."

Her smile grew incredibly slow when she realized what I meant.

"You were going to use sex?"

"*Am* going to use sex. I worked really hard planning the details of how I would present my argument. It's only fair that you allow me to do so. I have a very detailed list of places I want to put my mouth on your body."

"*Or* maybe we should talk some more."

"There's nothing else to talk about. We both want this."

"We do, but—"

"Don't say it's too fast or doesn't make sense because both are true, but it feels right." I delivered a sequence of kisses along her jaw as I spoke. "We spent one week that was more meaningful, getting to know each other than most people have in years, but truthfully, I didn't need the entire week." By the time I reached her lips, she was leaning into me, which was a good sign. "I'm pretty sure you stole my heart the minute you rushed into the kitchen and tried to club me with a stuffed elf."

Noel smiled against my lips. "You threatened to call the cops and have me thrown out of my own apartment."

"But I didn't, did I?"

Because I wanted you to stay.

"No." She smiled wider.

"May I present my argument now?"

"You can, and we'll deliberate further when you're done."

"Deal."

I wouldn't be done for a while, but I agreed, lifting Noel up. Her legs wrapped around my waist. She clung to me, snaking her arms around my neck while I carried her to the bedroom. My argument was about to be long and strong, so I hoped she was ready.

Noel.

EPILOGUE—TWO YEARS LATER.
CHRISTMAS MORNING.

"**I**F I GET down there and our daughter is wearing something velvet paired with patent leather Mary Janes, I won't be happy."

Kanton placed his hands on my hips and yanked me forward until our bodies were flush against each other. His head lowered enough to force mine back so his face was angled over mine.

"If our daughter were in Mary Janes, they wouldn't be patent leather. My mother would rather land comfortably in an early grave than have anything to do with patent leather. Now, it's very possible she had some custom made with Italian leather and had them flown in."

"Kanton . . ."

"I'm kidding. A *little*." He kissed me, and I swear this man's mouth felt like home. Everything good and naughty began and ended with those lips, and his tongue, and his . . .

"My mother knows the rules and promised to adhere to them."

Matching pajamas, only thoughtful gifts, and most of all, no outside cameras. Only our phones or personal ones if that was what we chose to capture the moment.

"She knows but has been fighting this the entire time."

"This is new for her. She's adjusting."

"I know," I huffed.

Lauren Joseph was a brazen woman who was just as stubborn. I wasn't sure which one of us would remain standing when we first met because she was determined to prove that I wasn't worthy of her son, and I was determined to prove to her that I was, something Kanton had made clear wasn't necessary.

He loved me, and if she couldn't accept that he and I were happy, she would have to remain outside our happy little bubble. I thought she would surely accept her fate, but a year ago, Kanton and I married on Christmas Day.

She wouldn't dare be outside of that, so she called a truce and decided I wasn't a fight she would win with her son. She didn't. We learned to coexist, but then the pregnancy announcement came, and she was overjoyed.

They said babies made the world a better place. Well, they indeed made Lauren a better mother-in-law. It wasn't that she was terrible. She was nice, and I liked her, but she never really warmed up to me . . . until I was pregnant with McKenzie.

Kanton also noticed it and put his mother in her place more than a few times about our relationship, but I always urged him to leave it alone. I would be fine as long as she loved him and embraced our daughter.

My parents loved me enough, and Lord knows they loved Kanton, but now, Lauren and I were close. Something shifted in her when Kenzie was born, something I could relate to because the same happened to her father and me.

She was so perfect, and she was a combination of all things good from Kanton and me. Maybe Lauren also saw that, but either way, she and I were closer. I wasn't upset that it happened because of Kenzie. I learned a long time ago to meet people where they were, and, well, meeting Lauren where she was meant accepting that she was who she was.

"Are you ready?"

"Are you?" I glanced his way, lowering my eyes to the T-shirt he wore that read, "*This is as jolly as I get*" while mine read, "*OCD Obsessive Christmas Disorder.*"

He kissed me again. "I'm ready for anything that involves you, Noel."

"Good. If this doesn't go as planned, you're on my side, not hers."

Kanton chuckled and brushed his lips over mine. "If a choice has to be made, it will always be you, but she promised me to behave, so we don't have to worry about that."

"Did she promise to wear the pajamas?"

"She did, and as much as it's going to kill her to do so, she will for you."

"For Kenzie," I corrected.

"For you, Noel. She loves you. You know that, right?"

I huffed a sigh. "I do."

"Good. Let's go."

As soon as we descended the spiral staircase, I stopped in front of the massive tree that stood dead center. It was at least fifteen feet tall and beautiful. Although professionally decorated, I wouldn't dare frown at how much I loved the decorations.

The theme was a winter wonderland, so the tree was draped in clear and gold crystal ornaments of all shapes and sizes. There were strategically placed basketball-sized ones that mimicked snow globes with green trees inside them to give a subtle hit of color to the decorations. Everything else was gold and crystal—simply breathtaking.

"As much as I hate to admit that I love this tree, I really do."

"See? There's nothing wrong with hiring a team to pull it all together." Lauren smiled smugly as she approached with Kenzie in her arms. Our baby girl wiggled, extending her arms while opening and closing her tiny fists to summon her father. He, of course, went right to her and lifted Kenzie into his arms while she giggled and squealed from the way he hugged and kissed her.

"I'm not opposed to having a team. I just prefer to do it myself."

"While wearing these." She tugged uncomfortably at the T-shirt she was wearing. I almost laughed at how appropriate the saying I'd selected for hers was.

"Well, yeah, every detail counts."

"So you say." She smiled and walked to me, throwing her arms around me. "Merry Christmas, Noel."

"Merry Christmas," I returned, relaxing into her hug. It was welcoming and friendly, but she rolled her shoulders back the minute she stepped away.

"How long do I have to wear this?"

Kanton chuckled, kissing my cheek as he navigated around me with our daughter in his arms. I looped mine through Lauren's, and we headed to the living room toward the tree that we all decorated a few nights ago.

"Long enough for Kenzie to open her presents and us to get some pictures and video, and then you're free to change."

"Thank God. I can't believe you're making me wear this ad. Don't think I don't know mine was intentional." She narrowed her eyes at me and smiled widely.

"I have no idea what you're talking about."

She shot me a look and then walked to Kenzie, taking her from her father. "Come on, sweet girl. Let's open your gifts from Glammie and Pop first."

When she carried Kenzie to the tree, Kanton's father walked up beside me to kiss my cheek. "Merry Christmas, Noel."

I offered him a gentle smile. Our relationship was very different. He was a quiet man who remained in the background. He didn't challenge his wife but didn't share her flare for being in the spotlight. But he was kind and embraced me from the moment we met, and I loved him for that.

"Merry Christmas."

He leaned in and whispered, "The shirt is perfect."

I grinned as he glanced at his wife and winked, walking over to join Lauren and Kenzie. Kanton moved behind me, wrapping an arm around my waist, which he used to move me closer, nuzzling his face in my neck. "You didn't want to go with something friendlier?"

"What?" I pushed my head back against his chest, and he lowered his eyes to mine.

"*Resting Grinch Face,*" he said, repeating the saying on his mother's shirt.

"It's cute."

He chuckled. "It's payback."

It was.

But still cute.

"Do you have my phone? I want to take a few pictures." He nodded, and I remembered. "Oh, and yours too. Mom should be calling soon, and I want to make sure they can watch Kenzie open a few presents."

With my family and his, we had to decide how to navigate the holidays. This year, we spent Thanksgiving with my parents and Christmas with his. Next year, we would switch, and we agreed that everyone would come to Atlanta for Kenzie's birthday so that we could celebrate with both families, as well as Simone, Lewis, and Cleo. Family was important. We were building our own.

After capturing a few shots of Lauren on the floor with Kenzie, who cooed and smiled, not really understanding the entire unwrapping gifts concept, I held up the phone, swiping through them, smiling bigger before turning the phone to Kanton.

"Perfect, right?"

He peered at the phone. "It's very Christmassy . . ."

It was. The visuals of the tree we decorated with his mother and father sitting on the floor in snowflake-covered fleece pants and matching holiday shirts were indeed Christmassy. Add in our daughter, who wore a similar outfit with "*Santa's Little Helper*" printed on the shirt, and you had a perfect holiday movie theme.

"You love *Christmassy*."

I shoved him playfully in the side, and he pulled me back into his chest.

"I love the woman who makes it feel like I belong in the Christmas photo."

"Good, because she loves you more."

I turned against him, closing my arms around his waist. "Merry Christmas, Mr. Joseph."

"Merry Christmas to you, Mrs. Joseph."

This man had done the impossible. He replaced my favorite day of the year with the day I tried to club him with a stuffed elf because that was the day I captured his heart, and I was pretty damn sure it was also the same day he captured mine.

THE END.

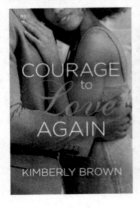